OVENMAN

A TIN HOUSE NEW VOICE

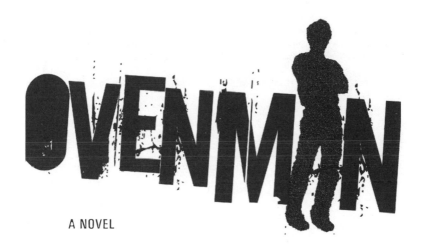

OVENMAN

A NOVEL

JEFF PARKER

TinHouseBooks

This book is a work of fiction. Names, characters, places, and incidents either are products of the author's imagination or are used fictitiously. Any resemblance to actual events or locales or persons living or dead is entirely coincidental.

Published by Tin House Books, Portland, Oregon, and New York, New York
www.tinhouse.com

Distributed to the trade by Publishers Group West, 1700 Fourth St., Berkeley, CA 94710, www.pgw.com

First U.S. edition 2007

Printed in Canada

Library of Congress Cataloging-in-Publication Data
Parker, Jeff, 1974-
 Ovenman : a novel / Jeff Parker. -- 1st U.S. ed.
    p. cm.
 ISBN-13: 978-0-9776989-2-9 (alk. paper)
 ISBN-10: 0-9776989-2-0 (alk. paper)
 1. Food service employees--Fiction. 2. Florida--Fiction. I. Title.
PS3616.A74523O94 2007
813´.6--dc22   2007018924

Title type by Megan Oiler
Interior design by Laura Shaw Design, Inc.
Interior artwork by William Powhida

An excerpt of this novel appeared in slightly different form in the anthology *Life & Limb: Skateboarders Write from the Deep End* (Soft Skull Press, 2004).

FOR YULYA

Intro

Welcome to *Ovenman*. This excellent novel comes in many flavors, or, better yet, toppings: strip-mall bildungsroman, punk-skater picaresque, comedy of (bad) manners, quasi love story, service industry send-up, and military-industrial satire among them. But what about the pizza itself, you might ask, the dough, the sauce, the cheese? Good question. I'm glad you might have asked. The pizza itself, in this case, is made of only the best quality ingredients, namely: Jeff Parker's huge heart, Jeff Parker's beautifully tuned ear, and Jeff Parker's impeccable comic timing. (Which of these wonderful attributes is the cheese, which the dough, and so on, is beyond me, and, perhaps, beyond the capabilities of the classic pizza metaphor.)

Ovenman follows the travails of When Thinfinger, who, despite his extraordinary name, seems your average bright guy working nowhere jobs. He tends a barbecue pit, manages a pizza parlor. He lives in a medium shitty town in Central Florida and sings in a medium shitty band during a fairly shitty moment in the history of the United States. He makes some perhaps unconscious medium shitty decisions, too, which threaten to have awful consequences. *Ovenman* is a funny book, but despite the surface play, it's not exactly lighthearted. It's as serious, perhaps, as the myocardial infarction you might have—will have, probably—after too many of the calzones and garlic knots When and his colleagues bake for a living.

This novel is about people working and trying not to work, about people drifting, people stuck. It's about the pain of wanting a bit too much from what's around you. It's about motorized skateboards and lousy tattoos and trying to be in love and being drunk too many nights in a row and getting weird letters from the father who deserted you. It's about all that plus the pride one can take in mopping a floor correctly or operating a Hobart industrial mixer or devising a groundbreaking method for distributing sliced pepperoni on a large pie. Anybody who has toiled in establishments like the ones employing When knows how important this pride can become, how ferociously one may defend his or her need to maintain it.

Slackerdom's one thing. Slacking is quite another.

You could say this pride, this commitment to excellence, is the who, what, why, and how of When Thinfinger. It's also, in some ways, the engine of this novel, and what makes When's interactions with the many memorable characters in this book, from the self-wounding Adonis to the menacing philosopher-dentist to When's lovely but literally broken girlfriend, so charged, so compelling. Our hero has not checked out. Against what is often his better judgment, he's still trying to be a reasonably decent (if a bit mischievous) force in an increasingly dangerous and indecent world. But it's never so simple as that, is it? Things can get more complicated—philosophically, emotionally—than we care to admit. That's where a fiction-maker like Jeff Parker comes in, when life can't be wrapped up with a glib gag. Parker is a very gifted writer, wise and funny, a worthy night manager of our dreams, and here in *Ovenman* he's served up something uncompromisingly tasty.

Savor it, and don't forget to tip on your way out.

SAM LIPSYTE

Twelve ounces of courage
Makes the world look better

—DAG NASTY, "Under Your Influence"

THE ROB I

For a moment, waking up after this caliber of drinking is like birth. There's all this nothing. Then my eyes pop open. The Florida sun hangs there in the open window, blinding me. My hand finds a yellow Post-it stuck to my elbow on which I seem to have written, *You dont no much*.

But I do know something: I've lost the Haro with the kinky triangular frame. I can't really even say *know*. More like *got a feeling*. Like, I've got a feeling my bike, my long-range vehicle of choice, is gone. Like, I've got a feeling I've been fired from Ken's Barbie-Q, where I've spent five mornings a week for the past year as Butcher/Pit Cook, quartering chicken, yanking out pork bones, spraying green stuff off racks of ribs with bleach water before splitting them. I've got a feeling me and Blaise went out to celebrate my premiere firement. I've got a feeling we celebrated.

I sit up and find myself polka-dotted with yellow Post-its, some of them blank and some of them scribbled on, nearly illegible markings that are trying to tell me something, but it's hard to know what. I take one from the top of my foot that seems to be a doodle of a U-lock with the words *vehicular misplaisement* underneath. My spelling, already bad, goes downhill fast on nights like last. A crumpled note is tangled up in my chest hair, longer than a standard Post-it, and on closer inspection I see that it is a yellow notice to appear and not a Post-it at all. Two boxes are checked: "Disorderly Conduct" and "Open Container." Below this, in the comments section: *Subject was witnessed kicking around city property (pylons) in the east wing of City Lot P with a half-full can of Natural Light. Subject then urinated on said pylons, the newer hard plastic ones. Subject informed me that the line inside the bar was too long and "I wouldn't be doing this if I didn't hate orange." I encouraged Subject to head home.*

These are my fourth and fifth misdemeanors and will no doubt mean trouble. Last time I went before a judge—that time to take care of over two K in parking tickets, a figure he dropped to five hundred, a figure I've yet to pay—he said to me, "Son, this represents a serious *caricature* flaw." His Southern made certain words come out more syllabled.

"Yes, sir," I agreed, considering myself lucky. When your arms are covered in faded blobs of green tattoo and you have been unsuccessful in locating your single long-sleeved shirt and you discover crust in your eye at the very moment the judge demands—his double chin pulsing—to know just what type of citizen it is you *preport* to be, you expect much worse things than tries to your caricature.

As for the pylon business, I do hate orange.

I am knotted tightly into stale white sheets, aware of my hunger, aware that I am alone because Marigold sleeps on the couch in the living room. She dreams that I murder her and prefers to sleep out there, she tells me, where she stands a chance. I am aware that for some reason my underarms smell like warmed hot dog bun. Aware that I feel mighty good.

So I stand and shake the rest of the Post-its off me. I collect them from the floor and cram them into this overflowing shoe box. I don't even bother reading them anymore. Then I do something I've been meaning to do. I stroll into the living room, passing Marigold, who, in her sleep, clutches the quilt to her chest and twitches. I go to the phone and order this motorized longboard with off-road and street wheels out of the back of *Thrasher*.

Days go by like surgery while I wait. It takes a week. I survive on the remains of the Barbie-Q funds, which I keep stashed under the mattress. Banks don't take my money. (ChexSystems blacklisted me after countless checks to "Cash" bounced at Publix.) Then the motorized longboard arrives, supplementing what's left of my once impressive collection of vehicles: a Vespa (gone), a vert board (still have), a street board (still have), the Karmann Ghia (still have but must use sparingly because of parking ticket situation), and the Haro with the kinky triangular frame (now gone).

The motorized longboard has racing-stripe grip tape and cutouts above the wheels so you can really lean into your carve. It makes up for every vehicle I ever lost. I ride it downtown kickpowered to the lawn mower store for that special two-cycle oil-gas mixture it requires. Then I'm shooting down Thirteenth, going twenty-three miles per hour in the wrong lane. So the speedometer says.

I believe.

Halfway home I detour to the skate shop to show this beautiful specimen around. I barge in, brandishing this fine thing, and there's Blaise catwalking the Haro with the kinky triangular frame.

"Lose something?" he asks.

"Pretty sure I had," I say.

"You were right. Some slickdick came in here looking to sell it. I reclaimed it for you, dogbrother."

But it's never that cut and dry with Blaise. Turns out he less reclaimed it than bought it back for, he says, ninety-eight dollars. Blaise is my best friend. Still, he requires me to buy it off him. This is how we deal with each other. There really isn't any point in arguing. When he says the figure, ninety-eight dollars, how much he supposedly paid for it, the other guys in the shop turn their backs to us and pretend to alphabetize the skate videos on the back wall. They're his friends. I'm tolerated because of him.

I tell him, man, I'm still broke, still fired, plus I just coughed up for the longboard and this special goddamn fuel. "Plus it's my bike."

"Correction," he says. "At the moment it's my bike, reclaimed on your behalf."

I ride the Haro back home while Blaise blasts along beside me on the motorized longboard. I retrieve the last of my Barbie-Q funds from under the mattress, telling myself that ninety-eight dollars is a real deal for this kinky a bike. I pay him and he counts the bills and says, "Pleasure doing business with you."

"I'm on the market," I say, opening the door and kicking him out. "Catch you on the flip."

I admire the Haro with the kinky triangular frame and the motorized longboard leaned against it in my living room. My vehicle collection is once again impressive, but plan Find a New Restaurant Job has moved from imminent to immediate.

I search for my long-sleeved shirt, my only long-sleeved shirt. It has a picture of a corpse face on it. I go through the tangle of covers Marigold leaves on the couch when she pulls shifts at Wild Hair. I search the empty spare room that is cold and hollow and used only as a place for our dirty clothes, which my dog Left claims as bedding. I finally discover the shirt in a corner at the back of the room, where it must have been since the day I got the job at Ken's Barbie-Q. Its smell is total MoonPie wrapper.

I formulate my plan of attack. I have never had to deal with a firing, have held numerous restaurant jobs and always rocked them. Need me to clean the toilet? It'll come out shining like you've never seen. What's your fancy special? Graham-cracker-breaded catfish? I ran the whole Barbie-Q on my own some days and it never ran so smooth. But thinking about the firing makes me want to smash somebody's windows. I am trying to figure out how to cover for a yearlong employment gap on the applications I'll soon be filling out. So I need to not want to smash windows. I need to be practical. I need to get the scent of MoonPie wrapper off the long-sleeved shirt.

I plop down onto the papason to count my laundry change and about impale myself on this fourteen-inch knife sticking out through the cushion, one that I stole from the Barbie-Q, the one I used to bust ribs. I pick up the cushion and pull the rib buster out. Pieces of white fuzz come out with it. There's a pile of knives underneath the cushion. Practically every blade in the house. My pocketknife, eleven or so butter knives, some serrated steak knives, a box cutter, and the Leatherman, which is mostly pliers but has a small knife in it. This indicates I am now, apparently, murdering Marigold with knives. Last month I couldn't find the Q-tips. I'd buy some—because I have to have Q-tips—and put them in the medicine cabinet by her tampons. The next day they'd be gone and I'd go around all day trying to dry my ears with toilet paper on an index finger. Trying. Of course, I could never remember if I'd actually bought them. Maybe I'd just intended to buy them. So I bought box after box. Then I strolled into the shed out back for a bungee cord and found six boxes. That's how I was murdering her last month, driving Q-tips into her brain. The sound, she said, was the worst part of it all.

I ride the motorized longboard to the laundromat and drop the long-sleeved shirt in a washer. I beg a half cup of detergent off the Chinese lady who runs the place. She has always been nice to me. When I had a paycheck, I once paid to have my laundry washed and folded and left a bag of weed in my pants pocket. When I came to pick it up, she handed it to me over the counter covertly, at the bottom of my stack of freshly folded clothes. She nodded and winked. When I smoked it, it tasted like generic industrial laundry detergent, the kind that really cleans.

The rows of plastic chairs alternate between orange and blue, but all the blue ones are taken. So I stand. When the long-sleeved shirt is done washing I put it in the dryer. A quarter buys eight minutes, and I'm trying to conserve the last of my change. So I drop in one and get back to the row of plastic chairs just as a guy with a big neck evacuates a blue chair in front of the Galaga machine.

I snake it and read a *Thrasher*, pop mini-ollies with the long-board, which makes a sound like a cork popping on the loose linoleum. There's an article about soldier-skaters in the Saudi Arabian desert. They storm the sands all day and teach the locals tricks at night. One guy talks about how the sand's real hard on bearings. Another says, "Arabs are so far astute rippers."

There's a picture of a guy in fatigues launching over a line of Saudi kids on a plywood runway in the sand. Then there's a sidebar that says Saddam Hussein calls Kuwait's oil pricing "economic warfare." I jot that phrase on a Post-it. I wage my own economic warfare on the restaurants I work in. I plunder and pillage. They pay me jack and so I take my own.

In the restaurant world, this is The Nature of the Way Things Work 101. And if there was any restaurant that should have had a grip on 101, it was Ken's Barbie-Q, run by two brothers from Starke, neither of them named Ken. They had me butchering from seven to nine, when I'd light up the pits (I get flashbacks to those pits), scrape them, cook the meat I'd butchered all morning, and set up the line for lunch, when this old woman named Beaches came in to scoop fries onto plates. I ran meat through the slicer, busted hip bones out of pork butts, cut my fingers open on the slicer blade, got sunburn from the pit heat, and re-upped for the dinner rush, when Skinhead Rick would show to pinch-hit. We'd get out of there around midnight five days a week. That set me with fifteen-hour shifts at minimum wage with no overtime. One of the brothers kept telling me, "Gosh, When, I sure wish I could get you some more money."

Right. Implicit deal, bro: I was taking my own and everyone knew it. That's why those twenty-four-hour surveillance cameras pointed everywhere but the beer keg I drained long and hard before locking the place at night. And, man, who can watch twenty-four hours of footage? Maybe you look at an hour here or there. The system's designed to fail, and a system designed to fail is one that gives you advance permission. So one night all Blaise's friends come up and we empty a keg and guess what? The hallway where you take the old keg out and put the new one in *is* within camera shot. And since I do all the work, it turns out the brothers from Starke *do* have enough time to fast-forward through twenty-four hours of camera tape while licking flecks of pork rib from their knuckles. There's me and Blaise and Blaise's buddies cruising through on skateboards, knocking over bus tubs of pork and beans in fast-forward. It turns out the system is not designed to fail, basic understanding is not understood, economic warfare, a minor battle, lost. When the shift was on, I took care of the place like nobody's business, like it was my own. They owed me those beers and pork and beans for me and my friends and they owed me the use of their kitchen as a power-slidable skate surface after hours. I'm sorry to have lost the Barbie-Q gig, but what can you do when people don't observe simple understanding?

You leave them off your future employment applications is what.

X

"Can't you fucking understand simple directions?" the guy with the big neck yells at his son, who's maybe fifteen, about how the jeans are still wet. They are standing together at the orange and blue folding counter. The son reacts like I used to react. He looks strangely at the damp pair of jeans he just folded. He did not realize wet jeans are a problem. He assumed, maybe, they'd dry folded. Or maybe that's how things come out of the dryer, jeans maybe, this being his first time folding. He does not respond.

Neck goes on: "If you could follow simple directions we wouldn't have to waste time loading the dryer back up, spending more money since it's got to heat up again. Now we have to sit here wasting our fucking time because you don't pay attention. Wasted time. Time."

I jingle the two remaining quarters in my hand. The kid puts the jeans and some towels back in the dryer. Neck sits down in the orange chair across from me. I don't look at him until he lights a Marlboro Red. With my shirt off, and the tattoos down my arms, I can be intimidating—the one good thing about them. People tend to think I've been in jail, that they were done with a razor blade instead of a guitar string. I won't say anything, 'cause I don't have the knobs, but if I did, it'd go:

"Hey, Thickneck, jeans don't dry easy."

"Which is none of your goddamn business," he'd say.

I'd barely turn my face from the *Thrasher* to eye him. He'd scurry across the room, glancing back to see if I was coming, and I wouldn't hear from him again except when he checked if I was still eyeing him.

My own eyes drift then and he catches me looking his way but does not scurry. He stares right through my face. I'm in the middle of my tough-guy fantasy and, for some reason, I bare my teeth.

"You going to bite me?" he says in the same tone he used with his kid about wet jeans. He stands slowly. Everyone in the place turns—from fluffy half folds—to watch.

"Have a taste of this," Neck Junior says, wagging an adolescent fist as he comes around the counter. He is no longer the little kid, unsure how to dry jeans. He's actually bigger than his father, I realize, as he approaches, swole about the throat.

I stand and stumble over the motorized longboard, dropping the two quarters. They roll between my feet and under the Galaga machine. There I am, quarterless, my dryer buzzing in the background. My long-sleeved shirt still, no doubt, hopelessly damp inside.

I stare at my *Thrasher* and shake my head. I have a couple options here. I could pull a wig-out, a tactic I used in me and Blaise's high school Slayer wannabe band. Blaise mastered the drums, the hard part about mimicking Slayer. All I had to do was figure out how to garble "Aggressive Perfector" and develop some stage presence. That's where the wig-out came in. It involved full-on flip-out, widening of the eyeballs, flaring of the nostrils, tattooed arms over head, screaming something like, "I am Satan! I am Satan!"—basically trying to look insane and dangerous.

In an acting class I mostly skipped back then, the teacher said if you wanted to look like a particular emotion you needed to think something that gave you that emotion. I couldn't really think of anything insane—the emotion I was going for—that had happened to me, so I imagined my step-dad Luke peeing on my feet when I was a kid, which he'd do every night in the shower. I practiced in front of a mirror. Slowly my eyes would transform from a shy singer's glance to something murky. Then I'd start reliving that trailer lifestyle, the both of us in the shower stall to save a few bucks on water, a roach the size of a possum swaggering up the wall, and Luke letting loose on my toes. I could feel it when I thought about it. It was warm, about the same temperature as the water but more viscous, a bigger liquid feel. Technically I was just mad, but it was a weird kind of mad, like, *I'm raged because you're peeing on my toes, dude, and there's nothing I can do about it so I'll just let the feeling well up in me day after day after day* . . . Even small and bushy headed, I could look like a scary motherfucker when I thought hard enough to relive that warmth on my toes.

The wig-out served me well later, when the black kids or rednecks came after me. I adapted it to the streets. Instead of jumping on stage, I jumped on car hoods—washing machines would work—anything that made a loud racket, clanged, disoriented. So, say someone is about to start something, rather than risk an actual fight, I start jumping around, flare out the nostrils, pound my chest, pull my hair, scream "I am Satan!" or "I am a skateboarder!" and jump on something people don't ordinarily jump on. That usually takes care of the problem. Usually.

The other option in this case, with Neck and Neck Junior in my face, is to do nothing, the sober option. To stare at my feet, where my quarters rolled away from me just moments ago, wondering why I'm not a little more like the person I can sometimes appear to be. Why couldn't I be dangerous and insane for real?

"Lose your quarters?" Neck says. "I can cram you under for a better looksie-daisy."

Then Neck Junior jumps in: "What kind of limpdick tattoos you got? Bushes? Homeboy got a hedge line. Hee hee!"

The Chinese lady who runs the place flutters over and calls them off. "Alight," she says. "Alight." I sit back down. Neck and Neck Junior go back to the orange and blue counter and watch to see if I'll get up. I thumb through my *Thrasher* for a while so I won't seem like a total pussy, even though there's no reason for me to be here anymore.

Neck Junior says, "What I thought."

I look around for a coat hanger or something I could get the quarters with, but there's nothing. So I open the dryer and put on my damp long-sleeved shirt and head out.

"Later days, fucknut," Neck Junior says.

I forget about them. I ride the motorized longboard and drop applications everywhere, maintaining low expectation. Any place that will pay me to wash dishes and not ask about where I wasn't working for a year, I'll be happy.

I don't even make the question stage. I fill out the application and then they tell me there's nothing available. After. I blame the damp shirt.

I'm just about home when I stroll into Piecemeal Pizza By The Slice. I'd always suspected that working here could really change things, to have access to the best pizza in town, and to work at a place with such prestige. I'd applied previously but wasn't cool enough for the Manager. That guy's not around now. It's some ordinary chick named Wendeal, who offers to take me on. Gives me the old "Can you start tonight?"

This, as anyone in the industry will tell you, is a sign of desperation. Something's gone on here that's left them needy. No one hires anyone to start that night, even someone possessing my resume—startling with regard to pizza, and mostly legit. She's thinking I'm a real catch.

"Can," I say. "Will."

X

In celebration of my employment, me and Marigold go biking. I don't mention the knives, wanting things to be good.

I ride the reclaimed Haro. She rides this two-dollar garage-sale Huffy. I'm still trying to teach her bunny hops. She learns slow but something in her burns. I recognize it. I put that there. Most of the way we tool along this little path near an alligator-infested lake on campus. I tell her not to take the corners too quickly until she gets that bunny hop down. I tell her it's a matter of life and death out here. "Alligators sun themselves on the trails!" I say. "Be ready." She doesn't listen to me. She is not ready. She tries hopping the barely protruding roots of oak trees and crashes over them. I do tire taps on stumps. I nose-wheelie the berms.

I have been trying to teach her the principle of the bunny hop for months. We practiced with pinecones. She has succeeded so far in almost clearing the smallest of cones with the front wheel, only to pulverize them with the back. Her body convulses, the bike stutters. I try to find something redeeming there, her own personal style or some shit, but the repetitive failure enrages me. And now she decides to use my approach, the confidence approach, another thing I've been trying to teach her: "Be the bike."

As we're riding home, she bolts, kicks it across the busiest street in town, in front of an Econoline, approaching the curb at a diagonal because, perhaps, she thinks if she puts herself under enough pressure she will somehow manage to clear the curb. In this moment she is trying to become the bike and the bike is resisting. The Econoline is closing in. To change course now would mean death-by-van. I'd say she might be able to make it, even if the shitty bike does weigh almost as much as she does, simply out of her desire to please me, to fix us. And maybe that's right. If she could be the kind of woman who could hop a curb, even if she lost her balance on the landing, it just might.

I stop in the median and watch. The van actually speeds up, breaking her concentration just enough. There's an abrupt acceleration in her pedaling. The gear slips. She convulses and leans too far forward. The front wheel rides directly into the curb. She leapfrogs the handlebars and soars, her bright yellow hair whipping out behind her. I realize then I never taught her how to fall, to go to her shoulder.

The Econoline honks and swerves around her unmanned bike, blocking my view as she contacts. I flip the van off and imagine her landing on her collarbone with her feet buckling over her head. I visualize it as clearly as if I could see it. I even hear what I think is a crack.

I hop the curb and assess the damage. She is writhing face-down on the pavement. She rolls over and screams. She is bright red and crying. Her white pants, the kind that are supposed to end just below the knee, are hiked up to her thighs, her knees bloody and skinned. Her perfect, tanned legs long ago ceased to do anything for me, but in this moment, all gnarly and fucked up, they're beautiful. She says, "Owie, owie," over and over. There are small granules of pavement in her unruly chin.

"Where was my hop?" she says, shudders.

"You should have gone to your shoulder," I say. "Fatty, absorbs the shock."

"I think I broke my back."

"Naw," I say. "Can you sit up?"

She looks at me like I'm grapes. "Get me some water," she says. Then she sits up most of the way, propping herself on her elbows.

"It's not broken," I say. "You couldn't do that if it was broken. Just need to walk it off."

She shrieks that me lying to her does not make her feel any better, which I have to admit kind of puts me off. There is not much blood. I pull her bike onto the sidewalk next to her.

"It's just tweaked," I say, then wander away. I phone her bandmates from a nearby florist, explain the situation, and buy her a Pepsi. She is crying less when I return but when I give her the Pepsi she starts in again. She wanted water, which again pisses me off, and I throw the unopened can onto the sidewalk and it explodes just as her bandmates pull up in their band car—the Rhododendron orange Pinto—and scowl at me. They contend I don't treat her right. They suggest to her on many occasions, in my presence, that she deserves better. So it's perfect timing.

They swarm about her. One of them produces a chilled bottle of Zephyrhills spring water and Marigold manages a smile.

"Hospital," she says to them.

"Hospital?" I say. "Why hospital?"

I become the object of disapproving head movement all around.

"Hospital," I say.

They hoist her up by her shoulders, I get her feet. We load her into the passenger seat of the Pinto. Then I make my move. I kiss her thin yellow hair and tell her I'll try and get off early, but I can't miss work. Not on my first day.

Her mouth forms a Q, a strange lip thing.

I smile and slam the door. "You're in good hands here. It's my first night, Marigold. It's just tweaked."

The Rhododendron orange Pinto screeches away. I leave her bike right there in the street, the piece of shit.

I arrive at Piecemeal fifteen minutes early. I don't wait for orders. I punch a time card. I tie on an apron, tuck in my yoke, glance around the dish room for cameras or other surveillance, see none, head for the dish sink. There I encounter a tall, skinny hippie. "Jafari," he says, holding out his soapy hand to me.

"Thinfinger," I say. "When Thinfinger."

His sink is a disgrace. Pepperonis cling to the side. The sprayer dangles, knocking him in the head when he leans over to cut off the faucet. The entire station is begging for an Ajaxing.

"I guess I'm taking over here," I say.

His eyes cross and uncross. I reach over him and lock the sprayer into its hook. "You want the dishes, brother? They're here for you," he says. "They all yours."

Wendeal appears in the doorway to the kitchen and orders me to stop right there. "Welcome aboard, Thinfinger. But don't touch that dish sink. You're Ovenman." I've never started in a position higher than Dish Dog. I've worked my way up, sure. But this . . .

"My Ovengal had to be fisted or fistee somewhere. You're the only replacement I've got. The hippie *just* washes dishes."

"Almost got them off my back," Jafari says. He laughs and bobs his head, pretends to hit a joint. "Squander."

I arrive at the oven and, in complete honesty, there are only about thirty minutes of instruction before I start working it. Before I am like the best fucking first-night Ovenman they've ever seen. A natural. The main Ovenman duty: running the Bakers Pride Y-602 double-deck pizza oven at five hundred and fifty degrees and cooking the thin pies and calzones brought over by the Thin Pie Guy. (The oven is so deep that manning it seems not all that different from gazing across what seemed like miles of half chickens at the massive Barbie-Q pit.) I slice the pies and calzones when they're done—by far the most difficult part—and send them out in boxes or on platters. I open the Bakers Pride doors for the Front Girls as they trot slice orders over for warm-up. Even though they are nowhere close to pretty, I am polite and cordial and waiting with the oven doors open when they arrive. I perfectly caramelize each specialty and line pie. I puncture bubbles in the dough before they disrupt the landscape of the toppings. After the cheese cools, I cut the crusts all the way through. Different sizes get different cuts, as do pizzas destined for tables and pizzas destined for slices—a lot to remember, but I get pretty damn near one hundred percent. Calzones I position in the hot spots just long enough to color the crust a deep mahogany brown. Every time my arms contact the oven doors, long oval welts appear and transform into pus-filled cockpits.

The entire kitchen staff orbits around Ovenman.

"You're doing exceptional," Wendeal says, stopping whatever she is supposed to be doing in the middle of a crazy Friday night rush to tell me. "Skordilli is the owner. He'll want to meet you. Remember that name. When you see him, pretend you've heard of him, his brother Dr. Bob too. They like that kind of thing."

It won't be a problem. I have heard of them. The brothers who owned Ken's Barbie-Q complained about the slickers who locked down the lucrative university-area properties, where they could control the high-traffic food business. More than once the brothers from Starke talked about coming down one night with masks and baseball bats to strike out the imbalance of power.

When the rush dies down, I'm called to the phone on the other side of Pasta. A personal call is a major no-no on your first night. But knowing who it is, I take it. "You were wrong," Marigold says. Then she tells me about how much of an asshole I really am. She's going into surgery in a few hours. Her back is *frack*-churd, she says. Her dad's flying in from Long Island—which is bad because she recently returned from there and an abortion Dad paid for because the Barbie-Q paid me jack. I better get my ass off work and down there, she says. *He* has taken off work at the bunting manufacturing plant he owns, and he's flying one thousand miles to Florida because he cares for her. That is what people who care about people do, she says. "People matter to people."

This is the position I'm in.

"It's broke," I say. "I was wrong. I can't believe it."

"I'm waiting for you."

"If he's coming there it means that I will meet him?"

"You will meet him. Yes."

"I'll be there as soon as I can."

When I say this I really mean it. I intend to devise some lame excuse for having to bolt early. While it is too soon to kill off a grandmother, I could do it. I can. But now I am nervous about meeting a man who knows I was the cause of his daughter's abortion, not to mention her broke back, a man who manufactures something I have never heard of before.

And these Piecemeal people, they're just so impressed by my ability. I kind of sink into scraping burnt cheese off the brick—it's so calming—and the next thing I know there's pans to be oiled and boxes to be folded. The phone is ringing again. I ask the Front Girls to tell anyone calling for me that I'm in the middle of shutdown and can't talk and don't want to even know about it.

I box up two slices for Marigold. I'm not looking forward to seeing her. I'm embarrassed, embarrassed I threw a full Pepsi onto the sidewalk while she was splayed.

The final Ovenman duty is mopping the floors, a restaurant duty I have always cherished. Out back there's a fenced-in hose area about the size of a shower stall. I treat the mop head to a much-needed bleaching. Then I scour the mop bucket to its brand-spanking-new yellow condition with steel wool. Taking the time, doing it right makes me feel better about things. The water pressure here is strong. The hose has a good, tight nozzle seal. I mix bleach (just enough to disinfect, not enough to streak) with a drop of blue squirt soap, and the shit chemical-smokes. This, my secret mixture, dissolves any grease. They tell you not do this, but when I inhale and feel the lung-choke come on, I know it's the right concentration. Fizzy, I go to work.

After all the chairs are neatly arranged upside down on tables, I start in, covering every inch of the floor with broad, aggressive strokes. The first step is to coat the place in a thin layer of water, starting at the back door and moving through the dining room to the counter separating the kitchen from the dining room. Then I squeeze the mop dry and go back over everything, sending its sopping tentacles into tight corners, under table legs. The trick here is back and arm strength, which brings out the polish. You don't need wax for the floor to shine. I rinse and scrub the bucket again and dump the dirty water down the parking-lot sewer drain. I rebleach the mop head and hang it to dry on an old mop handle in the hose area.

I have a look at the parking lot, almost empty of cars and quiet except for the splash of a strange fountain on the patio to my left. To my right there's a wooden fence running the edge of the parking lot, separating Piecemeal from the Chevron station. The hose area and the walk-in butt up against it. At the far end, next to the dumpster, there's a little brick half wall. Behind that are three barrels designated for grease. They're the kind of barrels bums make fires in. When you empty the fryer vats, you dump the grease in one. Then a special grease collection service is supposed to come by and pick it up. But apparently Skordilli doesn't want to pay for the pickup, so the barrels sit overflowing and the shit gets poured down the sewer. At some point, a crow got in one of the barrels and drowned. Half its greasy corpse sticks out from under the lid.

I enter the kitchen from the back door, where the fountain and patio are. In the middle of the fountain there's a cement stand with nothing on it. Algae clogs the water. The back door bells clang as I come through, stroll across my floor. The crew is standing at the counter. They have each poured themselves a beer. They are staring at the floor in amazement. I look over it myself, reaching down and running my hand across the reflection of my own pieboy face.

"You know a thing or two about work ethic, Ovenman," Wendeal says.

"Aye, aye," I say. As the film evaporates under the ceiling-fan breeze, the deep-down clean is there. It's there. Everyone knows it. They admire me. I think, That's *my* floor.

The phone rings. I am standing right next to it. As instructed, I say, "Piecemeal, Pizza for the People."

"What exactly is your dysfunction?" says Penny, Rhododendron rhythm guitar, serial bitch. "Are you retarded or, let me guess, a complete heartless prick?"

"You got me."

"Marigold's going into surgery, When. *Sur. Ju. Reeee.* For whatever unfathomable reason, she really wants you here."

"I'm en route," I say.

"You've broken her," she says, with a long pause, "back."

X

I cruise to the hospital on the longboard. Nearly the whole way is downhill. I approach thirty miles per hour.

I arrive just in time. Marigold is panicked. "They're putting metal in me," she says.

"What is a bunting?" I say.

"You've got to try, When," she tells me. "It's about deciding here's someone you're going to treat with the same selfishness as you treat yourself."

"Marigold," I say. "They made me Ovenman."

"They did what to you?" She reaches for my wrist.

"They started me on cook."

Her look tells me she's just not getting this, and that's okay. I didn't expect her to. I offer her the pizza and she says she can't eat.

"I cooked this," I say.

The nurses arrive. (I note that nurses do not wear paper boats in their hair. Why did I think that?) They scowl. They explain, like I am a two-year-old, one does not eat prior to surgery. I sense there has been talk among the women.

I hadn't realized the surgery was serious enough to warrant these kinds of facial expressions. Still, it's not like she's in danger of dying or anything. And you don't not show up for

the first night of work. Me and Serial Bitch follow the gurney.
We hold her hands as they wheel her to this olive-colored set
of swinging double doors. She is scared and because of that I'm
a little forgiven. The nurse asks her if she is okay. She breathes
deep and says no. She jerks my thumb. We kiss and I kiss deep
because I feel the tremors in her hand. I tell her I'm sorry I
threw the Pepsi. She lets go of me quick.

"Bunting is like little flags," she says. "For cheering teams on
and shit." Then they wheel her away.

"I thought those were called pennants," I tell Serial Bitch,
who's wearing a ribbon in her hair and a scarf around her neck
in exactly the way Daphne from *Scooby Doo* did.

She doesn't respond.

"I assume you're going to be here when she wakes up."

"Yes," I say.

"I hope so. We have to leave. We've got a gig."

Lately Rhododendron has been playing across town at the
Covered Dish, a club into packing the house with tools from
the college.

"How can you play without your singer?"

"We're not the ones who made her jump her bike."

"Bunny hop," I say. "The maneuver she attempted was a
bunny hop."

I return to her room and try the TV. No Discovery, so I
review the slice counts in my head: A small gets four pieces,
that's two cuts in the shape of a plus sign. The medium gets
six, which are first cut like an oblong X with a single vertical
cut through the center. The large gets eight, a plus sign with a
regular size X through it unless it's a slice pie, in which case it
gets six big ones using the same technique as the medium.

I make a Post-it to help me remember:

—small (4 slices) = +
—medium (6 slices) = x, |
—large custemer pie (8 slices) = +, x
—large line pie (6 fucken BIG! slices) = like med.

Piecemeal has one of the expensive wood-handled rocking pizza cutters. The kind you get your whole body into. The kind you smack down and rock all the way through so no layer of crust goes uncut, a serious pizza defect. The calzones get three slits on top. Slices go in the bottom oven, one minute each to put the heat on.

I reread the Post-it. I recite it. I make it the chorus to a song, and it actually sounds pretty good, better than a lot of other things. I get up and strut to it a little bit. Then I wander down to the cafeteria to see what they've got going on. It's all white coffee cups and casseroles. There's no one in line and the cook is leaning against the cash register.

I lean on the three metal bars where you're supposed to set your tray. "You guys make anything but casserole back there?"

"We make meat," he says. "Meats and casseroles. Beans and corn. There's some rolls and a salad down there."

"What's the sickest person you ever saw come down here for some casserole?"

"That's an interesting question." He runs his finger under the band of his white cook's hat. "Usually the sick ones fed in their beds. We bring the casseroles to them."

"Just wondering," I say.

"Now that I think about it, there was this cat would come down holding a flap of skin to his forehead. He had some skin cancer. And the doctor would cut into him like three sides of a square to get at the cancer, then tell him to wait awhile so they could see if they got it. That cat didn't want to wait without him some coffee. That's what it was. He'd come down here and

order coffee—so it wasn't casserole, it was coffee. Everyone
had to wait because he fumbled with his wallet one-handed,
the other hand holding that flap to his head under some white
rag. But what are you going to tell him?"

"Tell him to get that flap of head back to his room," I say.

"I heard that," he says. "Of course I've seen people come
down here when they were fixing to die."

"I got a girl in surgery right now," I say.

"I'm sure she'll come out of there all right," he says.

"That's right," I say. "That's exactly what I've been thinking."

X

I wake up draped across the armchair in Marigold's hospital
room. The nurses wheel her in and leave after scowling at me
some more. I creep over to see if I can get a look. She is turned
on her side, out cold. I pull the string, undoing her gown, and
try to make out what's what. Every single notch of her spine
looks like the head of a little screw. There's a line of pink stapled
together where they went in. I realize I've never really looked
at her back, and it's clearly the most incredible part of her. Her
spine is so knobby, each notch so pronounced. It reminds me
of staring across the pit at the Barbie-Q or scanning the oven
brick at Piecemeal, vast yet detailed surfaces. There's so much
to see there, so much to take in, so much to make sense of. I
reach out to touch.

"How's it look?" says a tall, dickheaded voice behind me.

"I don't see anything, yet I see so much," I say. We shake
hands. His swallows mine and crunches my fingers together.
He is tall, like his voice, taller than me. I step aside and the
first thing he does is cover her ass with that hospital gown so
I don't get her pregnant again. Then we maneuver around the
bed to face her. He presses her nose, rubs her head. She wakes
up but doesn't acknowledge either of us. I see a familiar red

buzz lurking in her eyes. She falls out again. I notice she is in a kind of contraption, a huge metal frame arranged around her, something I'd thought just moments ago was a part of the bed. He suggests that we leave her alone. We walk out beside each other. He's got an easy six inches on me.

We sit on an uncomfortable bench with no back or arm rests outside Marigold's room. I cross my arms on my chest and the sleeves hike up, showing my tattoos. He stares out the corner of his eye.

"I'm told you're a racquetball man?" he says.

"Me and my friend Blaise play sometimes on the courts at the park." Actually what we play is less like racquetball than a version of the game Butts Up, with racquets, the object to hit the ball off the wall and into the other person, after which he takes the butt-up position at the front wall for some target practice.

"At the park? Outside?"

"Yeah."

"Outdoor courts don't have ceilings." He chuckles. "You're not playing racquetball without a ceiling. What kind of a name is 'Blaise'? Now 'Blasé'"—he throws his arms up, nearly hitting me in the face with his elbow—"that'd be a name."

"It's kind of cool, sounds like with fire, you know."

A doctor buzzes by, stops, looks us over, determines he's the father and I'm nobody. Marigold's father stands and the doctor leads him across the hall to talk. I make out the phrases "minor fracture," "simple surgery," "a single precautionary reinforcement," "better safe than sorry." I wonder if her dad knows I'm the guy. He knows I'm the guy. I picture Marigold, trying to think up something to tell him about me that's good on their way to get the abortion. She came up with racquetball, a game I don't even play.

He sits down beside me again and neither of us speaks. He does not offer to tell me anything the doctor said.

I want to say something interesting to him, to ask him a challenging question. All that comes to me is *You flew here then, sir?* which is absolutely fucking inane. Of course he flew here, asshole. You want him to think you're a naïve, poorly tattooed, knocked-his-pristine-daughter-up prick *and* a moron? He looks at me expectantly. He smells my struggle.

"So you make little flags?" I ask.

"Bunting," he says. "The company I own makes bunting. Yes."

When we first met, Marigold massaged my scalp for five dollars plus tip with an exciting tenderness that chilled my calves. I became addicted to haircuts, every other week minimum. I craved her, but mostly I craved her fingers all over my scalp. She had this way of sliding hair between her fingers three times before cutting it. Attention to detail, which I admire. I drank pitchers at the Salty Dog, and then I walked into Wild Hair. She'd always take me, even if she had to bump an appointment—she called me her "patient"— and she was the most sought-after stylist at Wild Hair. We had elaborate interactions in silence. We exchanged meaningful, flirting looks in the mirror. She trimmed my sideburns extra rough, teasing the hair on the side of my face. She rubbed her tits against my shoulders—I could feel her third nipple, a mini just to the right of her main nipple, through her shirt.

She had this yellow hair, a real yellow, none of this honey bullshit. I mean Crayola yellow. It wasn't done up like you'd think a hairstylist's would be. It hung flat and dead, thin and limp, frayed flybacks at the sides. I loved everything about it.

One afternoon she told me about her penchant for memorizing songs.

"What's a penchant?" I asked.

"A knack."

She said she spent her spare time listening to and transcribing songs. She sang them to herself until she had them memorized and then waited for that particular group or performer to come to town. They always did because all the tools from the university make ours a ripe town to play. Her plan was to ask if she could get onstage and sing along since she knew all the words. Then she would be discovered. This was something. I made songs, and in her way she made them too.

"How many times have you succeeded?" I asked.

"None, yet," she said.

Maybe if I had asked exactly what music she liked, what bands she hoped to sing along with, I could have saved us all this. I regarded her penchant then as sweet, and I referred to her as The Flower. I brought her potted marigolds the first time I asked her to accompany me to the Hardback. I brought her to bars. She was new. She was pretty. She was a hairstylist. I didn't even think to ask.

She'd been christened a manager of sorts at Wild Hair (which I envied, such power) and had keys. Once after a couple hearty King Cobras at the Hardback, which got her really frisky, she said, "You, sir, need a trim." Then we hopped on our bikes and pedaled like mad down to Wild Hair, where we turned the AC all the way down and groped each other to one particular stall somewhat hidden in the back. It belonged to one of her colleagues, a fat gay guy named Reggie who combed his red hair into a greasy rooster comb. His mirror was decorated with pictures of him—always the same hairstyle—riding different animals. He had ridden horses, zebras, elephants, giraffes. There was even a much skinnier version of him mounting somebody's giant Harlequin Great Dane.

We turned the lights on at this particular stall and left the rest of the place dark. We stripped all our clothes off, then Marigold tipped my head back into the sink for a lukewarm shampoo while I devoured that third nipple. She wrapped my hair up in a towel, spun me around, put some very heavy music on the CD player, and snipped, combed, snipped. She took the clippers to the clump of soft hair on the back of my neck. Then she crawled over and around in front of me, standing on the arms of the vinyl barber's chair. She combed my bangs down the front of my face, scraped my nose roughly, then sat down on me as she trimmed them ever so slightly into a neat wet triangle. Eventually we wound up on the floor, rolling around on top of my freshly cut hair.

We went months itching. No matter how many showers, we couldn't wash it all off.

In my house the windows stay wide open and the ceiling fans on high at all times. When she started sleeping over we lay on top of my down comforter—the only thing I own that is soft and luxurious—naked and sweaty with the fan pushing hot humid air all over us. That is life in Florida without AC. After a couple weeks of this I remember saying something ridiculous to her like, "I like the feel of you. I dig your snip." She started crying and whimpering.

"I have an eating disorder," she said.

"Which one?" I said. "The A one?"

"Nope," she said, "the B one."

"Well. That's all right. You know, robins and even hyenas feed their young like that."

"Oh, When," she said, "I just don't want you to think I'm a silly girl."

That was about when I began to think of her as a silly girl. On the nights she slept over I woke up in the morning to small specks on the toilet seat, and though I never caught her in the act, I noticed her graying teeth and all I could think about when I kissed her was stomach acid. I've called these supposedly free counseling services all over town asking what I can do for her. How can I teach her to stop, and how do *I* deal when I know it shouldn't repulse me but it does? They act like I'm asking dumb questions. They say I can come pick up some literature but she should consult a doctor. "I see why your services are free," I say.

All I imagined when I considered dumping her was me two years down the road, drunk with regret after realizing I hate most things about any woman after a while, my hair falling out due to a lifetime of ball caps and bar-soap shampoos, calling her up at her husband's house and her saying, "I'm sorry, Thinfinger, I'd like to meet you for pizza but I have to massage my new man's hairline." So I moved her in with me and Left. I decided if I couldn't let go, I'd grab hold tight. I moved her in when what I wanted was for her to magically disappear. I thought if I put everything together like it should be put together things would fall into place, as things sometimes do.

No dice. We cohabitate miserably in our small two-bedroom house. Her third nipple no longer does it for me. Its lack of aureole, its flimsiness when the properly stationed nipples stand erect—it has come to resemble a mole. The Wild Hair sexual pyrotechnics are a dim memory. She got together with some girlfriends and put her penchant to work in Rhododendron, an embarrassing band that covers pop songs. She spends her time off from Wild Hair and band practice trotting around in front of the mirror, her thin yellow hair hanging limp at the sides of her head, singing lyrics to the latest Top 40 hits, the kind of music people laugh at. She listens to Casey Kasem religiously and records Rick Dees.

She's decorated the entire place in bone—bone planters, bone picture frames, bone ornaments, bone knickknacks. And there are skulls everywhere. She bleaches them and plugs translucent marbles in the eyeholes. Some are easy enough to peg—cat, rat, rabbit, horse—but some I don't know what they are, and I don't even ask because she wants me to.

She falls asleep on the couch watching *Animal Planet* and dreams that I murder her. For each night I don't come home she adds another animal skull to the décor.

So the morning after her bike wreck, I set out to do a certain number of things right. I awake to four Post-its stuck to my stomach. One is a stick-figure bike in midair over a curb. Another is a close-up of a front wheel clearing a curb. In another a stick figure Marigold lies facedown on a sidewalk, a tear dripping from her face. In the last the bike is underneath a van. I shudder. Another Post-it, this one stuck to my forehead, says, *FRACK-churd*. The notches in Marigold's spine.

I purchase potted marigolds with tip money the Front Girls divvied up with me. Cruising past the hospital cafeteria I catch her dad sucking on ribs like candy canes. I duck around the corner so he can't see me and peek at him. I am involved with a woman whose father enjoys bone marrow at eleven a.m.

I sneak past and am there holding the flowers, soil between my fingers, when she wakes.

She smiles.

"Where exactly is what's wrong with you?" I say.

"Do you see this cage I'm in?" she says. "I've been peeing into a drip tray."

"And how is that working out?"

"I'm soaked."

"I want to understand your injury."

She smirks, turning her mouth into that Q thing. We have not gotten on this well for twenty seconds since the haircut-in-Reggie's-booth days. I open my eyes as wide as possible to look completely interested.

"The doctor says it's a small problem but needed correction because of pressure against the spinal cord. I'm going to need a special kind of bed. I will not move from it for a month or so. But 'It's not nearly as bad as it could be'—whatever that means." She tries to move her head side to side as she says this and closes her eyes, tenses her mouth. "I don't even know, When. My father says he's taking care of it"—which a little bit makes me want to take care of it—"What else my father says is these Florida doctors are hacks and he's bought a row of seats for me on some plane to Long Island, where his friends are the best doctors in the country. We leave later today."

This may be it, I think. This may be what we need. A turning point.

"Screws down all of your spine?" I manage.

"There's just one," she says. "Somewhere. You can't see it, though. It's tiny. Those bumps *are* my spine."

"They are your spine," I say.

I kiss her and I'm able to kiss her well even though her breath tastes like pee-drip tray. I haven't been able to kiss her much for a long time. Now there is none of that. I kiss and kiss her. She is shocked at all my kissing. I jostle the cage playfully and feel the suppressed wince in her dry lips.

X

Then she disappears, whisked away to a better place by a bunting man who can take care of things.

And I am Ovenman.

With Marigold out of the picture for a while, I dedicate myself to the job the way I need to dedicate myself. Prime time. Solid gold. I master the oven and all its duties. There is no challenge I cannot meet. I can fold twenty boxes while cooking six pizzas, squeeze in calzones, and leave a space up front for slices so the Front Girls don't burn their hands—I still open the oven doors for them.

Whenever I dip back for supplies, I am so fast no one has a chance to miss me.

I transport the caramelized pies to the cooling section on a perfect rotation for the Thin Pie Guy, a long-haired bone-in-his-nose rocker dude named Greg, who takes too many smoke breaks and is erratic in getting the uncooked pizzas to me. It's like rowing a canoe with a guy who is a lot weaker. I do what I must to keep the boat straight. I sync up, slowing to Greg for the sake of the pizza.

I cool them just enough so the cheese won't stick, then I slice them apart according to the specs on my Post-it, now nailed above the slicing table only for emergency reference since I just chant that instructive chorus if I forget for a second.

My slices: immaculate, near-identical acute triangles.

That first night with Marigold gone, Blaise and I celebrate after work. There is drunkenness and there are wig-outs, the suggestion of violence to deter actual violence.

I awake the next day and my only memory of the night is a video still frame. All of my memories these days are like video stills; I can't see forward or backward from any one particular moment. Just one fuzzy screen shot, paused, in which I'm out of my body, looking down at myself: I am hanging one-armed from a refrigerator-sized amp. A crowd cheers and jeers below me. And the audio, skipping around in my head, in my own voice, goes, "I am Ovenman!"

The Post-it note stuck to my chest reads, *You dont want to no.*

I work seven days straight and on my day off, Blaise calls. "Thinfinger," he says, "want to come over and watch the war?"

"Are we on?"

"I've got a feeling," he says, "tonight is the night."

"I've got to wander the dog right now," I say.

"Wander by the beer store on your way," he says.

There is a letter sticking out of the mailbox, and that's a strange thing because people don't mail me. At first I think it must be from Marigold, but it's addressed to my old name, When Then.

"Thinfinger" was assigned to me when Luke, who came on the scene shortly before I can remember, adopted me in the fourth grade. Mom announced one afternoon we'd be going to the judge to change my name, and I figured great, who will I be? I wanted "Cougar." Then on the drive Mom said we were only changing my last name to Luke's. We were seated uncomfortably on vinyl seats in the back of Luke's GTO, breathing insulation because insulation was what Luke did and the trunk was full of the stuff. My ass was sweating and scratchy. Up until then I didn't even know what Luke's last name was, so I asked. In one of the only intimate moments I remember with the man, he turned to me in the backseat of his GTO and explained: "When my father first got to this country from Poland, he came to North Florida. His name was Wudcinski. People in North Florida didn't like Polish people then, basically like how we don't like black people now. He needed a new name, When. He looked around though at all the jackass Americans who didn't respect him and realized he didn't want an American name. He remembered a sergeant in his basic training commenting on his thin, dexterous fingers, a source of great pride to him. So he decided to take that rather than a common American name. Now you and I, we're common Americans, and we'll share a name, one made up by my father based on a part of his anatomy, a name that no one else in the world has. Thinfinger."

"Can we make my first name 'Cougar'?" I asked. It was becoming clear that Mom wasn't taking this absurd name.

"When, you just wouldn't come out," Mom said. "You were a month late and then after infriggingduced birth you held on for twenty-six hours. I kept saying, 'When? When? When? When will you get the hell out of me?' And when you finally came out I realized I'd forgotten whatever it was I'd initially planned to name you. I was only sixteen, you know. I gave up my life for you."

"Can I get 'Cougar' as a middle name?" I said. It seemed reasonable to me. "Other kids have them." Having a middle name myself, I figured, would allow me to go by it at some point, a back door.

"'When' is a very nice, unusual name. 'Cougar' sounds like a dipshit," Luke said.

I tear into this surprise letter. It's written on plain notebook paper, in blue ink:

> *Dear When, your mother knew me several years back in high school. She has told me about you over the years and sent a picture every now and then. Even though I haven't been there, you've been in my thoughts.*
>
> *You should know that I married some time back and have two kids. They are my life. I am a statistician in Columbus, Ohio. But I was wondering what kinds of things you're interested in. Me, I never thought I'd be a statistician. I majored in botany, which I really enjoyed but which didn't offer me any job opportunities. Then I went back to school some years later and got into numbers. You just never know. My advice would be to do something you're interested in that you can make a living at.*
>
> *I'll leave you with this: you've always got a friend in me. Now it is morning and I have to go shovel the snow. A problem you Florida people don't have. Dan.*

I pocket this thing. I'd always known there was a Biodad, but it had never crossed my mind to try and contact him. I hadn't even spoken with my mom and Luke in a decade, so why would I bother with this dude I don't know, who writes trying to get all fatherly advice on me? But the prospect of siblings was something I hadn't considered. I'd always wanted one or two of those. Also, maybe the guy would send me money. A statistician made money, didn't it?

I fill up both sides of a Post-it:

> *Dear Biological Father (or should I call you*
> *Statistishim?): I know humins are fucked-up animals.*
> *So dont think I have any weird notions about my real*
> *father. I realise writing you now may be causing you*
> *trouble with your current family and I'm sorry, if. I*
> *would like to contact brothers and/or sisters thouh?*
> *When Thinfinger.*
>
> *PS: My last name was forsibly changed to*
> *Thinfinger. I dont care for it but its silly to go back*
> *now. Simalurly, a crazy coked up tattooist etched shitty*
> *tattoos down my 15 year old arms while I was passed*
> *out. What do you think of that Statistishim? Biodad?*
>
> *PPS: I'm broke, but am all about something I'm*
> *interested in.*

I walk Left the usual route. The old dog is half black Lab, half pit. He has a neurological condition and he only moves in a leftward direction. If he needs to move rightward, he circles around to his left. He's covered miles of extra ground in his lifetime for no good reason. I let him pull me on the street board because it makes him happy. We hit the post office and the beer store, and then, recognizing Blaise's yard, Left charges in, dragging me over the grass until my back truck catches a root and shoots me, clutching the beer to my chest, into a pile of sawdust. His doorstep is strewn with bedding and mattress springs. The door itself is plastered with stickers that say, "POLICE OFFICER spelled backwards is SUCKASS LOSER."

The couch is empty, so I follow a trail of bedding and the murmur of television down the hall through a maze of dressers, a drafting table, TV stand, and recliner that have been pushed into the hallway. The glow of the TV is visible at the bottom of his bedroom door. I knock. "Hold on," Blaise says. Something that sounds like a power tool falls.

"Check it," he says, and I open the door. Blaise's room is small, but he's carpeted it calf deep with four or five old queen- and full-size mattresses and box springs. He has cut two rect angles in the mattresses to accommodate the entrance and the bathroom door, but every other inch of floor surface is bedded. Without frames it's low, and it's layered in paisley flannel sheets and down pillows. The TV is propped on a piece of plywood on the mattress in one corner. Blaise is on his knees in the far cor- ner proudly wielding a power saw and a twelve-pack. Shaka Bra sits with his back propped against the wall.

"Way better than couch," Blaise says. "Way better." He holds a beer out to me, and I step onto the world's biggest bed.

"Shaka," Shaka Bra says. We beer-can toast.

"It came to me in a dream," Blaise says. "The more gratify- ing my sleep, the less likely I am to narc out." He's low-grade narcoleptic and claims he falls asleep only when he hasn't slept well the night before, but I've seen him go down even after primo rest.

"There it is," Shaka Bra says. "It's on."

CNN runs a grainy green picture that occasionally lights up with bomb blasts and antiaircraft fire that looks like catapulted lightning bugs. What you are seeing is live footage of Operation Desert Storm, the news announcer says. I prop myself against the wall next to Shaka.

"I'm going," Shaka says. "I am so-shaka, there-shaka."

Shaka is six-five, blond, salty, and easily the best surfer in Florida. He splits his time between here and St. Augustine, where he keeps twenty-five girlfriends. I have never seen him in a shirt. He's the kind of person you'd pick to be if you could choose. He tends to make words out of his name. He is a punk rock Greek god, burly and rollicking, but when you see him you don't exactly think "soldier."

"My dad got blown up in Vietnam," Blaise says. "That's why I'm sitting right here on this room-bed. I got a get-out-of-jail-free card on combat for a lifetime. That's how it goes when you take one for the team. Your line is untouchable."

"The military is, like, inconceivable for me," I say. "Unless they got some cook positions opening up. I'll give all new meaning to the word 'gruel.'"

"You could go in the navy, Thinfinger," Blaise says. "You'd make an awesome deck swabber."

"Think about the rush, men," Shaka says.

We stare at the live footage for a while, then we stare at the replays of the footage. I realize I am doing this thing I always do when I watch TV, holding one hand close to my face and tracing the edges of the TV screen with my finger. It's not a conscious thing. I don't know why I do it. Seems to happen when I concentrate. Just as I'm getting bored of seeing those little fireflies shooting around on the screen, Jenny Raygun comes in carrying a stack of books.

"I need your assistance here, boys," she says.

She has the look of a woman coming off a hard night, which she is. No one knows—not even Blaise—what her real last name is. Her purple panties ride way up her back. Her and Blaise don't ask each other annoying questions like, "What's your last name?" or "Where have you been all night only to show up here again at five p.m. the next day?" They're that kind of couple.

Jenny Raygun joins us on the bed and has a beer. The news announcer says the same things we've already heard twenty times. Shaka can hardly take his eyes off the screen, but we pass around the books, which have pictures of veterinary oddities, looking for Jenny Raygun's new tattoo. She decides on an enlarged pig's heart shaped vaguely like a prairie dog.

She asks when I'm going to get the shit tattoos on my arms covered up. But they're a sore point between me and Blaise so he changes the subject by wondering out loud how likely it is that someone will skate a bowl filled with rattlesnakes before he does. Blaise always has a plan. Last year it was he'd return to school for public relations. "I'll publicly relate," he said back then, but his zero-point-six-five community college transfer GPA was not received well by the admissions officers. His new plan is far more elaborate. He's leading a political movement, lobbying the city for a skatepark. He's screen-printed these yellow and black bumper stickers that say, "Support the City Skate Park. Call Your Comish." He's been going to the city council meetings with a group of skaters. The local paper, the alternative rag, and the college paper have all interviewed him. Of course he has a hidden agenda: once the bowl of his own design is built, he'll fill the flat bottom with rattlesnakes and stage the photo op he thinks will score him the cover of *Thrasher*. He's already been in touch with them about it, and they've expressed interest, another reason he's worried.

If we lived on the West Coast or even somewhere down south, Blaise would be pro by now. But here we occupy a no-man's-land: North of us is North Florida, the Redneck Riviera, the capital—essentially South Georgia with some beach and buildings. South of us is South Florida, where all the real bullshit goes on. We're in between the two—a little bit of each and a little bit of something else. We've got rednecks and old people and cocaine dealers, some music stars, some actors. All the action is either above or below us. So Blaise has resorted to poisonous snakes and begging for facilities, which he resents. Now he is worried that if he doesn't get it together quick, someone will bite his idea.

It's a shame really. He's too good to resort to gimmicks. I have lost it over the years. Skateboarding is something different now. Everything miniaturized. Wheels got tiny. Pretty soon launch ramps disappeared from all the magazines, and the touring pros were either vert or street. Just going fast wasn't enough anymore. Blaise worked it. He was able to take all his stylings and make them work on street and vert. I never could. I only had enough space in my life to be good at one thing at a time.

Used to be, little sharp-tranny launch ramps were the thing. I'd sky, going blazing fast. Christian Hosoi was my hero. I'd try doing everything he did, nearly as high maybe: big judo airs (front foot kicked out), airwalks (both feet kicked out), Christ airs (everything kicked out). Even Blaise couldn't launch as high as me. After my launching phase, I fixated on curbs. I still get excited over an odd-shaped curb, a little taller than usual, or flatter, or the kind at gas stations with a metal lip coated in slick yellow paint. I'd lop up there and stop, contorted in any crazy position—smith, blunt, five-o, tail—and hold. That's what skateboarding is really all about, those pauses in between moments of high velocity. Stuck up top a curb you've got time to think. You can't think when you're moving; that's all instinct. But once you're up there, paused—and some of these curbs are two feet tall and you're like, *I could hold this pose forever*—you've got all the time in the world to imagine your way out of it: some kick-flip thing to nose, shove it, or just reach down, grab the board, and yank right out.

"We're making progress with some key commissioners," Blaise says. "They're scheduling a vote. But I shouldn't have said anything to those *Thrasher* people, not until it was a lock. People are stealing great ideas left and right these days."

"What is that?" Jenny Raygun asks, pointing at the TV.

"That's our war," Shaka says. Then he says, "Cat's eye,"

and bolts out of the room. A minute later Blaise goes to the bathroom and Jenny Raygun elbow-crawls across the bed to whisper in my ear. "I have a suspicion," she says, "that Blaise wipes his penis after he pisses." She is especially breathy on my lobe. We slide over to the door and listen for the sound of the postfountaining toilet-paper roll. She looks down to make sure her underwear is showing.

If her suspicion is true it would confirm something I've thought for a long time, that underneath it all Blaise is something else. He always seemed untouchable to me, always had a way with the world that I did not. Punk rock and badass. But a decade ago we made a trip to Panama City and he revealed himself. We'd heard there was a skinhead named Blue who would tattoo us even though we were underage if we followed a set of codes. We pulled off at the designated Jax Liquors and parked in the specified parking space. We backed the car into the spot and flashed the brights on the appointed double-wide five times, and waited. Our sources had told us that Blue would come up to our car, but nothing happened. After a while, we flashed the brights five times again. Nothing.

So we got out, walked up the porch steps, and knocked on the screen door. I followed Blaise, feeling sketchy about the whole thing, but to calm me I thought about how Blue was a pretty nonthreatening name and all. Suddenly he was there, nude except for combat boots. The ears and eyeballs of an elephant tattooed just above his trunk of a dick. He was holding an ax handle.

He didn't move for clothes, just stood there. A puppy attacked the screen door and he kicked it. "What the fuck do you fucking want?" I couldn't speak. Blaise stepped up.

"Tats," he said. "What we want is tats."

Blue pushed open the screen door and said, "Well entrée, gentlemen."

He tossed several albums of flash art on the coffee table, then sauntered down the hall. The walls were papered with Skrewdriver flyers. I got the sense that the skinhead who sent us there didn't have our best interests at heart. But we were fifteen and driving on learners' permits illegally. Who else was going to tattoo us?

Blaise didn't need to sift through the albums. He had already drawn what he wanted, a little batlike thing with a tail. I needed to find something. I thought about something bandlike, maybe the Misfits skull, but while I admired Danzig, I realized their dark music just didn't mean as much as the more weepy beer-drinking choruses of the Descendents. I turned to the tribal stuff. I was going to get whatever I chose on my shoulder, where no one would ever see it unless I wanted them to. I felt stupid. I wished I'd asked Blaise to draw me something.

I settled on a little twisty fragment of tribal about three inches long, kind of like vines but more jagged. Blaise played around with the puppy. When Blue reappeared in cut-off jeans, he had a small tackle box in one hand and the ax handle in the other. He said, "I'm only going to tell you once: never pet that dog again."

"My bad," Blaise said.

"Kick it away from you now."

Blaise looked, unable to kick it.

"If you don't kick it right now, it won't understand that you hate it. It must think that everyone, every human being, every canine, every microscopic skin fleck in the air hates it."

Blaise shoved it away and it came right back at him.

"Get out right now." Blue held up the ax handle.

Blaise kicked it across the room but the pup was relentless, it chortled back at him. "Now you've got it thinking you like it. Now it thinks you want to *paalaaaaaaay*."

Blue herded the puppy down the hall and closed it behind a door.

"All right," he said, "which of you's I'm-no-more-a-pussy party starts first?"

I didn't like the looks of things, but one of the points of this was that you didn't like the looks of things. You didn't like the looks of things but you went with them anyway. Besides, he had a professional-looking dentist's chair. Blaise wasn't saying anything, which was unlike him, so I said it. "Mine," I said. "Mine."

"Well you're the next contestant. Come on down."

Then he pulled out his gun. It was nothing like the shiny sixteen-needle whirring instruments we'd seen in tattoo shops. It was a model-train motor minus a casing. A ballpoint pen tube was electrical-taped to it. A crooked steel guitar string acted as the needle. The train motor buzzed reluctantly and the guitar string moved up and down through the pen tube. I was already in the chair. I pointed to the design and where I wanted it, well above the elbow, coverable by T-shirt sleeve so Luke wouldn't massacre me.

"I can freehand that," Blue said. "It's not a problem."

I guess I looked freaked. "Look, I've been doing this for twenty years, kid. My work's been in all the mags." If I'd known then what I know now I would have recognized the cocaine in his jitter, the red in his whites. All I really knew was case after case of Natural Light and toilet-paper-roll bowls. He might have been up for days ax-handling that puppy before we got there.

And still part of me blames myself. Nothing might have happened at all if I hadn't passed out. Supposedly it happens to thirty percent of all people who get tattooed. As Blaise told it later, just as Blue finished outlining what I'd asked for, I began to vibrate a little. That part I remember, the muscles in my arm tensing, then humming. Blaise said I went ghost white, then a shade of green, and then I went out. Blue stopped for a sec, and then he held my chin and turned to Blaise, said, "Kid, your buddy just died." That was all it took to take a fifteen-year-old Blaise off his game.

"A joke," Blue said. "Come here and hold his face. We'll finish him off while he's out of it."

Blaise held my head up, still unsure if I was dead or what. He didn't look down, he said, until he felt the pulse in my temple, but when he did, he didn't know exactly what to do. Like so many meaningful moments in my life, I have no memory of it myself. Blue didn't hold the pattern at three inches, just above the edge of my shirt sleeve. He extended it, tracing the extension, quickly, all the way down my arm. Below the elbow, he lost the jag and got curvy.

"I don't think he wants that?" Blaise said he said.

"Hold his head," Blue said. He was taking the design to its natural extension, he explained. He talked to Blaise as he did it. He told him he was saving time, that tattoos are more addictive than crack, that I would be back in a matter of months to have it finished off and I'd be thanking him when I woke up that he'd just taken care of it now since I was obviously still such a pussy. He'd seen this happen hundreds of times. He traced the pattern down to my wrist, then started on the other arm, working his way backward, up from the wrist. He said to Blaise, "You're an artist aren't you? An artist sees lines that aren't there. Don't you see the lines that aren't there?"

"I know he doesn't want the other arm done," Blaise said.

"I'll fuck you with my puppy," Blue said.

It was amazing how fast he laid the outline, Blaise said, especially with that low-rent gun, the kind of thing that looked like it was meant to power miniracecars around a miniracetrack. Watching him do it, Blaise said, was actually beautiful. At the time, the lines seemed true to him. He went right through the thin blond hairs on my arm. He must have known if he didn't get enough done, I would have a decision to make when I woke up.

When I did wake up, it was from an extraordinarily pleasant dream. My whole body was numb. It took me a minute to realize where I was. Blue was still working. Blaise was still holding my head, and when he saw my eyes open he tipped my head back. His eyes looked panicked. Then I felt the needle for the first time, on the bony part of my right elbow. Blue was zigging the tribal design around the elbow, drawing a loop there.

I still didn't get it. Blue stopped and looked at me. "Welcome back," he said. "Any poontang out there?" I was looking into Blue's eyes but thought I was looking into Luke's.

I looked at my arms. It took a minute before it all clicked. I remember blinking a lot. There were only the outlines, no fill yet. But curved lines tracked both my arms.

I jumped out of the chair and flew out the screen door.

"You're a new man," I heard Blue yell. Blaise followed.

Standing in Blue's driveway, he told me the story. "I couldn't stop the guy," he said. "Dude's looped." Blaise never said that he couldn't do something.

The Jeffersons blared from Blue's TV. At that point I knew there was no one else in the state who would tattoo me until I was eighteen, another three years. I could either walk around with hastily drawn outlines or let Blue finish the job.

When we walked back in, Blue was sitting on the couch, laughing at the TV and eating a bologna sandwich on white bread, drinking some import, which I wouldn't have expected from him.

"Done bellyaching?" he said.

"I'm done," I said.

"Try not to faint on me again."

I took the seat, Blue licked mustard from his hand and went to work. Three hours later, I strolled out of there not recognizing my own arms. Dark black . . . well, bushes, blotches, blurbs covered them and ended at my wrists.

Blue said he'd give me a deal for all that work. A hundred and fifty dollars. But I'd only brought seventy-five, and so Blaise chipped in his seventy-five, which was fine, I figured, since he definitely wasn't taking a seat. Halfway home he asked me when I'd be able to pay him back. I told him to yank himself. "You owe *me* now," I said.

We both angled for the bright side. They actually looked pretty cool in the sense that they were tattoos and we were in high school. The whole way home I kept my palms facing up. From that angle, my arms still looked like mine. And we agreed not to tell anyone about my passing out, or about Blue jacking me for the dough.

The second I came home Luke kicked me out of the trailer. Mom had only questions: "What did you do to yourself?" "Why do you make yourself a target?" "Where are my cigarettes, my glasses?"

At six that morning Luke drove me down to these little apartments on Apalachee Parkway in Tallahassee. He walked me in and signed a lease on my behalf, laying down the first two months' rent himself. He told me I'd better get a job soon if I planned to make that third month's. He said that if I fucked up his recovering credit I was really going to have a problem on my hands. In the apartment, the first time ever being on my own, I fell asleep feeling lonely, and when I woke up, my tattoos had scabbed and begun to peel. But the ink was watered, and the gun was single needle, if a guitar string even counts as a needle. In less than a month they faded from the killer tribal black to a washed-out gray and finally to an olive green.

Blaise flushes before he's done peeing, and me and Jenny Raygun fall back onto the room-bed together.

"You sleeping with my girlfriend again, Frailfinger?" he says.

"You left her in bed with a strange man," Jenny Raygun says. "Maybe you deserve whatever you get."

"Look," Blaise says. He reaches for my hand and turns it palm down. "Look at those thin, frail fingers." They are that, awkward, bent at weird angles from having broken them as a kid. It's like I inherited them from Luke's father except I'm not related to him. It's like I grew into his name. Now that I have a Biodad and, more importantly, brothers or sisters to grow into, I want to check out their hands. "These are fingers," Blaise says. He holds up his own hands, with fingers that are well proportioned and straight, sturdy and thick.

I reach for the bong to change the subject, and we all go to the kitchen for a light.

Shaka stands next to the stove, melting a red-hot butter knife into his chest. The gas burner's flame is turned up full blast. He sucks air as he presses the knife into his pectoral and breathes out as he pulls it away. Strings of skin stick to the blade.

"Open a window, you maniac," Blaise says.

Jenny Raygun's eyes go wild. She's excited by this. Shaka leans against the stove, holding the knife in the burner flame again. She puts her hand on his lower back, slides it inside the waistband of his shorts.

Shaka steps away from the stove and Jenny Raygun moves with him. He pushes the knife's edge into his chest again and turns the blade as he goes so it's burning lines thick and deep. He grits his teeth and his nose trembles as he loudly sucks saliva. The knife melts into his skin like it's butter. The skin strings peel off his chest and then break. He leans against the stove again.

The kitchen smells of burnt hair and skin. Jenny Raygun has draped herself around him. Blaise is fumbling through the kitchen drawers looking for a lighter, ignoring this.

"One more detail," Shaka says.

He turns to face us. The deep burns make a horizontal oval around his titty. This time he holds the knife loosely between his thumb and pointer finger and rolls the blade vertically from the top of the oval to the bottom so that it burns through the nipple, just like a wooden-handled pizza blade through a slice pie. His tan skin goes stone white and his eyes dart back into his head. No question, if it was me, I'd hit the floor. Not Shaka. He turns off the burner and pulls away from Jenny Raygun. He washes the butter knife with a green sponge over the sink and the piles of however many months of Blaise's dirty dishes. He sets the knife on the edge of the sink and swivels around, his hand on his hips and chest jutted out.

"Cat's eye," he says.

It's a serious wound, red and deep. Little blood droplets rise up and hold. The edges of what remains of his nipple are jagged and wet.

Blaise lights the bowl. "Keep the knife, Shaka," Blaise says, holding in a hit. "It's yours."

"It's beautiful," Jenny Raygun says, her fingers reaching to touch his chest. He winces when her nail grazes the edge of the eye. She can't seem to keep her hands off him.

"Got to get a good night's sleep for my enlistment," he says, then staggers out the door with the butter knife. He's hunched, which is wrong for Shaka; just as wrong as good posture is for me.

Blaise says, "Imagine licking peanut butter off that knife ever again."

We stand there shell-shocked for a while, inhaling the lingering smell of Shaka's burnt skin and passing the bong until the smell of weed has killed the burnt smell and the buzz has smoothed over the shock. Then we start pounding beers, and Blaise breaks out this croquet set he picked up at a garage sale for one dollar. We arrange a croquet derby course in his front yard, over sawdust mounds, downhill bunkers for two wickets, and up an incline to his front door to hit the stick and win. We croquet in the dark. Left pursues the balls and we keep taking them from him because we're scared he'll break his teeth trying to eat them.

I make it through fast and furious and I'm two wickets away when Blaise luck-shot taps my ball and opts to crack it into the next yard so I come in last. This pisses me off. I boot wickets out of my path, barge inside. I snatch off my shirt and tumble onto Blaise's room-bed.

"I'm sleeping here," I say.

"Take it sleazy," he says.

"Latro," I say.

And Jenny Raygun laughs and laughs and laughs.

I dream that I'm a little gold-plated windup Buddha installed at the front of the Piecemeal pizza line, next to the vegetarian slices. Wendeal slaps me on the back of my flat bald head, winds me up, and I say, "I'm something of a golden child around Piecemeal Pizza By The Slice. I'm something of a golden child around Piecemeal Pizza By The Slice. I'm something of a golden child around Piecemeal Pizza By The Slice."

I wake up to Jenny Raygun and Blaise fucking on the bed beside me. Left is lying at my feet watching them. She is still wearing her purple panties. I fake sleep a little, turning away until she starts getting loud. Then I split with Left towing me on the nonmotorized skateboard back to my empty house.

For the second time that night I dream, which is strange. More often my eyes close and then they open and if I happen to remember anything it's one of those still frames that is either something from a dream or something from actual experience but it's hard to know which. I dream that I wake up covered in Post-its written in a foreign language. I walk into the living room, and Marigold is waiting for me on our couch with a set of three candleholders made from hedgehog skulls. She's back. Left barks to say I'm in trouble. The dog fears for his own head here. Marigold meows. In her voice the hedgehog skulls chant, "We've got to make progress."

I wake up to Left barking. I'm annoyed by the dream. Progress. Right. When she is stashing all the knives in the papason. Is that the kind of progress we're looking for here? I walk around the house examining the skulls. None of them seems to be a hedgehog.

I go in for an Ovenman shift and decide to implement one of my trial runs while Skordilli is lurking around. I want him to see this. The first time you steal from a restaurant you steal something small, and you steal it deliberately. Make no motion to conceal. If you are busted, you claim ignorance. You were under the impression employees were allowed an occasional low-value food product. The first time I steal from Piecemeal Pizza By The Slice, I steal a grapefruit. We do not serve grapefruit, but for some reason the prep room has a little bit of everything. I palm one and head directly back to my station. Skordilli is blowing on a frothy Café Girl special. I walk right past him bouncing the grapefruit off my forearm and catching it again. I insert it into my Quest pack, zip the pack shut, and go back to the oven. No one, not him, nor anyone, says a thing. This tells me volumes.

After work I rage with Blaise all night. I wake up the next day on Marigold's couch with Left on the floor beside me. There is a Post-it note stuck to his collar that says, *Thinfinger 1, Piecemeal 0—brakefast to be had!*

And I'm appreciative toward my fucked-up self for reminding my sober self about the grapefruit. I remove it from the Quest pack and give it a squeeze. It pushes right back, just like the juicy ones are supposed to. I get excited about it. Then I pull out the empty silverware drawer and remember the knives are in the papason. I remember that they're there and I also remember that no one told me they'd be there and I wouldn't know except I almost committed suicide by sitting down on them. I wouldn't know and I now wouldn't be able to have this grapefruit the way a grapefruit is supposed to be had: severed in half, the lines perforated so the fruit spoons out in meaty bites. I would have to peel it, which is the absolute most unsatisfying way there is to eat a grapefruit.

I dial Long Island to talk to her about her knife hiding,

something I meant to do the day she fell off the bike. Bunting Guy answers. "Is Marigold present?" I ask.

"Oh," he says. Then there's like ten minutes while her dad tells her it's that Thumbnail from Florida who she's living in sin with. By the way, he doesn't necessarily mind her living in sin with someone, except that it's me, and why doesn't he just tell me not to call anymore and they can send someone to pick up her stuff and be done with it. She tells him I'm better and more thoughtful than I seem. He says with those ridiculous shapes down my arms my look is *loser*. She says she told him already those were accidental. He says I'm naïve, irresponsible, clearly going nowhere in life, and dragging her down with me. She says he's the one who forced her to go to college in Florida. He reminds her she is no longer in college and that she cuts people's hair for a living. She is a people groomer, he says.

"Hey, When," she says.

"What are the knives doing in the papason, babe?"

"Oh," she says, in exactly the same way her father had.

"I was hoping to eat a grapefruit."

"I meant to put them back."

"It's one thing to dream this kind of shit—we can't control our dreams, I know that. But doing something about it in actual, in real physical life . . ."

"It's not like you grocery shop. And they're different now, When. The dreams, you're different in them."

"What's different? Guns? Lightning bolts? Nail clippers? Let me guess: salt. You're a slug and I murder you with salt."

"I don't want to think about that."

"Do you agree that I should be able to find a knife in my own house?" I say.

"You never eat at home. There's nothing to cut."

"There might be, Marigold. A grapefruit is here right now needing cutting. Vitamin C is here to be had. Sitting should be safer, by the way."

"Where did you get a grapefruit?"

"It was a gift, okay? The owner of the restaurant, who highly respects me and my ability and my work ethic, which is a thing that some people in this world feel is an important thing in this world, he gifted the grapefruit to me as a sign of apprecia tion." Marigold does not condone the economic warfare. I once convinced her to lift some special shampoo from Wild Hair, but later I found the receipt in her back pocket. She paid thirty dollars after the fact rather than keep what was already hers.

"Before the surgery, it was just, like, normal stabbing, like you'd see on TV. You'd stick the knife in my gut, I'd fall down, we'd stare into each other's eyes, everything went black, end of dream."

"Okay."

"The stomach, kidney, liver, sometimes the neck, a couple quick thrusts. Then I'd fall down. And when you stuck me, I would come out of my body. So I'd be watching it all from overhead or to the side, which was freaky but not unpleasant. It was bad, but it wasn't that bad."

"I dreamed you were home already."

She makes the sound with her tongue on the back of her teeth. "I don't know," she says. "You're creepy sometimes when you're drunk, When, always calling yourself 'Satan' or 'A fuck-ing skateboarder.' It's like, where's my restaurant worker, my hardcore front man? So after the surgery, it's been different. Now, you take your time. You hold me facedown and open up my back like a fish. I feel every movement of the blade. I'm still alive, and I don't wake up, and you twist this huge screw out. I don't come out of my body while you're doing it either, which is what's really scary."

"Well then it sounds to me like you're different in the dreams now too. Maybe it's you."

"Maybe it is," she says. "By the way, in that real physical life you're so concerned about, I'm getting around. My back is healing nicely," she says. "Thanks for asking."

I hang up and retrieve the rib buster from the papason. I bury it in the grapefruit, which is nothing like what I expected. The rind is an inch thick. What pulp there is, it's dry as bone.

Coming into a new restaurant there are always things you know that they don't. But the restaurant inevitably has certain techniques on you. The dough, for instance. I have always been partial to pushing dough out with a roller. But when Skordilli—a strong, smoky man with a head like a horse's, who sometimes requires that staff gather to discuss the latest issue of *Pizza Today*—notices my prowess in the oven arena, he trains me himself on thin pies. He teaches me to throw. "It's all in the fingertips," he says. "You've got to be the fingertips." This is something I can relate to. He puts his hands all over mine to position them correctly. He forms me as I form the dough. It doesn't take long and when I get it right, my assignment is to stand there, being my fingertips, for two hours at the beginning of each shift, wearing the Piecemeal slogan—*Make Food. Not War.*—on my bandana and T-shirt, throwing out dough so the customers can watch me. This enriches their dining experience. Me, no longer Ovenman, now Thin Pie Guy.

Right before I'd been hired, there was a Piecemeal Purge, when Skordilli fires the entire staff for no good reason. So after mastering Ovenman and Thin Pie Guy, I was trained on the other positions pretty quick. I took to each one with equal, natural taking-to. Thin pies took a week, because there's some nuance to working with the dough, but the other sections, a couple days each, max. Pasta Dude was nothing. You fill the steam tables with water and set two pots in, one for the meat sauce and meatballs, one for straight marinara. Drop the noodles in the water, slap them on the plate, make the call: "Mari up!" Front Girl—the cash register was any old cash register. Salad Bitch, well, salads are salads—the Greek gets a calamata and that's that. The fryer scares me a bit, the way it fizzles and pops, but still, I can work it.

One night they even made me Café Girl and I served cappuccinos and chocolate-covered espresso beans. Normally that's Uschi's gig. The café's only open a few hours each night and she works those few hours every day of the week. She has big hair and big boobs and her station is in perfect view of the Ovenman station (making Ovenman all the more coveted a job). All she does is smile and wear low-cut blouses and work that coffee machine like a champ. She seems different from the rest of us. She's well dressed and has good posture and doesn't smoke and seems perky rather than pissed and doesn't partake of beers after work but sits sipping one pro bono espresso after another out of little cups, her pinky outstretched, lost in thought. That's why she's Café Girl, I guess.

A couple weeks pass and I'm called in and randomly assigned a spot, take your pick, and Skordilli skulks around. Sometimes I catch him and Wendeal looking at me and then looking at each other, nodding. Skordilli calls me in back all the time to slip me twenty, forty, sometimes sixty bucks cash bonus on top of the weekly check. I've never had a boss bonus me, and because of it, I'm confused, have temporarily halted lifting anything, no grapefruits or six-packs or miscooked special-order pies. But it bothers me because according to all tenets of my economic-warfare policy and with the grip this guy has on the university area, I should be cleaning him out.

When I signed on, Piecemeal was running in standby mode. Wendeal is heavily into the dyke community, organizing marches and other events marked by pink triangles or rainbows. She worked for Skordilli some years back and following the purge came in—as a favor—with her lesbian friends to run a holding pattern while he put a new staff together. Basically I was working with the lesbians, Greg, Jafari the hippie, and a few useless others. The lesbians and I did all the work and they sort of took me in. I figured they'd really like this NOFX tune I have on a bootleg about a woman's first homosexual encounter, "Liza and Louise." Lines like *She said I'll never forget the first time you kissed me / Now I want you to fist me*. I brought in a tape my second week to play for them. I thought it'd be an endearing thing, a way to say that I was cool with them without actually saying it. But it just pissed them all off. They asked if I would mind not bringing in any more of my music until they were out of there, which would be soon, Wendeal said.

"I work in here a few weeks whenever Skordilli blows his top and cans the whole staff. I bring my girls and we get the place back into shape good. Then I invariably remember why it was I left the restaurant business in the first place. It sucks."

I didn't understand how she could feel this way about restaurant work, but we connected on other levels. They let me in on the soup call. Every restaurant has a version. "It's a responsibility," Wendeal told me. "No matter how busy we are, if something worth looking at comes in: 'Soup's up.'" Piecemeal doesn't make soup, of course. But with its prime location on the main drag near the university and the infinite hottie traffic that comes with that, at almost any time of the day you could hear someone crying out for soup, and everyone in the kitchen would look up from what they were doing to see a nice piece.

X

Wednesday is officially the deadest night of the week at the Hardback—even deader since we took over—and the only night they'll book us now that I'm the vocalist. You're lucky to get a dozen or so gutterpunks drinking King Cobras and a clique of slutty, untouchable girls who shoot pool, intentionally krangoing balls off the table to get attention. They giggle and knock boots together and go home alone. And that's all the excitement to be had.

Wormdevil is Blaise's band and was enjoying some ascent in the local scene until their singer quit and he brought me on against the bassist's and guitarist's objections. The deal is I am only allowed to sing my own lyrics to one, maybe two songs per show. For all the rest, I'm bound to one word, the name of the band. Blaise explained it like this: "You just kind of tweak the word around, make it a chorus, sing it, scream it, huff it. Go high pitch, low pitch. Show your range, basically. After a while these restrictions will be lifted."

I personally do not think I'm so bad. In recycling old Post-it notes into songs, I may actually be on to something. But having a popular local band isn't about how on to something the music is. It's about how liked the people in the band are. Blaise is respected and liked by everyone. The other two are cool, but older and sort of distant. They work construction jobs and don't hang out much. They have that mystery thing going. I am not mysterious and I'm not well respected or liked either.

I am not sure why that is. Aside from his unibrow and the fact that he's a far better skater, a natural really, me and Blaise are a lot alike. People confuse us. We're the same height. We both failed out of the community college. (I for failure to attend. He for inability.) We are not-tall, brown-headed, bow-legs. I regularly plunge headfirst into sand when dropping in on the wussy Gulf waves. He frontside inverts. We are both rare un-tan Floridians. My arms are covered in faded amoebalike tattoos often confused for bushes. He is tattooless, the main difference.

I show up after work, a little late, on the motorized long-board and the wormy door guy gives me shit again. Normally I make a point to get here early and carry in a cymbal stand or something to appease him. He knows I'm in the band, but he tries to get me to pay. Blaise doesn't have this problem, cymbal stand or none.

"Three bucks," he says.

"I'd love to pay," I say, "but I'm actually the entertainment here tonight."

He stares at me. He has a rattail and wears a gray Members Only jacket on a cool seventy-five-degree night.

"I get this kind of shit all the time, all the time," he says.

"Is Blaise in there? I could go get Blaise and he could con-firm that I'm in the band that plays here every Wednesday."

"That would require you getting in. Getting in requires three bucks."

"Do you seriously not recognize me? I've been playing here for the past seven Wednesdays running. Am I so forgettable?"

I pay three bucks, the whole of my share of the tip money, to hear myself sing.

And surprisingly I'm not the only one. The bar is almost packed, nearly twelve people. The untouchable girls, the gut-terpunks, and some others I recognize from other bands around town. I immediately start flipping through my Post-it notes since I haven't prepared. I brought a handful from the shoe box for this show and see the stack I got into goes way back. These are some of the first ones I wrote, when I started noting the important things Mom and Luke said to me.

"Tonight's show is about family," I announce from the stage. "And by the way, we're Wormdevil."

Then Blaise busts into it. The older guys get to rocking and I start my bob. I do this thing I saw another singer do that looked pretty cool: jump around onstage like a frog, bringing my feet way up to my ass, crushing them back down to the stage, turning three-sixties. This is one of the songs I'm supposed to sing all "Wormdevil" to, but fuck it. The bass player is trying to say something to me but I'm too into it. One by one I yank the Post-its from my pocket and read them in time—I just follow Blaise's beat. I can't even hear myself and I close my eyes and sing Post-its from memory:

> *Mom said speed is not a thrill,*
> *When I started driving*
> *Mom said adults drink socially teenagers drink to get*
> *drunk,*
> *When I started drinking*
> *Mom said I gave up my life for you,*
> *When I first called her a bitch*
>
> *Small pizza four slices plus sign*
> *Medium six slices ex eye*
> *Large customer pie eight slices plus sign ex*
> *Large line pie six big slices ex eye*
>
> *Step-dad said you're cruising for a bruising buddy,*
> *All the time*

He said you don't spit in another man's wind,
When I spit in his wind
He said tell him to get his ass home right now,
The first time he found out I was stealing his weed

Small pizza four slices plus sign
Medium six slices ex eye
Large customer pie eight slices plus sign ex
Large line pie six big slices ex eye
ex ex eye, ex ex eye, ex eye

I open my eyes, expecting to see people feeding off me, but they're all still sitting at the bar, facing the other direction. The untouchable girls are shooting pool. One of them struts over to the jukebox, glances at the stage but looks right through me, drops a quarter in and selects some Slayer. The bass player keeps gesturing behind me.

"What?" I say.

"The mic plug, siltshit," he says. Then I see the thing, my mic plug atop a set list on which the guitarist has written in brackets: *MORE INSTRUMENTALS*. I must have yanked it out before the song started. So I plug it back in, and then I can hear myself again.

"Can you hear me now?" I say and at least two people out there flip me off. It's hard to see exactly how many through the glare.

I sing the word "Wormdevil" as the lyrics to every other song. I try to tweak it as much as I can, sing some happy Wormdevil, then a tragedy. I do some slapstick comedy Wormdevil, punching myself in the side of the head and moving across the stage like a mime. I do one song in which each utterance of "Wormdevil" has a question mark on the end of it, then I switch to exclamation points midsong. One of the untouchable girls says something to the bartender and he turns up the jukebox.

We quit early and join everyone at the bar. People talk to Blaise and ignore me. I hear the bartender tell him he's trying to bulk up Wednesday night and next week will be our last gig. There are no more days available at the Hardback for Wormdevil. The bartender tells Blaise he's sorry about that.

Some guy asks me how I got the idea I could sing and I don't answer. I scrape out the dough caked under my fingernails with the corner of a tooth.

X

The Lesbian Song Rift is soon irrelevant. Wendeal remembers that working in restaurants sucks and decides to walk immediately. She will use her English degree to go back to school for computers. The lesbians walk with her. And I'm called up—even though I shouldn't be too flattered, because bone-in-his-nose Greg is too.

Spooky Greg is a self-declared witch who specializes in performance bullshit. He's all over the restaurant doing everything except what he should be doing. He hides in the Naked Woman Poster Corridor to gross out the Front Girls—when they turn the corner he is there licking the crotch of one of the poster women. He wastes precious pre-dinner-rush minutes gyrating his hands over thin pies, "blessing" them. On top of that he's always running around the restaurant hollering in a Chinese accent, "You fired. You punch out now."

In the first few days of my Piecemeal employ, I mistook him for a Specialist, the kind of restaurant worker I could relate to. Then I happened to be down at the café one day when he got off, and we decided to smoke some weed at my house and watch Discovery. We were in my living room passing a joint, and I was trying to explain to him what being Ovenman meant to me; it was the first position I'd found that perfectly defined me. "The designated Ovenman closing duty is even mopping," I said.

He suddenly stood up and said, "You mind if I undress?" with the joint pinched in his lips. I thought I misheard him and shrugged my shoulders. Then he dropped his painter's pants, stepped out of them, and sat again. His crotch was so thick with hair his dick was not visible. He unbuttoned his flannel shirt with one hand and tossed it on the floor with his pants. He pulled his legs onto the couch and sat there Indian-style, then he passed the joint to me.

"What are you doing, man?" I said.

"I'm passing you the joint," he said.

"Your naked ass is on my couch."

"You said you didn't mind."

"I'm too stoned and didn't understand what you said."

"So you mind?"

"Yeah, I mind. My girlfriend sleeps here."

"It's nothing. I just like to be naked when I'm stoned and watching TV. I'm not gay."

"I'm not gay either," I said. I took the joint. It was slick with his spit and stuck to my finger.

"Those are good omens," he said, pointing at Marigold's skulls. "Where'd you get them?"

"They're my girlfriend's." I hit the joint.

"The one who sleeps on this couch?"

"That's the one."

"Strange thing for a girlfriend to do."

"She dreams I murder her." I passed the joint back to him and he reached over for it.

"I know a guy who deals in skulls—well, he calls them talismans—if you ever need some."

"I'm all right," I said.

"Just let me know," he said.

"Did I say earlier that I mind?" I said.

"Oh, yeah, that's right." He stood up and stepped back into his painter's pants, tied them, and sat down. "Is it cool if I leave the flannel off? It's kind of hot in here."

"Sure," I said.

I have no idea why Skordilli chose Greg.

As for me, there's a few dudes who've been there weeks longer, but after they sit out back toking up by the fountain, they come in and slack, whereas I mop the floor every night and take special care to scrub the sinks down with Ajax when Jafari forgets. I'm bitter each night I'm not assigned Ovenman, and I hop on the position every chance I get, encourage whoever's working it to take numerous smoke breaks. When I'm on thin pies I pull rank on any poseur Ovenman and coordinate my own oven-placement strategy. Sometimes I take the peel out of his hand and spin my own pies, moving them into position for optimal caramelization. And if he doesn't take the topping cues I give him, say he cuts through a perfectly placed tomato wedge designed to center on a slice, I take the rocking pizza cutter and cut the pizza for him. It's obvious why Skordilli chose me.

Greg will manage morning shifts. I get night. And when Skordilli puts me in charge, when he teaches me to both X- and Z-out the register, I vow that I will not be the lazy Manager who struts around not doing jack. I will inspire by example. I will push that yellow mop bucket all over this restaurant every night. I will mop and I will manage.

My first night as Manager I bring on my buddy Skinhead Rick as the new Ovenman. Having him in my natural position makes me feel a little bit closer to it. You might say that I made Skinhead Rick. He was the Barbie-Q's Senior Pit Cook just one year ago, a weak little ponytail coming off the back of his neck, announcing to anyone who'd listen that *his* song was CCR's "Someday Never Comes." He was regular Rick then. He lived with his parents in Lakeland, which is populated mostly by rednecks and students of the Golf Course Maintenance Certificate Program there. He often talked about bringing me with him to the hair-transplant clinic if he ever got his inheritance from his senile grandmother. He said he wanted to point at my shagged, unwashed hair and tell the doctor, "Give me that." But he never got the money.

I started bringing him out after work and introducing him around. He cut the ponytail off straightaway. He started crashing at either my place or Blaise's. He bought a skateboard. It was like having a free bodyguard. Then I turned him on to the music, which really changed him. He took right to hardcore, and before I knew it his shorts were down to his calves and he had a collection of old skate shirts that made me jealous. He started mail-ordering CDs and moved into a little apartment in town.

Skinhead Rick had shot steroids for five years before he nearly killed four men with a bowling pin. He went to jail for a year on charges of aggravated assault even though there were four of them. The way he describes it, they cornered him. Four black guys, so I'm sure he said something. He had a woman in the car and he claims he had to show her what he's made of, but I know he was really just scared for her. Behind all the bluster and skinhead, there's a real dude back there. Like one night at the Barbie-Q, I opened my finger on the slicer. I'm a complete pussy when it comes to clean cuts and I went green and fainted, almost landed on the pit. Rick caught me and helped me over to a booth. He saw that I was hurting and broke my balls a little, but he closed down my station for me. He wiped the meat and my blood off the slicer. He did everything. Then he came by and said, "I picked up your slack a little but now you got to get back on there. It ain't that bad a hit." So there were parts of him you had to admire even on top of everything.

Now he's still shooting steroids and going to mandatory weekly counseling. He listens to Rush Limbaugh and stockpiles guns and any other weapons he can get his hands on, which is illegal because he's a convicted felon.

When I got myself fired at the Barbie-Q, he went down with me. Though he was uncomfortable with it, he had hung out and partied with us, the whole time saying, "I can't believe we're doing this." (The only guys he's ever been scared of are the Barbie-Q owners, and I don't know why. You'd think Rick could handle them.) He got himself caught on the Barbie-Q cameras just like the rest of us, whipping through the kitchen on a skateboard with a bus tub of pork and beans.

So I owe him one.

I train him myself on Ovenman, which is a strange reversal of roles. At the Barbie-Q, he trained me. He taught me to butcher and the correct way to build up the fire under the pit. He showed me forearm workouts so that I could tolerate the eight consecutive hours reaching back over the heat with the prongs to line up half chickens in tidy rows. Now here I am, teaching him to finesse the peel under some inadequately corn-mealed thin-pie crust.

He gets this. His style is less refined, but he has a natural talent. He's a former Alabama Golden Gloves champ from the few years he spent in Alabama. He shaves his whole body. He carries a grenade to work in case any frat boys fuck with him. Small tattoos of SS shields are only half hidden under his ankle socks. He constantly tells people that if he didn't have that felony on his record, he'd be on his way to guillotining towelheads right now. He'd go Conan the Barbarian in the Middle East.

Skordilli tells me the first order of business is to build us a staff.

Rick says, "We need to get us some good-lookin' straight bitches in here."

Skordilli smiles and pats him on the back. Rick does not like that shit, but takes it from Owner.

Rick cleans the oven and Skordilli calls me and Greg in back with him and Dr. Bob, an ex-dentist and Skordilli's massive half brother. The office is a narrow space off the dish room where we keep our paper products. By themselves, Skordilli and Dr. Bob take up the whole office. Me and Greg fill in between them.

Dr. Bob picks up Rick's grenade. Rick keeps it in the office, sitting out in the open on the baker's rack where we stash the laundry and everybody's personal shit. There's a row of purses, dirty aprons, Rick's grenade, four duct-tape wallets, and a broken peel.

"Nice," Dr. Bob says. "Who's the merchant marine?"

"Rick," I say.

Dr. Bob laughs. "It's not live right?"

I shrug. "He's into weaponry."

"He should cast spells," says Greg, who claims that casting spells helps him keep his mind off the stresses of life. Everybody's like, suck it, Greg.

"Probably it's live," I say. "It's Rick's."

"That guy keeps a live grenade in the back of my restaurant?" Skordilli says.

Him and Dr. Bob buckle. "I like that shit," Dr. Bob says.

"Moxie," Skordilli says. "Some nuts." Dr. Bob puts the grenade back down on a pile of aprons. Everything gets solemn and quiet. Skordilli crouches down and removes a pizza box panel that hides the black box, the safe, which is just wide enough to fit three stacks of cash register drawers. You can hear the jukebox up front and the long pull of Rick's scraper down the oven brick. I look up and around, scanning for cameras or some other kind of surveillance. There is none. Skordilli goes over the process for counting the drawers, wrapping twisties around packets of bills, writing the totals on a Post-it, then crouching and stacking the bills in the black box.

We need a new combination, and he asks for suggestions. I tell him I've got one: 23-3-7. Greg wants something else, he says that it's bad luck to have two of the same number between a two and a seven. But I say it's the only combination I can ever remember without writing down. On a phone, it spells "beer." I insist, and Skordilli sides with me.

Then Dr. Bob wants to check our teeth. "Open," he says. He points a flashlight into my mouth.

"One word of caution," Skordilli says. "If you ever fuck with me, this fella here goes to work on your teeth."

"The cheese. People don't talk about it—murder on the gums," Dr. Bob says.

They buckle again, laughing far too long at what Greg and I cannot identify as jokes. They dress in expensive suits and coats with high collars. I wear nothing but shorts and T-shirts. We are given our restaurant keys as we're officially anointed management. To celebrate we drive around in Skordilli's Infiniti smoking bright red weed that he says costs five hundred per ounce. I don't feel I have a choice but to be trapped in the backseat of this Infiniti, and I don't see what any of this has to do with what's important about working in restaurants: mopping the floor, getting your hands in the food, working it like you know you work it. I am nervous and giddy and I keep my hand in my pocket, fingering the key while considering my new station.

I immediately see my advantage. The temporary halting of the economic warfare is over, bonuses or none. In this town of fifty thousand starving college students, pizza is power. All love Piecemeal Pizza. After the shift, I go from bar to bar, making arrangements. Are they interested in some free pie every now and then? Guess who's the new Night Manager at Piecemeal? How about some fizz? They are skeptical at first, but when they show up on schedule—after Skordilli's five p.m. departure six nights per week—they place their orders up front. I nod at the Front Girls. Then they're sent aside. Just like a normal customer minus the paying part.

We bring on a staff. I assemble my cast, mostly gutterpunks from the Hardback. They accept humbly. The Piecemeal crew is respected. When we walk into a bar, people know who we are because they've seen us toiling, pierced, tattooed, angry, and hot. Long-haired and no hair. Dyed hair. Scullions. Sweaty, grubby, short pants and sneakers, jump boots. Piecemeal is not the kind of restaurant where the staff comes out clapping and singing for your birthday. It's the opposite of that, you're lucky if we look at you. As Night Manager I command prestige, and I take my own bonuses.

X

I feel sorry for Greg. During the day shift, Skordilli comes in unannounced wearing a chef's hat and starts getting in the way. But for all his hands-on during the day, Skordilli is hands-off at night. Nights, we rarely see him. I run the show. Occasionally, he'll saunter in, have Uschi whip up a cappuccino or a smoothie, maybe he'll have some middle-aged babe all titties in the Infiniti. And then they're off again.

After the night shift we congregate around the fountain out back. It's secluded enough to keep out the cops. We huff lines, bowls, leftover portabello white pie. We pound the Newcastle from the Piecemeal taps. Then we're off to the Hardback by way of a hotel bar manned by one of our regulars. We arrive at the Hardback for Wormdevil's last show and Members Only lets me slide by even though I am ready with tip money to

pay my way. I sing the same songs and the gutterpunks form a
little half-moon around the stage. They bob their heads to my
pizza chorus. The untouchable girl in the back drops a quarter
into the juke and the bartender—Pepperoni Stuffed Pie, extra
cheese—cuts its power.

The owner, who likes his veggie lasagna with lots of sauce,
tells Blaise there's been a change of plans. Wormdevil can have
Wednesdays as long as we want.

X

I wake up and my Post-it says, *the feeling is paind joy.* I know
what I mean. I stand for a while in the bathroom, where I like
to stand because bathrooms remind me of my mother. I haven't
talked to her since Luke booted me. Bathrooms are where we
spent the most time together. She'd be clipping my toenails by
way of showing me how to clip my toenails. Or cutting my
hair. Or teaching me how to clean the bathroom when Luke's
friends were coming over. Sometimes I'd pass out, just like I
did during the tattooing. And I'm not sure why, just all the
quiet and the white and the boredom. I'd faint for thirty seconds. I'd wake up and she'd be panicked, pissed off, asking me
what I was trying to do, scaring her like that.

It's part of what makes me and Blaise such good friends. I
pass out at almost anything: drink, blood, bud. He's narco.

Now, standing here in my bathroom, with Marigold far
away in Long Island, I can sense her in the faucet gunk. She is
everywhere and nowhere. She is in the absence of knives in the
drawer, the presence of them under the papason cushion. She is
in the skulls. My feet find her toenails knotted in the fabric of
the bathroom rug. Red speckles from deep inside her still cling
to the toilet rim. I rub at them with dry toilet paper. I wet it but
they still don't dissolve. I make plans to borrow the big-leagues

scraper and some industrial bleach from Piecemeal. I will big-leagues scrape them off.

I need her actual physical self back. That is the thing. Without her self here, I'm left with only the things I dread about her, which isn't going to fix us at all.

There is a shuffling sound from the porch and Left attacks the front door. I open it and find Biodad Letter II in the mailbox. I tear it open and unfold it on the kitchen counter. The letter sticks to a spot of old Pabst. It's written on the same obscenely big notebook paper as the last one, a short note, a waste of so much space.

> *Dear When, It was great to get your letter. I wondered if I would hear from you. I don't hear from a lot of people. I hunted you down with a $200 payment to a private detective. He gave me your address and said you sing in a poorly regarded band. I hope you don't mind.*
>
> *As for me, don't worry about messing things up in my world. I never married, and I never had any other kids. Not that I didn't want to or wouldn't want to. I just never found myself in the situation. I guess it's getting pretty late.*
>
> *See, I can never think of anything to say. Dan*

I read it through a few times then go dig the last one out of my shoe box of Post-its and compare lines. *I married some time back and have two kids* versus *I never married, and I never had any other kids*. These phantom half siblings I'd created for myself—they had taken shape, grown faces—suddenly melt away. I was imagining brothers a lot like Blaise but without the always-showing-me-up part. I didn't have a family before and now I don't again. What I have is a Biodad who sends lies via letter from Ohio, a real champ. I have a dysfunctional broken girlfriend. I have a best friend who sells me my own bike back for a profit.

Left watches me comparing the two letters in the the kitchen light. He whines and I realize I haven't given the poor bastard water in days.

I'm cruising by Piecemeal, a little early for work, when I see Skordilli swinging Greg out the back door by his hair. He chases Greg to the parking lot drain and kicks him in the face with his fancy porous-tread breathable sheep-hide restaurant shoes. Before I know what I'm doing, I'm pulling Skordilli off and he's gargling, "All right all right all right all right."

Greg limp-runs away, muttering spells under his breath.

"That one," Skordilli says, "said the wrong thing." He is out of breath. He holds up his hands in front of his face, and Greg's hair, threaded through Skordilli's fingers, glints in the sun. "The wrong thing."

He climbs in the Infiniti and peels out. I try to get the story from Skinhead Rick, but all anyone knows is that Skordilli was lecturing Greg all day about playing around too much. Greg's main focus seemed to be the witty labels he affixed to each product. "Squid Mayo" on the calamari chipotle dip. "Play

Dough." "Gasp-Gaspacho!" "Bloody Mary-nara." It was getting on everybody's nerves, all the "You punch out now!"

I can't imagine what you could say to Skordilli to make him kick you through the parking lot. But it doesn't matter because everyone is glad Greg is gone. And to celebrate, we start drinking off the taps. It helps because we're training some newbies. There's Gutter Boy on Pasta Dude. He's doing all right except I don't think he washes his hands. There's Ashley, a short Hialeah girl who says she just got a boob reduction and is still trying to recapture her equilibrium. She keeps tipping backward when she reaches for the boxes.

I wash dishes myself because Jafari is building some kind of statue on the stand in the fountain, which he's weeded and cleaned. He's also stocked it with several schools of spotted guppies. The statue is an assignment from Skordilli, and everyone is cringing at the thought of what idiotic thing he might construct.

After the shift, I covertly remop Rick's floor, get the tentacles into all the spaces he missed. Then I sweep up the cigarette butts from the fenced-in hose area, where Jafari's underwear hang, drying on the ends of broken mop handles. He uses the hose area as his shower. I give the mop head and bucket a good bleaching. The whole crew congregates to watch Jafari play with Legos on the cement pedestal in the fountain and snort Gutter Boy's dirty blow cut with roofies, which is like hitting powdered Vicks VapoRub.

"Does that fountain dissipate?" Ashley says. She points to a narrow stream running from the corner of the fountain. It trickles across the parking lot to the sewer drain near the dumpster.

"Yeah," Gutter Boy says, "it leaks."

"Whatever that's going to be," Rick says—he tosses his grenade into the air like an apple and points at the Lego model of a helicopter that Jafari is assembling on the pedestal—"I can tell you that I hate it."

"If you're going to be sitting out here so much," Jafari says, "you need something beautiful to look at. I've only got to figure out what it is that will be the something beautiful you look at, which I'm making." He is standing in the fountain and the guppies are circling his bare feet.

"I'll tell you what I need," Rick says. "I need something to explode." He pretends to throw the grenade at the fountain and Jafari drops to his knees.

"You almost made me flatify a guppy," he says. "Oafus."

The crew convinces me to open the restaurant back up and we heat slices and lasagnas. We pour off more pitchers. I go over the floor one more time when we're done, buffing out all the staff footprints back and forth to the keg. Then I march into the office, slide the pizza-box panel to the side, and slip a twenty out of the night's drawers. It's the same amount Skordilli gave me as a bonus when I came in today. That's how I will work this. Whatever he pays me, he will pay me double. I rewrite the Post-it accounting, to reflect twenty bones less, and pocket the dough.

X

I am up by four p.m. The Post-it, written on both sides, reads, *No one actualy knows what there doing. Song about this.*

I wander to Piecemeal early and sit at the outside part of the café, eating chocolate-covered espresso beans and trying to buck up Uschi, whose tears are trotting down her blouse. She turns thirty today and it's set her off. "I'm freaking Café Girl," she says. I'm hardly listening but instead planning to take home a whole mushroom and anchovy pizza for Left tonight, a little penance for neglecting him in Marigold's absence.

"Oh, 'Woman of Advanced Age,'" Uschi says. She went to

the doctor today and glanced at her chart, which defined her this way. "I should have known there was a reason not to look at those charts. Never look, When. You don't want to know what they're saying about you."

"I don't think you can be drafted anymore," I say. "At this age, assuming there was one."

She hears me but doesn't indicate. She dips back inside. Her station is the only one that has inside and outside sections. She whips up some foo-foo coffee drink that's mostly Cool Whip and slurps it down.

Then Rick's calling me from inside. I poke my head in. He says, "We still hiring?"

"Nada," I say, and just then, as the entire day kitchen crew calls out, "Soup's up," Rick gives me the Funky Fish Eye. I realize the person he's asking the question for is standing across from him at the counter, looking, calmly, at me. She's hard to see at first because of all the metal in her. She's reflecting so much light. I move a little and see she is wearing a tank top and has double quotation marks tattooed on each shoulder. Words start popping into my head, I see them written across the blank of her chest: *mitre saw, mutton chop, belly button harness*.

"Except for that one Front Girl position," I say. "That solitary singular opening we are still filling with someone."

"Mea," she says. We shake and she gets me almost as good as Marigold's dad did. She is small but her hands are actually bigger than mine. She smells of watermelon rind.

She looks me in the eyes, and the piercings in her eyebrows, nose, lip, and tongue wink. There's one through her belly button threaded with a hiplace. "I've got to be frank with you, I have a day job and I go to school, but my nights are free and I could sure use the extra cash."

"Let's interview," I say.

"Fabulous," she says.

I tell her to go have a seat in one of the booths at the back of the dining room while I step behind the counter for a clipboard, an application, and a pen. Rick whispers, "Twinkie." Once I have my clipboard, I'm prepared to manage the situation.

I throw my shoulders back, but she takes control: Her day job is at a leather and tattoo shop where she does piercings and assists with minor duties like running tattoo needles through the autoclave and mopping blood off the tile floor. Her mother raised her vegan so she's never eaten a cheeseburger or a slice of pizza. Pure, unadulterated, fair-skinned Mea, an art major at the university. She says all the wrong things: another job, works with blood, no experience in food, never eaten pizza, student.

"How does it feel to have never ate cheese?" I ask.

"It feels pretty anticlimactic," she says.

"How do you mean?"

"I mean, it's like the feeling of never having been pierced for you."

"How do you know I'm not pierced?"

"It's written all over your face."

"You've really never ate cheese? Seriously? I admire the meat thing. That's dynamite, but with cheese, you know, like, the cows need to be milked, man."

"Cheese is gross," she says.

"Cheese is God's apology," I say. "Do you think you're capable of selling a product you don't consume?"

"I think I can handle it," she says. Then she gets up and leaves our interview table. She walks straight into the kitchen. I trail her, puppy-dog-style. Ashley is taking some guy's order. He asks for a pepperoni slice. Ashley turns to heat it, but Mea taps her shoulder. "Mind if I give it a whirl?" Mea asks. "Knock yourself out," Ashley says, fumbles for her lighter in her back pocket, and goes outside to smoke. Mea grabs a spatula, nimbly edges it under the slice, and walks over to the oven, where Rick lowers the oven door and bows at her. I watch this act with jealousy, wanting to be the one who opens the door for Mea. She deposits it, turning to Rick and asking, "Is here all right?"

"Here is just fine," Rick says.

She curtsies to Rick and turns back to me. "Is that approximately what we're concerned with my handling?"

"When you start is tomorrow at five," I say. I hire her in spite of all the wrong things, in spite of the fact that we have ourselves a staff.

"What should I wear?" she says. In the space where the application says, "For Office Use Only," I write, *What should she wer?*

"I'll get you a Piecemeal T-shirt and bandana."

"I've always only dreamed," she says, laughing. Then she walks out of the kitchen, turning back at the door to salute. I look down at the app and find that her name is written as an acronym, M.E.A.

"Wait a sec," I say. "If you want a paycheck we'll need to know your actual name."

"What do you mean?" she says. "Those letters are my name. You can call me Miss A. or Mea. It's your choice."

X

Mea's first shift starts out like this: There's some rugby tournament, and all the rugbyers come in for pasta. Since I'm still training Gutter Boy on pasta, Ashley is teaching Mea Front Girl. My only other experienced Front Girl coughs up blood and has to go home early. And Jafari, in for Greg, didn't prep me enough angel hair for the dinner rush. So on top of it all I'm boiling noodles and trying not to stare at Mea, who is already more competent than Ashley, who needs help doing a simple thing like place-matting a stack of trays.

This ornery bald woman orders a Diet Coke but Ashley pours Coke. Figuring no one knows the difference, she serves it anyway and forgets about it. Thirty minutes later the woman faints into the jukebox. She's diabetic and could've croaked, her husband tells me. I give them their money back and two coupons for free garlic rolls and admonish Ashley, who's like, "Yeah, yeah, yeah, I'm sorry, I'm sorry, I'm sorry."

The rush finally dies down a bit. Mea says, "I think I'm getting it," and Ashley says, "Can I take a cigarette break now?" They both go smoke and I watch the front.

The phone rings and Ashley dashes through to answer it. Then she comes and gets me. Her eyes are wide and she's tittering all over the place.

"I need to talk to you in back, dude," she says.

We step outside. "First off, I'm wicked sorry about the frigging Coke thing. Truly. But oh my God, you're not going to believe this."

"What aren't I going to believe?"

"I have to go. I'm afraid I'm going to have to split early."

"I see," I say.

"My sister," she says. "She just called me. She's got to get an abortion and she's all, 'I need you.' She's my sister, When."

"She needs an abortion right now? At eight p.m. in the evening?"

"Okay, I know it sounds weird, but you're going to totally have to trust me on it. When women need abortions, especially little sisters, they require immediate attention, like now, I mean."

My Dead Grandmother Radar is off the charts, but I am not the dickhead manager type. No way. I have looked into the eyes of too many dickhead managers with the same desperation. "You punch out now," I say, in my best Chinese accent.

"Thanks, When," she says. She slips as she runs to the time

clock, steadies herself, then scurries out the door. It's possible, I
think. If she was lying, she has a real gift. Her eyes had a look
of pure surprise.

I assume my stand-in position as Front Girl, which is conve-
nient to Mea. The bartender from the Salty Dog comes through,
followed by Shaka, who is decent enough to drape a shirt over
his shoulders when he enters an establishment, but he doesn't
button it. Peeking out from behind his breast pocket is the corner of the cat's eye, slick with pus.

"What can I do you for?" I say.

"Salad-shaka," he says. "Greekeecheski."

I hook him with a fresh salad, extra calamata.

"Basic training going away party," he says. "Be there or be
somewhere better."

Skordilli swings through and orders a latte with cheesecake
from Uschi. He acts like he's some Godfather. He calls Jafari
from the dish room and they discuss further renovations while
the dishes stack up. They're talking sheet-metal cutouts on all
the patio surfaces, maybe one of those green, plastic, corrugated
roofs. Jafari hangs on against my will. Skordilli has a thing for
the worthless, the removed, the inappropriately stationed. He
tells me, "I like working with people a little bit different. I like
you types. You remind me of myself." The one thing he has in
common with Skinhead Rick: they both hate frat boys.

The Jafari story goes like this: Apparently, one day following the Rainbow Gatherings in the nearby national forest,
Jafari showed up at the restaurant carrying boxes of sculptures
crafted from wood scrap, old floor trim, crates, benches, and
construction debris. Skordilli's first instinct was to boot him
like he booted all the rest of the hippies who emerged from
the forest after the gatherings, but Jafari won him over with
some choice weed and a redesign plan that could be had on the
cheap. Skordilli was stoned and commissioned him to decorate

the restaurant, to give it a "deco, yet bohemian atmosphere."
He gave him space on the roof for his shop. That was nearly six
months ago. He works on something on the roof then brings
it down through the trapdoor into the Naked Woman Poster
Corridor and installs it somewhere. He's turned the whole
place into one of his sculptures—a low-rent Taj Mahal. In
other words, if you're not Jafari or Skordilli stoned, the place
looks like it's falling apart. There are purple-pink archways
and uneven, wooden partitions with stained windows separating the booths. The fence separating the parking lot from the
Chevron is a bright collage with a chain of words stretching
its entire length: *Peace, Sun, Happy, Day, Friend, Dog, Nice, Be,
Wonderful, Smile, Play, Pizza, Understand, Unity, Taste, Nurture,
Piecemeal, Make Food Not War.* He convinced Skordilli to keep
him on as a house artist-dishwasher. He's like thirty-eight and
I'm his boss. He accepts this and built me a magazine rack out
of an old motorcycle rim.

Skordilli finishes his latte and books out of there. I stop him
at the door. I look at my feet and confess the Coke story. He
tells me not to worry. "These things happen to stupid cunts like
that all the time," he says. He puts his hand on my shoulder and
squeezes so hard my hand spasms. "Free garlic rolls?" he says.
"Very astute move."

This and my treatment of Ashley's abortion emergency rein-
vigorates the manager in me. I make Post-it checklists for all the
new people at their respective positions.

Front Girls: Fill up the napkins, clean the soda-fountain
nozzles, wipe down all the surfaces with bleach water, divvy
the tips, put all the leftover slices into the cooler, sweep your
station, punch out, get a beer.

Pasta Dude: Clean everything, put all the leftovers in the
cooler, punch out, drink a beer.

I tell Rick that he can forget about mopping the floor. "I'll be taking care of that duty from here on," I say.

"As your pleasure," he says. He walks back and forth through the kitchen and mutters, "Hippie suck" every time he passes Jafari at the dish sink.

Jafari says, "This hippie suck is going on a twelve-hour shift so what?"

After everyone's on the back patio, I meander through the restaurant with the yellow mop bucket, mop, then empty the bucket into the drain behind the restaurant and hose it down. I'm as careful about keeping this bucket bright yellow as I am about keeping the floor spotless. Day crew leaves it full of filthy water and covered in grime, and I polish it back to its like-new state. *Dirt dont clean*, I write on a trusty Post-it.

The new Pasta Dude asks us to call him Gutter Boy to his face—what we already call him behind his back. Most people wear goatees to hide their soft chins, his is designed to emphasize it. Rather than break at the chin line, he grows the beard down to a point just above his Adam's apple and sharpens both sides. Whenever he stands out back to smoke, the lizards come out of their cracks in the ceiling and push out their throats. His skin is scaly. He seems comfortable among them.

Which is why I flinch when I finish my mopping routine and join the crew out back, where I catch him running his marinara-stained paw over Mea's belly. I had taken extra-special care on the floor, wanting to impress her. He ruins my night. I find myself wishing they'd all just leave. I like it best at Piecemeal when it's dark, closed, and I'm here by myself. I come here sometimes after a night out, have a slice and some beer. If I'm really tired I sleep for a little while on the prep table. It's so peaceful, everything shiny and clean, except for the dish sink, which Jafari never Ajaxes. I leave the lights off and stand at the Front Girl station looking out on the main street. No one can see me in there, in the dark, no one would ever expect me. It feels like the place is mine. I want to protect it.

"Miss A.," I say to Mea, Gutter Boy's orange fingertips tucked in below her jean line. "Your first night then. Strong reaction?"

"It's not nearly as exciting as putting holes in people," she says, then orders Gutter Boy to retrieve her another cold one and he scurries. I told him to scrape the dried wheat noodles off the steamer five times tonight. He stared at me unblinking, and did nothing.

"It's not?" I say.

"You seem like my kind of people, Thinfinger. But I wouldn't say I enjoy this restaurant work," she says, and breaks my heart.

Skinhead Rick is in a good mood: he wants to celebrate the first Desert Storm ground battle in Saudi Arabia. "Come sit down, Hippie suck," Rick says. "Our people are going to the mat for you."

Jafari is standing in the fountain again. The Legos are gone. He's found a large tire, not quite big enough for a tractor but oversized for a big truck. He's twisting Phillips-head screws into the treads with a flat-head screwdriver, looking upset. "It's not working," he says. He plods out of the fountain, slaps the screwdriver on the table, and takes the beer Rick arranged for him. Rick raises a toast: "If I didn't have my felony record I'd be over there with you, my brothers." He nods at the sky. No one clinks his glass but everyone drinks. Gutter Boy fills up the table with little mounds of the roofie-blow mixture, and he and Mea fondle each other in the corner.

When I wake up the next morning, I've got a feeling I lost the motorized longboard. It is a strong feeling, one to be trusted.

The sun is in the window where it always is. My legs are knotted into the stale sheets. I am once again polka-dotted with scribbled-on yellow Post-its. So all is normal.

Then the phone rings. And here's the thing: No one calls me. Definitely no one calls me before the Florida sun clears the top of my window.

I remove a Post-it from my elbow. It reads, *DONT PICK UP*. A thick hair antennas off the note. I try to make sense of this: Maybe Marigold called last night and, no doubt pissed at my lack of sympathy for her broken back, told me she'd call again in the morning when I'm less belligerent. That could result in my affixing this note to my elbow before passing out. That could result in her calling way too early this morning to harangue me for my drunken lack of sympathy. Song title: *Its Likely To Be The Most Likely Explanation*.

I slip into the living room before the pickup ring, tiptoeing, and snatch the power cord out of the answering machine. Marigold's skulls, dozens of them, atop every surface throughout the living room, stare at me with their clear marble eyes. No matter where I stand in the house they're watching me. My latest morning ritual: I flip them all off.

There is a pizza box on the coffee table, but the box fold on this one—it's not right. Maybe I'll call a box-fold meeting. Or I'll have to get after someone about the box-fold technique, likely Ashley. I fear the girl is just not working out.

I observe an unofficial moment of silence for the motorized longboard, but—something like one month!—it ranks up there with the things I've kept surprisingly long, like that wallet on a chain that somehow, despite the chain's efforts, still got away from me.

I read another Post-it. This one says, *Prep dawg, occasional sacrifice*. And like that my own question is answered. Who would be calling me in the morning? Skordilli, of course. Boss. Restaurant Owner. And you don't want to not answer when he's trying to get ahold of you. Just last week he chased a frat boy out of the restaurant for spitting on the jukebox. Skordilli ran right out of his shoes, the ones with specially rubberized treads engineered specifically for nonslip traction on restaurant kitchen floors. When he caught the guy he sock-foot drop-kicked his head into the dumpster. The ambulance and police all acted like it was some freak accident, that this guy's head found its way into the side of the dumpster. Skordilli, Local Business Owner, has his ways.

He told me that with my new station, Night Manager, I would sometimes have to sacrifice. I would sometimes—if one of the Prep Dogs overslept or quit last minute—have to come check in the produce early morn. He brought me in one prep shift last week to meet the Produce Pecker and to see his game, how he buried the brown heads of lettuce at the bottom, the soft tomatoes in the middle, the moldy zucchini in the vertical rows. Marigold knows I sleep days anyway.

I truck to the phone. I pick it up and try to sound awake.

"Prepared for duty," I say.

"Rip me off? I'm not the bad guy here. I'm the local business owner." Skordilli's waxing postal. "The local business owner helps out you scumbags."

"Bossman," I say. "They feeding us rotten eggplant again?"

"We have new troubles this day. What'd you count last night?"

I got the feeling I've lost something besides the motorized longboard. And I lose a lot, but one thing I don't forget, ever, is the exact total of the night's drawers. "Two thousand fifty-six dollars and thirty-six cents," I say.

"Cleaned out," he says. "Gone. The all of it." My memory of the night is nothing except one of those video stills, I can't see forward from or behind the moment. This one's a fuzzy picture and my head screams BC Powder but I can barely make the image out: me and Jafari, of all people, just the two of us, me and the hippie handyman, amid a cluster of beer bottles in the office, and directly between us the night's drawers. I can't recall whether or not I put the money away, whether we cleaned up the bottles, how I got home and knotted into the stale sheets. Did I even lock the back door? "You locked up, Thinfinger? You locked up my restaurant, right?"

"There's the trapdoor in the roof," I say. Jafari comes in and out of the building through it. "I locked up, but there's the trapdoor in the roof."

"That hippie doesn't seal the trapdoor?" Skordilli shouts. "Canker!"

"I locked up," I say.

"Had to be bone-in-his-nose. Had to be."

"It had to be," I say. "Why don't I come down there in a little bit?"

"Why don't you come down now?"

I shower and keep thinking I can't believe that Greg would come back and rob the place. I come out of the shower hungry, starving for the only thing I starve for these days: pizza, my pizza, Piecemeal pizza. The Piecemeal pizza is the finest thing. I consume and consume it. That will make things right.

But when I skank out of the bathroom, beelining for the pizza box on the coffee table, I see that Left has got the same idea. He is circling, stupid big-dog-style, but he goes overballistic. His nose knocks the pizza box to the floor and what spills out is not the pizza of the gods. It is not my familiar salvation. It is stacks of cash, some of it bound properly in one-hundred-dollar increments by the all-too-familiar Piecemeal twisties, some of it loose.

Left sniffs it and looks at me with very confused eyes.

STRATEGICAL
STRATEGY

There is a moment when I think
about bringing the cash to Skordilli and Dr. Bob and explaining the situation, but it is only a moment. They would pull my
teeth out in the parking lot. I gather the stacks of cash, cram
it back into the pizza box, which is falling apart because of its
awful fold, and set it underneath a monkey skull in the living
room. I climb on the Haro with the kinky triangular frame and
cruise to Piecemeal, a faint hope alive that, like the Haro, the
motorized longboard will find its way back to me.

The Rob isn't part of my economic warfare. The economic
warfare concerned getting what I and all kitchen employees
deserve. Piecemeal is actually paying me above minimum. I
am entrusted. Skordilli always kicks me bonuses. I am using
the place to my own benefit. Sure. Everyone is. All the Front
Girls dole out freebies to their prospective boyfriends, and I
don't blink an eye at that. The Rob must have been an accident,
an obscene mistake, one I'll get by on only if I am lucky. It's

one thing to lift a twenty out of the doctored drawers at the end of a shift, to double the daily bonus, to funnel fifteen or twenty free pies to acquaintances, barkeeps, and pretty girls. It's another to wholesale rob the joint, an establishment you treat as your own.

But I am lucky. Skordilli has already convicted Greg, soundly and surely. I show up and find Skordilli in the office grinding his knuckles into the wall. The black-box door is wide open. Inside, the empty drawers and the nightly figures on my Post-its, in my handwriting. Now I just have to fill in the story. A creepy untrustworthy witch to begin with, one who had all the keys to the place, knew the comings and goings, the combination to the black box, and now had a revenge motive for robbing the place.

I know the restaurant better than Skordilli does. I know its rhythms and hooks. I take a broom and walk him through the Prep Dogs' Naked Woman Poster Corridor to the trapdoor in the roof. I pop it open with the broom handle and pawn this one off on Jafari: "The hippie doesn't seal the trapdoor," I say.

"He no longer works on our roof," he says. "Let's put it that way."

"Do we call the police?" I say.

"We handle certain matters in house," he says. He's standing very close to me, closer than ever, and he's tall, so his knees press into my thighs. His hair is cut close and spiky, a jarhead cut, and he looks tough for an old guy—athletic, square shoulders. I slump in his presence. He runs the steps at the football stadium twice a week. He looks down his long horse face at me. I take this to mean he's not comfortable with the idea of any law enforcement getting into the books.

Even though I don't know what exactly went on, I'm trying not to show what I don't know, remembering the convincing resolve in Ashley's eyes when she made up her sister's-emergency-abortion-support excuse: a technique I can learn from.

I climb the storage cabinet, which puts me in reach of the trapdoor. I poke my head through the Piecemeal ceiling. I plant my hands on the sandpapery ceiling tiles and push myself up. Skordilli follows. We are there on the flat roof, watching the traffic go by on Thirteenth. Jafari's workshop is a mess of products and gadgets, scraps and pieces of things, spools of wires, and table legs, all arranged around puddles. I wonder how he got all the shit up here. There's a sleeping bag under a little overhang with a clump of hair at the top. I walk Skordilli over to the back corner and show him how easy it is to shimmy down the wide steel gutter. I get to the bottom, step off, hold out my palms like it's plain, then shimmy back up.

Skordilli kicks Jafari's sleeping bag, and the hippie grunts, rolls over.

Skordilli and I walk back to the trapdoor.

"It's crystal clear to me now," he says. "We need to clamp down on our business around here."

"Agreed," I say. "I'm right there with you."

When I think back to the run-up of this whole thing, it's like, how could I have planned it any better? Only, of course, I didn't plan it. Like most important things in my life, I don't even remember it.

X

Because I steal nothing that day, my day off, I return home still hungry. It is inconceivable to spend the stolen money on something as insignificant as food. I will have to get rid of it, but there are bigger plans in store, designed for greater effect.

I've taken to stashing spare slices in the freezer at home. I'm on a mission for colder and colder pizza. I grab one now and accidentally knock over a stack of ice cube trays, behind which is a sausage, a beast.

I can handle this kind of thing at work, where it's just part of the job. But in my own freezer? I can't take my eyes off the thing. Why is it here? My appetite gone, I call Long Island for another tirade.

She answers and I let into her: "Haven't we talked about the issue of sausage in the house?"

"Is there sausage in the house?"

"That's another thing, why the freezer? That makes no sense."

"It keeps better. That you should know, Ovenman."

"Marigold, I believe I have related to you the story of the Hot Dog Bucket. At the Barbie-Q, after I hacked all the fat scraps off of everything, I scraped it into a hole draining to the Hot Dog Bucket. My boss used to spit his dip juice in there."

"Excuse me for enjoying the sensual pleasures in life."

"Sensual pleasures?" I said. "What sensual pleasures? It's liquid scrap meat sewn into guts."

"When," she says, "have you ever even zipped your own dick up in your zipper?"

"Many times," I say. "Many goddamn times."

"You know, you want me to be all punk rock, but then you don't want me to eat sausage. Sausage is very punk rock."

"Oh no, I don't buy that," I say. "Fishing is punk rock. Fishing, velocity, and girls."

"Good, I'm at least one of those," she says. "So get ready. I'm coming home."

"Oh," I say. "When?"

"Tomorrow."

"Why didn't you say so earlier?"

"Surprise, When, surprise."

Instead of eating, I clean. There are still some Marigold specks on the toilet seat. She has been gone weeks, and still. Whatever I have done, I have made good on my plan to steal the big-leagues scraper from Piecemeal and I go retrieve it from the Quest pack and the bleach from the kitchen. I splash bleach onto the specks, then I go after them aggro with the scraper. They don't yield at first, like hardened spots of concrete. Eventually they pop off and into the toilet water. When I am done, I am in tears from the bleach. I kick Left out of the empty room. Marigold's clothes—frilly blouses and skirts that are neither revealing nor long enough to drag on the ground—decorate the floor. I Windex the windows and scrub the floor in there. I have stolen special cloths and sponges and mop heads as well as detergents and bleach from Piecemeal.

When Left attacks the front door, I sense another letter from Biodad has come. This one encourages me to live my dreams. He is living his dream, and it is a dream, he writes, that not a lot of people understand, but that never mattered to him. He was able to understand early on that what mattered to him and what mattered to the rest of the populace were very different things. So he embraced his dream, that of becoming a garbage truck driver, and that is what he has spent his life doing, barreling through the early morning streets in a fifteen-thousand-pound truck, ridding the world of its waste.

I see more clearly what I am dealing with now. I take a fresh Post-it and write that my dream has always been to become a garbage truck, a fifteen-thousand-pound truck barreling through the morning. And what does he think about that because maybe our dreams are not so dissimilar, and then I write how much I appreciate him encouraging me toward mine.

Marigold is wrong about my wanting her to be punk rock. I understand that there is a certain kind of woman—the untouchable girls from the Hardback, Mea, Jenny Raygun—

that I just can't handle, as much as I might want to. They are too much like me. Would I like if she didn't sing in a gay Top 40 cover band? Yes. Would I appreciate her occasionally wearing a leather skirt as opposed to a flowered sundress? You bet. And her skulls are a nice touch. Why not just a little more of that is all I'm saying?

She doesn't get it, just thinks I'm harassing her. So there is reparation to be made. And when buying a top-of-the line bed with a pizza box full of stolen money, there is only one sensible accomplice. While I wait for Blaise, I remove the monkey skull from the top of the box and count. I have never in my life had so much money. I will be rid of it as quickly and efficiently as possible.

"Check it," Blaise says, as he walks in. "Skatepark funding approved. We break ground this weekend."

"Congrats, man," I say. "You're really doing it."

He throws in a Slayer tape and we watch Discovery, *The Search for the Tasmanian Tiger*, which has a double-hinged jaw and is supposed to be extinct. Our way is to watch the television with the sound down and the stereo cranked. The researchers encounter many Tasmanian devils and other striped marsupials but no tiger. It occurs to me that probably the skull of one of these animals is somewhere in this room.

After a while Blaise says, "Thin, the set square enough for you?"

I realize I'm tracing the square outline of the TV with my finger. I clamp my hands in my lap. "Brain flow lame toe," I sing. "Uh oh here we go / Fly high cruise by / As I let this feeling grow."

"What?" he says.

"What what?"

"*What* feeling to grow?"

"Probably the feeling of regret," I say. "Or the impending

feeling of impending regret. I leave that to my fellow musi-
cians to interpret."

Blaise doesn't know what it means either. He thinks for a
while. He plays some air guitar over the stereo cranking and lip-
syncs. "Like sanity or revolution?" he asks. He thinks for another
minute. "It'll fit perfect with this new one we just got going."

Then he high-fives me.

In celebration we rake the leaves in the backyard into the
fire pit and set them ablaze. We crowbar some palettes from
the shed and stack them over the leaves. He douses the pile in
lighter fluid and throws on a match. We back up to the house.
Left does counterclockwise circles around it, barking. Blaise
readies the hose.

"We have a mission this day, my friend," I say.

"Let me guess, you're finally ready to burn the Ghia? I'll
push it around."

"Are you nuts? That car is a classic. And as far as I know, it
still runs." I go inside and get the pizza box, set it on the porch
steps, and flip the lid. "This is our mission," I say. Blaise drops
the hose onto his shoe.

He reaches out cautiously for one of the Piecemeal twistied
stacks, like it might bite. He counts.

"We have the park funding, dude. The city's paying for that.
With this, we can acquire some top-quality rattlesnakes."

"I can't do that. I'm sorry."

"That Biodad send it?"

"That guy just sends lies. I've robbed my own restaurant.
I did not intend to, and I don't remember doing so, but it
seems to be done. There's no going back on that. Another sap
has taken the blame, so I'm clear." I tell him the whole deal.
I tell him about Greg and how he's the perfect fall guy and
how Jafari's roof workshop gave me the breaking-and-entering
excuse I needed.

"You robbed your own restaurant? Like, as in really robbed it and not just pilfered the fuck out of the joint?"

"That appears to be the case."

"Do you think that's a smart idea?"

"Sometimes, even when I'm stealing the smaller stuff, I think I'm stealing because I want to get caught. But I don't want to get caught. So why do I sometimes think that?"

"Who wants to get caught?"

"Maybe there are some limits to be tested. In a way, it's like Robin Hood."

"No one wants to get caught. That's stupid."

"Skordilli is rich and I am poor. And now I'm working on ways to rectify some areas of my life."

"Marigold?"

"Marigold."

"You know what I think."

"I know what you think."

"A sweet girl, cute, but too sober, loopy, not built for our world."

People begin stopping in the street because the fire is singeing the leaves of a dogwood. Blaise picks the hose up again. He sprays a light mist over the flames. We don't want anyone to call the fire department. We are not on good terms with them.

"I know what you think," I say.

"And the public welfare system of our fair country may never forgive you," he says.

"She returns tomorrow. I aim to purchase a good bed for her broke back. I'll get her off the couch and into something comfy, her own space. Women like to feel taken care of and what makes one feel more taken care of than a nest?"

"This is your strategical strategy?"

"I at least owe her a good bed, if nothing else."

"We could partake a load of beer."

"Piecemeal's got all the beer we could ever need."

"You promise?" he says.

"Promise," I say.

We hose down the fire and cut back through the house in time to catch a glimpse of what may be the last living Tasmanian tiger. We didn't expect this. It looks like a cross between a striped fox and a kangaroo, with a thin mouth like a possum's. I glance at the skulls and spot one that just might be it.

We cruise in Blaise's van to the bank and I convert to big bills. I tell the bed salesman that I want the high-end Sealy Posturepedics, the kind they bounce bowling balls off of on TV. Blaise says that those are the Simmons Beautyrests. The salesman takes a hard look at me and Blaise, then leads us across the showroom floor.

"It's all about spring count," Blaise says.

"Your buddy knows beds," the sales guy says.

At Blaise's direction, I order up the queen in Summerside Plush.

"This one?" the salesman says to us, surprised.

"I'll be needing a canopy as well," I tell him. Blaise goes to investigate light fixtures and I follow the salesman a few showrooms over, where I select an oak frame with a canopy and Mombasa netting.

"This one," I say, "also."

He has a douche-bag mustache. He's still looking at me like, "Come on, jerk-off," so I pull out the big bills and he gets all apologetic. He goes on to describe his process, how he starts people off in moderately priced showrooms and the goal is to work them up to where I started. He asks if we're interested in going with him, sometime, to a bar that has phones on all the tables.

"Negatory," I say.

At the checkout he hands me the "Important Safety Messages from the Sleep Products Safety Council" pamphlet and goes over the Full Cycle Rotation/Turning instructions and the limited warranty. Then I start to get nervous and giddy while counting out the hundreds and some guys in back supports, obviously confused as to how someone like me is buying such a bed, load it into Blaise's van.

Blaise wants to use the twenty or so dollars left over for beer. I make him drive by the Hare Krishna house and leave the donation in their mailbox. I don't really care for the Krishnas, but I have had my fair share of the free lunch they serve on campus and one thing I'm not doing is spending it on something I want, or on Blaise for that matter. When we get home we hurry the bed inside so it doesn't get wet. The Florida rains dump without warning. It's clear skies one minute and then a detonation of grape-sized droplets, a burst of rain that catches us halfway between Blaise's van and the house. We haul it into the empty room. We use his tools to put the canopy and frame together, then hoist the box spring and mattress into place. I peel Marigold's covers off the couch and fit them around the Summerside Plush. Ready and waiting.

Tremendous
torrendous
stupendous
hazardous

We arrive at Shaka's sayonara party and his dad meets us on the patio. He hugs Blaise and pats my head. Shaka's dad is covered in tribal tattoos. They're pitch black. Mine are green. His are vivid. Mine are blotchy. His were done by a world-renowned fakir. Mine were done by a coked-up skinhead in a double-wide. Shaka's dad is cool, but whenever his gaze falls to my arms he gets this sorry-for-you look. There's my problem: Among normal people, I'm a tattooed freak. Among tattooed freaks, I'm shit-inked—a serious defect, worse than if I wore Polos.

We arrive midjam and gather in the band room. I grab the microphone and don't let go, so I'm picked up as singer. Takes me a minute to catch the groove. It's a little hippie but so what. When I get it, I scream and pogo my head into the room's load-bearing crossbar. I hit the floor but don't slip out of the groove. I'm singing off my memorized Post-its as I climb up off the floor:

Give me a beer
I only bestow
One single vow
That I hold dear

I live by one rule:
Do what must be done
To keep my homey ass out of prison

I'd rather be
Impaled
No fucking fee
Just don't wanna go to jail

In my life
Take my wife
Or my son
If I had either one

I riff them in various formations to about three songs, until Shaka's dad stops and says, "Hey, When, can you go fill us up beers?" It's kind of abrupt, but I guess we're taking a break. And Shaka's dad is one of the oldest rockers on the scene. He called in a favor to get Wormdevil booked on Wednesday nights at the Hardback. So you do what he says. They shut the soundproof door behind me. It locks.

I round up all the cups and head out to the keg while they start up again, Shaka's dad singing. I return, fumbling eight tumblers of keg beer. I kick the door once but they can't hear me. I kick again, drop a tumbler of beer. Nothing. I wait for an intermission between songs and kick some more before Shaka's dad yells to leave the beers and quit kicking the fucking door.

I sit alone by the pool for an hour, consuming their product, until they're done.

When Shaka comes out, as a kind of apology he invites me to play Ping-Pong even though we both know he'll spank me. He spanks me. But I get my first good look at the cat's eye since the night the war started. It looks fresher than when he did it. It's so gnarly it doesn't look real.

We stand in a circle by the pool and smoke something Shaka brings out and then smoke something his dad brings out.

"Why'd you do this, Stephan?" his dad says.

"It gives me power," he says, "to see from my titty." He head butts Blaise. "Seriously," he says. "It's some shamanistic shaka shit."

The lines of the brand run a half-inch deep, red and oozing. He stands tall, like he always stands, but something about him cringes. His frame looks shocked. I figure he's scared. I never saw Shaka like that.

"Not your little brand," his dad says. "Why are you going over there?"

"To get me my war on," he says. "I'm worried only that I might miss it."

Shaka grabs a bottle of vodka and dives into the pool. When he comes up he climbs onto a blue float. He unscrews the vodka cap with his teeth and sips as he floats to the edge. He holds out one arm, says, "Toss me a light." Blaise tosses him a lighter. He snatches it out of midair. He kicks his feet a little, pushes off the side of the pool so that he floats to the middle. He upturns the bottle on his chest, pouring vodka into the deep ravines of the cat's eye until they run like riverbeds. He flicks the lighter near his heart, touches the flame to the cat's eye, and it catches. The humidity makes everything slow. He's splayed there for what seems like infinity, a flaming feline eye looking skyward from his chest, before he rolls over into the pool with a swoosh and a puff of smoke.

X

I'm awakened by the phone ringing. The sound makes my stomach hurt. I have to wonder if I did it again. But it's only Dr. Bob calling me in because the Prep Dogs didn't show. "Hurry it up," he says.

I hang up thinking this is not right, scramble out the door without brushing my teeth or changing into a clean Piecemeal T-shirt. The feeling persists when I unlock the back door to Piecemeal and see no one, not even Dr. Bob. Normally the Piecemeal kitchen is a mass of bodies and water, babble and gunk. This morning the place is dry, empty, the mice scatter at the crash of the steel door. There's one Front Girl I don't know bleaching the soda machine nozzles. I tear apart fifty heads of lettuce (Skordilli's voice in my head: "When you cut the lettuce with a knife, it browns. You've got to tear it with your hands, put those thin, thin fingers to work"), crisp them in an ice bath, and store them in bus tubs for the day. I drizzle olive oil into the Cuisinart for the Caesar, all over the anchovy paste, emulsifying. I shred boxes and boxes of mozzarella. I bow before the marinara pot, then mix without consulting the recipe even once, without measuring, sugar, salt, oregano, basil, and two cans of sauce, one can of paste. Find the lowest spot on the oven, where the gas is just a flicker, and slow-cook that shit.

I don't hear him come in, but when I return to the prep room, Dr. Bob steps out of the shadows in the Naked Woman Poster Corridor, where he might have been the whole time.

"There are only four words in the English language that end in 'dous,' Thinfinger," he says. "Tremendous, horrendous, stupendous, and hazardous." He reaches for my face, pulls my jaw open, and tilts my head up to the light. "How's that cap on the bicuspid?" He pushes on my tooth with his milk-white finger, wedging me against the counter with his belly. His finger tastes like chalk. He pushes on the tooth again.

He laughs a karate-chop kind of laugh. "It looks good." He lets me go. "It's very good work."

"Now tell me about our situation?" he says, sitting on the prep table.

"I've prepped most things already. I need to whip up a fifty-pound dough ball."

"Not that situation," he says. "We have confidence in you in that respect."

"You mean our Greg problem?"

"Always better to square things away multiple times, ensures clearer understandings. Skordilli told me, I just want to hear it from you."

I tell him the same story I'd told Skordilli, trying to seem sure, but not oversure. It's strange, this business: Dr. Bob opening up the place, asking me the same questions Skordilli had. I tell myself, Be ready to run.

"Sounds solid," he says. "You're our guy, When, but that's a few bucks we're out." He roughs up my hair. "Now come with me. The health inspector's coming, and I'm going to need your help."

I wondered why we'd had a recent visit from the Sysco guy. Apparently, he comes only in preface to the health inspector. He brings dish soap and cleaning chemicals, paper towels, those "Employees Must Wash Hands Before Returning to Work" signs, scouring pads—all the things that customers or employees steal within a week.

I run to the bathroom and swish dish soap to kill the remnants of Shaka's shipping-off party from my breath. The bathroom, which we call The Hague, is destroyed, meaning Jafari forgot to clean it last night. The room itself is a six-foot-by-six-foot brick box, with no windows. You turn on the light by pulling a too-short metal chain descending from the lightbulb and then the lightbulb flickers like in horror movies. The walls are covered in drip stains of various colors and, because of the Florida humidity, there's always a light cover of condensation on every surface. I invoke a trick my mom taught me long ago, when she was teaching me to clean bathrooms. Mom's trick for making a dirty bathroom look clean: Windex the mirror. The idea is, if you can see yourself clearly, you don't notice how filthy it is around you, because there are few really clean mirrors in this world. When you Windex-clean a mirror, you create a special moment for people. Even if they look bad, as most people do in The Hague, they'll appreciate the clarity.

So I take a dry rag and wipe the humidity off the mirror. You have all of about ten seconds before it forms again, and in that ten seconds I Windex the mirror and, while I'm at it, the faucet and the toilet flusher. When I come out, the health inspector, a small woman with black hair, is standing there with Dr. Bob.

"Our manager, Monsieur Thinfinger," he says.

"Pleased to see your help here so early," she says.

"I'm pleased to be here," I say.

As I follow them through the kitchen, which is really, aside from the floor, a disgrace, I understand Dr. Bob's utility: He keeps Piecemeal free of health-code violations like he's got The Force. When she starts writing us up because the sauce in the coolers is fifty-two degrees when it's supposed to be forty-two, Dr. Bob suggests that something might be wrong with her thermometer and she admits, "True, that is possible." When she says that the morning set-up Front Girl needs her hair tied back, Dr. Bob tells her that that's all thoroughly taken care of and she says, "Check. That's all taken care of." She notes that the dead crow is still in the third grease bin and all the grease bins appear to be full as well as not changed in some time. "Appearances can be deceiving," Dr. Bob says. "We just fill them up on a regular basis and that crow, that's not the crow you saw last time, that's a new dead crow. They can't keep themselves away from that grease. Check." Using the barrel lid he pushes the crow into the grease, like he's trying to make it disappear. It goes under for a moment, then bobs back to the surface. Dr. Bob shrugs. After the inspection, he offers her pizza, a fresh morning slice, and she politely declines. "Thanks, but I never confuse work with pleasure," she says with a look on her face that I know very well, one that says she's about to puke.

We truck back through the Naked Woman Poster Corridor and Dr. Bob hands her a bonus of her own. She departs and he hangs his heavy arm around my shoulder. He points up to the hole in the ceiling, which he has nailed shut from the inside. "Sometimes it's as easy as a few sharp nails and a hammer to take care of things," he says. "Sometimes it's easier than that."

As I walk out the back door, a four-cylinder engine head misses me by inches and crashes to the ground, nicking the curb. I look up and Jafarl is standing on the roof holding a ficus tree. "Oh, shit, sorry, man. I didn't know anyone was here. Hey, can you reach this for me?" He lowers the tree by its branches and I catch it by the pot. I set it down on the curb next to the engine head.

"Good thing you didn't clip the health inspector," I say.

"I'm in serious heat for this roof thing, man," he says. "Thought I was homeless again. Now I've got this." He points to the parking lot, and for the first time I notice a turquoise Westfalia van on blocks in the corner, by the dumpster. "My new workshop slash living quarters."

He shimmies the gutter. I carry the ficus and he carries the engine head. He's wearing baggy overalls with flip-flops and no T-shirt, the same thing he always wears. The hems of the overalls are damp.

He gives me the grand tour. Where the sliding door should be, a purple curtain has been hung. And inside there's a small table and two dining room chairs welded to the floor. The front seats have been converted into his sleeping bag platform and the camper top stores his junk. He sets the ficus down beside the table.

"Should you ever have any important customers looking for a private table, feel free to use this, after you make a reservation, of course."

We sit down across from each other at his table for two. I don't like the position I'm in, laying on the bullshit with Jafari. But right now, I need him. He's the last one I remember seeing before the robbery. There's this image in my head, one of those video still frames, me and him standing in the office. But nothing more, before or after.

"How's the tire idea for the fountain pedestal?"

"The tire didn't work out, wouldn't hold. The damn fish are always pregnant and slow and I couldn't stand the thought of crushed pregnant fish. No, that fountain pedestal is important, and I'm going to have to wait on some true inspiration."

"Look, I want to ask you a question. Would you have any idea why I woke up to something weird the morning after the rob?"

"I don't follow you, jockey."

"Well, there was this pizza box when I woke up, but it contained a nonpizzalike substance, a very peculiar type of thing."

"Can you describe the substance?"

"Well, it was very nonpizzaey, almost a, like, rectangular, rather than triangular product. You know anything about anything like that?"

"The morning after the restaurant was supposedly robbed by the Gregosaur?"

"What do you mean supposedly?"

He looks at me weirder than he normally does. Jafari's skin on his nose and face is rough, like someone buffed it with sandpaper. His eyes are dark around the edges, at the eyelids and underneath, like they're rotting. I can't tell if he's reading me or trying to sort something out in his own head. He takes his foot out of a flip-flop and scrapes the bottom on the edge of the table, props his elbow on his knee.

"Thin, this whole place has eyes and ears and noses and mouths. I'm like"—he gestures toward the purple curtain, and I see the outline of someone standing there—"I'm like, bow wow, bow wow how." We hear the clanking of metal under a footstep.

"True dat," I say.

"Word is bond," he says. He winks at me and nods.

Dr. Bob moves the curtain aside and looks around. His voice suddenly fills the van like a bass kick: "What a pad."

"Thank you, bossman," Jafari says. "Appreciation for your admiration."

X

With Jafari's relocation from the roof to the van out back, all his junk becomes way more visible. None of us realized exactly how much shit he had up there. The normally tidy parking lot explodes with it all. He gets as much as he can into the van but there isn't much room with the table-for-two setup. So he stacks his crap around the van in little piles: table legs and chair legs and support beams and fence posts and chicken wire, lots of wire in general, spools of wire, telephone wire, cable wire, electrical wire, trees, crab traps, crates, an old grandfather clock, engine parts, engines . . . He covers it all with sheets of clear plastic that he steals from construction sites so the rains don't ruin everything. But to my eyes, it all looks ruined already anyway, so I wonder why he even bothers.

X

There is a letter from Biodad in the box but the return address says Dan's Specialty Shoes. I know it's him because the same address in Columbus, Ohio, is written underneath. I cram it in my pocket and go to work.

It's February, but Rick has stripped down to his boxers because the Piecemeal kitchen is so hot. He leaves his jean shorts in the office with the grenade. I take the opportunity to tell him about the pasta station. From there you can lean against the cooler doors all night long. I tell him that a breeze from the dish room cuts right through the thin-pies station if he's interested in being Thin Pie Guy. He grunts. He ties on his apron so that it looks like he's not even wearing pants and goes to work on the oven. The fact of the matter is the Ovenman position should be mine.

Instead I'm running around all night planting little sticky cards in all the corners because we've developed a mouse problem. I advocated regular traps, but Skordilli got a deal on the sticky ones. So now the Prep Dogs come in every day to a bunch of panicked mice squirming and struggling to unglue themselves.

As I'm replacing the card in the prep room I come across a little brown one stuck on the trap behind the flour. I don't know what you're supposed to do with them once they're stuck, but I recognize this as my problem, a Manager problem. It makes me feel important, sure, but that doesn't mean I'm glad about having it. Skordilli busts in through the back door shouting my name.

"Hey," I say. "What am I supposed to do with these?" I hold up the blank card with the squirming rodent.

"Oh these are good fun," he says. He snatches the card out of my hand. "Their legs snap right off, like plucking a leaf stem from a tree branch." He pulls one of the mouse's back legs and it squeaks nervously. The leg snaps off, the foot stuck to the trap. Skordilli laughs. "How do you like stealing from my restaurant now, little cutie?"

He tosses the mouse in the garbage. It lands in a reject pasta mari, its face stuck to the card. "Come out here and help me hose this blood off my car," he says, rushing out again. I follow him out back to see what the fuck he's talking about. Dr. Bob is washing his hands off with the hose. I'm always nervous when these two show. It's strange to see them together, absolute opposites except for their height. Dr. Bob is fat and hulking with a round head. Skordilli's head is long and he's skinny. He's got a joint between his lips. I find the spray nozzle and twist it onto the hose. Skordilli trades me the joint for the hose and sprays off the hood. He points at the sky. "Look at those stars," he says. He takes the joint back and gives me the hose.

Dr. Bob opens the back door of the Infiniti and there's two small patches of blood on the white suede seat. "Any idea what will remove that?"

"I think I've got just the thing."

"Good man," he says. "Them blipping to-go pasta bowls you dish out." He winks. Skordilli and Dr. Bob laugh.

I find the specialty surface cleaner without bleach in the dish room, the kind I use for the stool covers at the café, and some wet dish towels. I scrub at the spots on the white suede until they lift away and the white rag is stained brown.

Dr. Bob squeezes the joint between his finger and thumb and tucks what's left into my T-shirt uniform pocket, where it smolders.

"If our witch comes around again, you better call me,"
Skordilli says.

He tosses me a chamois to wipe the hood down, which I do.
He is wearing a trench coat in seventy-five degrees.

"How have things been tonight?" he asks.

The hood is dry but I'm still wiping it. I want to ask if Greg
is alive or how bad they beat him, but it's unclear what is to be
left unspoken. "I'm going after the mice," I say. I figure there
would be more blood if they had killed him.

They stare up at the moon, which is a white smudge behind
gray clouds. "You know," Dr. Bob says, "our father had this
belief that mice will show up anywhere someone is stealing
from you."

"Well, there's not so many of them . . ."

Skordilli flashes me that gummy grin, says, "And we pull
the legs off thieves." Skordilli pops the trunk and hands me a
shoe box. "I almost forgot," he says. I open it. Inside are brown
shoes resembling Hush Puppies. But these are special restaurant shoes. They match his own, brown sheep's leather with the
membranous sole designed to hold fast to the slick tile surface
of the restaurant kitchen floor.

"I can't accept these," I say.

"I insist," he says. "Put them on."

I step out of my Airwalks and tie on these dorky things. I
have never worn shoes other than sneakers. They're stiff.

"Well thank you," I say. "Thank you so much."

"You're untoppleable in those," Skordilli says. They roar off
in the Infiniti.

The joint burns through the inside of my T-shirt pocket and
singes my skin. I fish it out and inhale a last puff, then flick
it into the parking lot. I wander back into the dish room, the
restaurant shoes sticking to the floor tiles like suction cups. The

sound reminds me of Biodad's letter. I take it out of my back pocket and open it up:

> *Dear When, I wanted to tell you about my new enter-*
> *prise. You're the first to know, you know. I'm starting*
> *a specialty shoe store. So many people have extra wide*
> *or extra long feet, myself included, that I know that*
> *it will make an absolute killing. I'm at this moment*
> *patrolling the mall for primary storefront placement.*
> *I need a partner. Did you ever sell footwear? It doesn't*
> *matter one way or the other. We can be a father-son*
> *op. Right now I'm calling it Dan's Specialty Shoes, but*
> *we can go any which way with that. I'm open. There's*
> *already one called Father & Son, but that's a chain.*
> *Ours could be Reunion Shoes. Just an idea. Kick it*
> *around. Ha! Dan*

I do not have siblings and he is not a statistician. Or maybe he is. I look at my feet in the silly shoes. They are of average length and width, perfectly normal-sized nine and a half feet. I crumple the letter and drop it in the trash.

Mea stomps back to tell me the customers up front are asking about "a meeping sound." I hadn't even noticed the mouse's tortured squeaking.

"Aye, aye," I say. I watch her calves, the black ink of her tattoos over her doughlike skin is the exact color of her hair. I pull the sticky card with the mouse out of the garbage, a wedge of tomato is dried to its head. I tug on him a little and he tries to bite me. The squeaking gets louder. There is no saving him. I go outside and submerge the card in the fountain. The guppies huddle at the other side of the pool, away from the little cloud of marinara. I count down five minutes. In this, the quiet of the fountain splash and random bubbles from the drowning mouse, I imagine the pummeling Skordilli and Dr. Bob laid on Greg. I pull the sticky card out and make sure the mouse is dead. I walk across the parking lot, through the drain puddle, and toss the trap into the dumpster.

I wander into the dining room and drink a beer below the new TV Skordilli installed. It doesn't have volume but I read the deaf-people subtitles. The news is on and they're saying something about the war. I bright side: I'm one hundred percent off the hook for the rob. Greg is bleeding somewhere. Yes he is. But, I will not be violating the single solitary provision of my personal philosophy: to not go to jail. The TV says that Saddam has been pumping millions of gallons of crude oil into the Arabian Sea. It's a smooth tactic, I think, and I immediately decide to implement a similar policy: to pump Piecemeal product into the community, no holds barred. It's the one thing I can do to make myself feel better for whatever caliber beating Greg just endured because luck made him the fall guy, because I used him for what he was worth. Up to this moment I have handed out single servings, a beer, a dinner, an occasional whole pie, sure. I have sanctioned the handing out by others of single servings, beer, dinner, an occasional whole pie. Now I get Blaise on the phone and offer up an entire box of sliced pepperoni for pickup. Who likes cheese? Who wants the wholesale sticks of mozzarella only the restaurants get? Come and get them. I am the one who signs it all in, checks it off, controls the inventory. I can say we went through a lot of product. No one keeps track of how much we're supposed to bring in per box of roni, per obscene slab of cheese.

I call up some of Blaise's friends who are always up for a party and ask them how they'd feel about having a keg party tonight.

"Fuck shit up," they say.

I say, "Well, come and get the keg, bitches."

When they show up I take Rick out back and we load a Newcastle into Blaise's friend Ginn's truck and tell them we'll be by later, after our shift. "Don't even think about tapping it until we get there," I say. I sign in the kegs every day, and I sign them out. Tomorrow, I'll forget to mark off that one keg came in. There is no one to say otherwise. I'm their guy.

But being Manager means that while waiting for the shift to end and the Piecemeal-sponsored party to start, after checking the mousetraps and walking through the dining room to nod at customers like four thousand times, I stand inconsequentially in back. Brain, the new Thin Pie Guy, is busy enriching the customers' experience throwing out the thin pies, being his fingertips. I'm the inconsequential one beside him. That's what customers do while they wait. They watch Brain throw pies, or they watch Rick spinning the calzones with my peel technique. They watch as Gutter Boy gingerly garnishes the tops of meatballs with parsley flakes. There is even something to admire in the choreography of the Front Girls, Mea and Ashley—well, in Mea. There's the way she double-spatulas four and five slices at a time from the display trays to the oven—where Rick is waiting dutifully with the door open—and back to the customers' plates.

Spinach
Tomato
Girl

Later, when I'm delightfully sloshed and counting down the drawers, I contemplate the twenty I want to lift out of habit. I could take it, have taken one night after night. I'm not sure why I hesitate now, but something about the look of the bill stops me. Part of me feels like it's one thing to bleed the place dry if it's kegs and pizza and other product, but in our post-rob universe something is out of line about explicitly ganking cash. I look around out of paranoia. No cameras are installed, definitely. That's not the way Skordilli and Dr. Bob operate. What is different if I take one now, versus taking one before The Rob? There is a photo above the black box of Skordilli and Dr. Bob shooting machine guns somewhere in some -vakia or -vinia country. Their constant bonusing me has nothing to do with me. They're buying me off, but I didn't ask for that. I didn't ask for any of it. If you think about it, it's essentially a tip. Treating me like a server, the most looked-down-upon of any employee type in the food industry. The Front

Girl positions are bad enough, and I specifically instruct them
to be as indifferent to customers as they can be. "Sometimes," I
say, "pretend you can't hear them when they order." Is it right
that some dowd who gets dressed and shaves and goes around
kissing ass makes more than the backstage guy who's doing all
the work? People ask me sometimes if I'd ever consider being
a waiter. People—mostly students but when you get down to
it everybody, everybody in the whole world—are always saying, "I'm going to be a waiter, I'm going to be a waiter." And I
say, "So what." Be a whore, and I'm no customer's whore and
no Skordilli's whore. So what if him and Dr. Bob are hooking
me up a little better, it still just barely clears the rent. So what
if they take me under their wing? So what if I rip them off
explicitly or on the down low? That doesn't change the basic
understanding: restaurant employees take what they can get
and Owner has to deal. I take that twenty in the name of Greg
and for all the nonwaiters in the world and for all of us who
are kitchen dogs through and through, and while I'm at it I
take another one in the name of Marigold, who has to put up
with me, and for that lying Biodad somewhere in the Midwest
and especially for my crew—and so what to that.

Mea appears in the office doorway as I pocket the second
twenty.

"Going to this party then?" she says.

"Where's your Gutter Boy?" My voice comes out too crackly,
revealing too much.

"Guttered," she says.

"Record timing."

"He's too hungry. But you didn't answer my question, Night
Manager," she says.

"Putting in a Hardback cameo, then I should be there."

"Me and my girls are going trolling for wang," she says. "We
may show up too, dependingly."

"I'll look for you," I say.

She clicks her tongue ring across her front teeth. "Where'd you get those, that work?" She points at my arms.

I take a look at her tats, dark and shapely, mushrooms and redwoods and skinny tree sprites.

"They're accidents."

"What are they?" she asks. "Raisins?" She inspects my right arm, touches it. "No, let me guess: pillows?"

"I don't know," I say. "They're mine."

"Single needle, pretty awful. You're in the sun a lot I bet."

"You hunting for a raise with all these compliments? I'm not authorized."

"If you wanted to get them covered up, I could get you a deal. The guys at Second Skin work magic with cover-ups, spinning crucifixions into leprechauns. How about adding some texture and shape, call them pepperonis?"

"I don't eat meat," I say, "recently butchered."

"I've never eaten meat," she says. "But pepperonis are cooler than raisins." She runs her finger down my arm. "They have topography, like hives."

"Do you know what that shit is made out of?"

"Everything's made out of something gross depending on how you think about it. And I'm not talking about eating pepperoni, I'm talking about its cool factor."

She takes my hand to her stomach and lays it on a perfectly smooth crook-nosed tree sprite tattooed under a fur coat of blond hairs, her blond stomach hairs.

"Here's a thought," she says. "What you could do is get them blacked out, your whole arms, wrist to shoulder. My boss is submitting black work for a *Tattoo Review* spread. He's looking for someone to get his arms done totally black. You'd be famous."

"Blacked out?" I say.

"You're one surly cool boss," she says, and she winks and turns away. "Namaste."

Brain back-flips into the pit. The band blows if you ask me so I drain King Cobras. One of the slutty-looking untouchable girls leaves the pool table and props herself on the bar beside me. Her head moves side to side, real cool-like, then it stops on me. She says, "The Piecemeal guy."

I turn and get my first ever close-up look at her. A guy like me doesn't approach chicks like her. In fact, I'd always only seen her and her friends as silhouettes, fluttering around the pool table in high-heeled boots and net stockings that stop above the knees, bending over so that skirts suggest asses. But when I look at her for the first time close up I see that I recognize her.

"The spinach-tomato-with-blue-cheese-on-the-side girl," I say. I know people all over town by their quirky lunch or dinner, if they like their slices cold, for instance. I know faces by pasta marinaras, ham and pineapple, ravioli with meatballs, chicken parmesan hold the parmesan.

"Flattering," she says. "My regular order."

"Yes," I say. "But quite an irregular regular. We don't generally prep spinach tomato. So every time you come in we've got to stop everything and make up a whole pie for your one pain-in-the-ass slice."

"Well," she says. "I didn't mean to cause you so much trouble. But—oh wait a second—that's your job."

"See, that's what you've got to realize, Spinach Tomato Girl, in a restaurant certain things come with certain things." I have passed the point in the night when my voice might crackle. I am spinning pure silk. "Burger King has done our industry irreparable damage. Why do you think when you're in a fancy place and you return the meal to the French chef requesting it cooked longer or new sauce or more something or other they get fucking pissed? You're questioning what they know."

"You know," she says. "In German, the verb for 'to know' has two forms: 'kennen' as in meaning to know or be acquainted with people, and 'wissen,' as in to know facts."

"We have two kinds too, 'know' and 'no.' I'm constantly confusing them, but it's as in, '*No*, we don't have any spinach tomato.' We make forty other kinds of pizza, though, that are on the menu right in front of your pretty face. And, Spinach Tomato Girl, loogey is French for what I know is in your food when they return it."

"Pretty," she says.

"Cooks don't do customer-friendly, but yes."

"Are you a cook?"

"I am Ovenman," I say. I get tapped on the shoulder and turn to see Rick standing there with Skinhead Katrina, his new girlfriend, who stands a good foot taller than him and is broad shouldered, built exactly like the Bakers Pride Y-602 double-deck pizza oven. Rick has his arm locked through hers and the look in her eye dares you to fuck with him, like anyone would anyway.

"*I* am Ovenman," Rick says, all smiles, then he grabs a pool cue and goes after some guy who's always up at Piecemeal trying to scam food. I usually give him some for the hell of it and he takes advantage.

"Yes, okay," I say. "He is Ovenman. I just manage."

"I'm Reiny," she says. "Of course continue to call me Spinach Tomato Girl if you want." She holds out her hand to shake. Her fingernails are plain, filed smooth, undecorated. I take her hand and hold on, checking out her icy grip. She reaches across our connected arms for my Cobra and chugs—far better than myself, an admirable distance drinker but can't slam a beer to save my life, can barely manage a shot without gagging—until I release her.

She says, "I heard to work at Piecemeal you have to sleep with the manager."

"That's true," I say. "It's an unfortunate prerequisite."

She makes a sound like *hum*.

"Are you looking for employment?"

"I'm trying to rationalize it," she says. "Is there free pizza *and* sleep with the manager?"

"Tons," I say. "All you can tremble."

I tell her about the party and then we're on our way out the door.

Rick has broken the pool cue over the guy's head and is pulling off his own shirt and here come his swastikas, like moths flashing their wings in predators' faces.

"Come on, slick prick," he's saying.

"Yeah, slick prick," Skinhead Katrina says.

"Hey, party at Tony's," I say to him. "We're sponsoring."

"Wait, where is that?" Rick says, shoving his hand to the guy's chest, balling up most of the front of the guy's T-shirt in his stout fist, and hoisting him into the air. The guy is still dazed from the pool cue. So, while I give Rick directions to Tony's house, he hangs there, eyes wide and confused. Rick's other hand is cocked back in midpunch.

"It's directly behind College Beverage," I say.

"Is that Second and Twelfth?" He lowers the guy so that he's standing on his own again. He immediately bows up at Rick.

"I think. Really just go down University and take a right at College Beverage. I'm not sure of the road."

"I think I know where it is," Rick says. The guy, recovered now, bolts. He ducks out of his shirt, leaves the rag empty in Rick's hand. For a second, Rick can't believe it. The guy runs out the back door of the Hardback and shimmies over the alley

wall onto Main Street with Katrina and Rick fumbling after
him. Rick isn't tall enough to reach the top of the wall. He falls
on his back, cusses, and Katrina boosts him up high enough to
reach, then follows him over.

"Your friends?" Spinach Tomato Girl says, fitting her hand
in mine, this time warmer, with a little bit of grab.

"My colleagues," I say and walk on, with my head high,
leaning into Spinach Tomato Girl to keep from falling over.

X

We ascend this elevated deck, and I introduce her around the
keg—of course they already tapped it—as Spinach Tomato
Girl. I stop on a blurry Jenny Raygun, who is standing beside
me in her low-riding army-green pants, a T-shirt that says, *2
Girls Fucks*, and that purple loop of underwear pulled over
each hip. She'd make a perfect seven-inch cover shot if ever
there's a Wormdevil seven-inch to be made.

She says, "I have something to show you, Thinfinger" and
her voice echoes around my head. Jenny Raygun has always
expressed absolute disdain and a slutty flirtiness toward me. I
usually avoid her when Blaise is not around, but tonight is a
night of triumphs and great volumes of beer on Piecemeal via
me. I leave untouchable Spinach Tomato Girl and follow Jenny
Raygun.

Sometimes you have to guess at what you're doing as you
do it. It's hard to say how exactly it happens. It's not that I
think Jenny Raygun is Spinach Tomato Girl, but I act like she
is. They kind of switch out for me. I trail her purple-harnessed
hips down the steps and into the bathroom. She closes the door
and inserts my hand into a big wet mess in the front of her
pants. She puts her hand down my pants, and then we're on
the floor. We don't say anything and I just push because it's like
fucking a mop.

The house used to be a beauty salon, and I'm reminded of Marigold, the multiple sinks with neck slots, the splintered ends of Jenny Raygun's hair. There's carpet in front of the sinks and a step leading to a shower stall. There is no toilet, just sinks and shower stall and carpet. Jenny Raygun's head is propped against the step to the shower stall in an uncomfortable-look-ing way though she doesn't appear to have any problem. Her face is a strange one, flat, freckled, and there always appears to be something moving underneath her cheeks.

At this angle, the floor is not quite big enough for our entire bodies. We can't fully stretch our knees out. I push, my feet planted against the bathroom door. The effect of fucking Jenny Raygun is a sobering one. The blur around the corners of my vision clears up, more from boredom than excitement. But I don't quit. That would seem rude, and anyway there's a certain momentum in sex. I keep my legs braced against the bathroom door and move only at the hips. The carpet stings my knees.

"This is your one chance at this, Thinfinger," she says.

"Oh, you're one of those talkers."

"I bore easily. But right. I like to see what guys say. Most of them don't say much."

"I'll say anything."

All I feel is wet. I lift up her shirt and put my face in her tits, thinking it may help a little. My lips roam her ordinary single-nippled boobs looking for something surprising. Even the taste of her skin is exactly how I'd have imagined it, like stale bread.

"When I was a kid, my non-Biodad used to pee on my feet in the shower," I say.

"Urine kills funguses," she says.

The sound of urethane wheels on hardwood floor thun-ders overhead, then the unmistakable rat-a-tat of a skateboard

coming down the steps, and then a knock on the door, and
Blaise's voice going, "Thinfinger, you down here somewhere?"

I don't stop and Jenny Raygun's blank face doesn't change.
Blaise cracks the door but my feet are fast. I rise into a push-up,
locking my knees and slamming the door. He pushes again, and
I think he knows. Then I think, Maybe just let him in. After
all, he was the one who was too scared to stop the coked-up
tattooist from crapping all over my arms when I passed out
in the dentist's chair. Maybe that's the reason I'm down here
doing this anyway. Who knows how things would have been
different if he had stepped up that time like he's stepped up
all the rest of his life. Luke wouldn't have kicked me out, and
I wouldn't have had to get my first restaurant job at Maxie's
Better Burgers to pay the rent.

But I don't let him in. "Making larvae," I say.

"Find me outside when you're done. In need of bouncing a
cool plan off you."

We hear him roll outside and pop ollies on the other side of
the shower-stall wall. For some reason, I remember hearing
once that the ollie, the most basic of all skateboard maneuvers,
was originally called the Ollie Pop because of the popping
sound the tail makes. And I remember that it was invented
in Florida by a guy named Alan "Ollie" Gelfand in the late
seventies.

"Blaise had an easy life," she says. "His father got blown
up in Vietnam so the government bought them a big house
and gave them money. Nothing bad has ever happened to him.
That's how he can be like he is."

"I admire Blaise," I say.

"You're the one supposed to do the talking," she says. "What
would your girly girlfriend say if she could see you now?"

"I think this is exactly what she expects of me."

"And why do you do what she expects?"

"I'm crazy about her, but it's the particulars that are giving me trouble."

"Then move on, young son. By the way, I can't feel anything."

"I'm retarded in moving on," I say. "I can't feel anything either."

We stop. We stand up. She says, "All right then." We zip our clothes and wash our hands in the sinks with slots for necks.

"Too bad that broccoli girl wussed out," she says. "Roughage." She cracks the door and peeks around and slips up the steps. I think I hear her say to herself, "I seriously require more drunk fuel."

I try to keep up with her but she's too far ahead. All the soberness I achieved from fucking her drains away. I can still hear Blaise outside, his urethane wheels squealing across the asphalt. I don't want to see him now so I make for the steps and trip over the first one. I go for the Post-it pad but it falls from my hand. I need to clue my morning self in. I reach for the pad, and a leather Harley boot crushes my finger. I look up and it's Mea, standing over me.

"Whirrrrrrrr," she says. "The sound of my trolling motor."

I **wake up on** the sidewalk across the street from my house, my cheek granule-pocked. I sit up and check the Post-it stuck to my palm: *purple panty putanesca*. I bang my head on the sidewalk. I punch my own cheek.

A *Star Wars* storm trooper with a bright orange helmet emerges from the front door of the house. Standing on the sidewalk opposite me, Left runs circles around it before I recognize that it's Marigold, her upper body a white, plastic exoskeleton, her hair dyed the exact color of highway pylon, an impossible orange. It no longer hangs limp and sorry at the sides of her head, but bounces in luscious curls.

"You forgot to meet me," she says. "The airport."

"Welcome," I say. "You're back."

"Yes," she says, "my back." She clomps across the street. I stand to meet her. We hug. She picks the granules out of my cheek as we walk into the house.

There is a contagious calm I get, waking in this condition.

No matter the message on the Post-it, things feel like they will be all right if I can just get some Gatorade and sit down on the couch. People even feel at peace seeing me. It fades fast. Inside, my eye goes right to the tip of a knife blade peeking out from underneath the couch cushion. A lemur skull glares at me from the top of the TV set, or maybe koala.

"What's going on in Left's room?" she says.

"Surprise, toots," I say. "Sealey Posturepedic. Summerside Plush. Get well soon."

"You moved me out of our room?" she says.

"I thought you'd need a good one. It's top of the line."

"I came back to you for this?"

"It's an arrangement, an arrangement for the sake of your body. Have you even looked at it? It's not like you've slept in the so-called 'our room' for months. You've been on the couch, cuddling a baseball bat."

"I looked at everything while you were passed out on the sidewalk."

"It's an awesome bed, pricey too." I pause, notice a physical change in her. She seems to be losing her balance. "Why did you come back?"

"Because you're trying, When," she says. "I stay, and I came back, because you are trying. Even though it may not appear that way, I know that is the case. I know. I need to lie down," she says. She is crumbling, collapsing at the knees. I catch. This is a surprise that she views me as trying. Maybe, but I'm more adept at locating some momentum in a certain direction and going with that.

I steer her to the room that is now her bedroom. It's nothing like I left it. The Summerside Plush is rudely pushed into the corner, one leg of the canopy collapsed so that the Mombasa netting is hung over the bed like fish netting on a dilapidated dock. In the center of the room is some fancy soccer-goal-looking thing with hammock netting stretched across it. She walks in front of me, her back encased in the white plastic, overstraight, like she's constantly falling backward.

"Insurance bought me a special bed, When. It's made by the Stryker company. Their guys came here and set it up. They even picked me up at the airport when I called them. I didn't know what to do with this thing."

"Can you ride it?" I say.

She climbs into the hammock face up and pulls another sling down on top of her. "This is where I'll be needing my roommate's help." She motions toward this crank, which flips her around as I turn it, her body sandwiched between the upper and lower slings. I crank until she is reversed, facedown. She has a *Rolling Stone* on the floor. She's reading an article about Right Said Fred. Left lies down to the left of the magazine.

"For weeks I didn't even move from one of these things. It's the perfect position to read in bed. I'll never go back. When you called me I talked to you from a lying position. Why does it smell like bleach in here?"

"What's the current status of your condition?"

"I'm getting around," she says. "I'm going to snip hair and I'm going to play shows, standing for only short periods at a time. As long as I have the Percocets everything is all right. I just need to sleep in this suspension thing, to not put too much stress on the screw. What's the current status of your condition?"

"I'm good," I say.

"I can see that you're not good."

"Okay, you're right, I'm not good. I'm running into some trouble with the manager side of things."

"You're moving up in the world."

Neither of us has anything to say after this. We both look at my shoes.

"What are those things?" She points at them.

"Special restaurant-grade, nonslip. Your hair is orange."

"Do you like it? It's racy. I'm so immobile I wanted a color that really flies."

I can barely look at her head, but I try to say something nice. "The curls are bigger than skateboard wheels. Bounceworthy."

"Wait," she says. "I need you to fill my prescription. It's on the TV, under the new skull. They make me so tired I can't even speak."

I shut her door. I have to pee but I inspect the toilet rim first. Sparkling. An upshot: it's difficult to retch straight-backed. Then I step into something soft, her panties balled up at the base of the shower, plain white. Something stirs in me at the sight of them. I wrap my hand in some toilet paper and trash them.

X

Blaise rumbles up in his van unannounced as I am heading out on the regular skateboard to the drugstore. The van is spray-painted black, windows included, and covered in stickers that say, *Drunk* and *Angry*. He rolls down the window.

"Hey," he says. "Get in."

What comes to me then is one of those still frames, like the one of me and Jafari in the office the night of The Rob. Only this one I can be certain about: me squirming Jenny Raygun and Blaise pushing on the door. My knees burn.

"I've got to get Marigold something," I say, holding up the prescription.

"I'll drive you. Come on, I need your help."

I hop in the passenger side. Something straightaway is not right. Blaise is wearing jeans, which is weird because it's always the same temperature here: hot. On the corrugated metal floor of the van are a stack of dusty cloth bags and two pitchforks.

He shifts the van into gear and it bucks ahead.

"I didn't see you last night," he says. "After you finished making larvae."

"Smashed," I say. "I was smashed, forgot to pick up Marigold from the airport."

"How'd she like the bed?"

"Not too impressed. She needs a special medical bed. Something like a hammock."

"A hammock," he says. "That's good sleeping."

He pulls into the Eckerd's parking lot and I hop out. I fish the prescription out of my Post-it-clogged pocket and notice a gaping blank, a screaming absence—right next to the brand name is a blank blank labeled *Refills*. Blank. A note for Percocet, a bottle worth about $250 to the people I know. How would anyone know if I filled it in? One refill. The note is written in black ink. I fish out the pen I keep in the Quest pack for Post-it noting, and it just happens to be black too. A sign. I put it against the brick wall and draw a scraggly line in the refills blank, drop it off, and we ride on.

I pick up one of the bags on the floor of Blaise's van. It's basically a pillowcase with a drawstring.

"They belong to the guy next door, a Little League coach."

"Are we hunting pillows?" I say.

"Snakes. We are snake hunting, my friend." Then Blaise stops in the Publix parking lot and says, "Since you wasted all your money on Silly Girl's bed, we have to pull the EBT to buy beer."

Working in a restaurant, I don't buy food. I have never grocery shopped, not in the traditional sense. Blaise is a different story. He doesn't work in restaurants and he doesn't work anywhere. He prints his own *Suckass Loser* and *Drunk* and *Angry* stickers and lives off that government stipend. We both qualify for food stamps. He takes them. I don't.

My mom used to get them, back when they were actual stamps, little fake bills you had to count out while all the people with real money stood behind you staring. Every month we'd go to the offices and wait in long lines to get them. I didn't mind that part; everyone there was in the same boat. It was the actual checkout line at the grocery that sucked. Mom counting out the little tickets and arguing with the cashier whether or not Nutella was an approved food-stamp item. All my years in elementary school I was the last kid in the cafeteria line so no one would see me use my free-lunch card. Restaurant workers don't have this kind of problem.

Nowadays you get an EBT card with a magnetic strip, like an ATM card. That should make checkout less humiliating, but they managed to preserve that part: You can't use the regular ATM card reader. They installed this obscene brown box so everyone knows.

When we pull the EBT we are not looking for food or anything else we want. We stalk the grocery store aisles looking for items with the deepest discount. It doesn't matter what they are. We'll be leaving them in the cart, in the parking lot. What we have planned all along is to bring Blaise's card in later to receive the discount, which is the only way to get cash from government assistance. Today the big item is Marshmallow Fluff, in the sixteen-ounce size, which normally goes for $5.99 but is on sale with the Publix Preferred Shopper card for $1.99. That is the kind of differential we're after. We take ten jars of that and head for checkout.

I catch the expression on the face of the dude behind us when Blaise swipes the EBT. It is a mixture of interest and pity and pride that I've seen a million times. The checkout lady asks for the Publix Preferred Shopper card. Blaise says, "Darn, I left that thing at home. Gosh." He pats his pockets all around. The dude behind us offers his, which he keeps on a keychain. Blaise declines. The dude insists. Blaise says that really wouldn't be appropriate. Dude keeps on. "I don't want your charity, pal," Blaise says. "Thanks."

"Why not save a few tax dollars?" the dude says.

He's bigger than me and Blaise put together, so I pull wig-out: "I am Satan, motherfucker!" I say. "I will eat your beak off."

The checkout girl smiles. She has a giant tattoo of a mosquito drinking from her jugular. The dude backs up, looks at me, then switches to another register.

"If you guys want, I've got a store card I can swipe for you," she says.

"That's not on our program, honey," Blaise says, winks. "Thank you, though."

"Whatever does it for you," she says.

Our receipt tells us the magic figure so we don't even need math: "If you were a Publix Preferred Shopper, you would have saved $40 today."

We wait patiently in the parking lot, about thirty minutes. Blaise swings a pitchfork around like a bo staff. Then he goes back in and presents his Publix Preferred Shopper card with the receipt. They can't give credit to the EBT card so they fork over that savings in cold hard. Blaise goes right to the coolers and buys a case from the same checkout girl. I take two jars of Marshmallow Fluff for Marigold and leave the rest in the cart in the parking lot. Blaise makes a point of backing the van into the cart and knocking it over.

Then we truck over to Maud's Fish Camp, where we are locals. Maud lets us bring our own beer. We pitchfork around in the woods near the fish camp for a couple hours without finding anything alive except roly-polies and centipedes. I muck up the special restaurant shoes good. Blaise keeps sneaking up behind thick-trunked trees and jumping out at me with the pitchfork aimed at my heart. He hisses when he does this. At one point he jumps out with this dead four-foot moccasin wrapped around his neck, but I don't know it's dead until he screams, falls to the ground, and throws the snake off him, and I start stabbing it and he rolls around in the leaves laughing. If ever I saw him trying too hard to act like everything's normal, it's now.

When it starts to get dark, we admit defeat. We use the left-over EBT money to rent cane poles and bait from Maud. We sit on the edge of the dock under the lights watching bobbers.

"A tyrannic disappointment," Blaise says.

"If we had found any, we'd probably have gotten bit. And where would you keep them until the thing?"

"You're being really negative. Just one little piece of that bed money and we'd have afforded oodles of good quality poisonous snakes. Just one little piece."

"I'm not taking it back. She can't sleep in that Stryker thing forever. The bed is a profound expression of comfort and warmth and security. That's all I need to say."

We sit there not talking and not catching any fish.

"Did I ever tell you about that time Luke took me to the Wacissa River early one morning? I jumped in and four moccasins came at me. I couldn't see them 'cause I was in the water. Luke could though. He was standing on the platform. He reached out his hand and said, 'When, quick.' I grabbed his hand and looked over my shoulder as the snakes broke the water. They almost had me."

"Where are those snakes right now?"

"Well, we couldn't handle moccasins you realize. They're too aggressive. Rattlesnakes maybe. Coral snakes sure. Not moccasins."

Blaise shakes his head. He throws the cane pole into the water and walks back to the van with the rest of our beer. He sulks the whole drive, then, a few blocks from Piecemeal, he pulls into a construction lot, the site of the future skatepark, and brightens up a little bit. It's a concrete slab, a former 84 Lumber yard. "Ready-made foundation," Blaise says. "Of course we'll be cutting into some of it." He outlines where the bowl will go, and the street course. "At this very moment the most experienced skatepark designers on the Left Coast are making their way through the South, to us."

"How's your scandal holding up?" He jerks his head, like he's taunting me.

"It's calmed down," I say. "Jafari's been booted off the roof, which is one plus. Though the owners seem to have found the witch and put it to him."

"He dead?" Blaise says.

"Wouldn't we hear about that if he was?"

"Who knows, dealing with these people. Could be."

"I'm trying not to think about him. I never meant for anyone to get hurt. But I do like to think about Jafari making his home out back in that little van when he yearns for the roof."

"Sucka," Blaise whispers, and I assume he's talking about Jafari.

We finish off our case in the van, staring at the concrete slab that will soon realize Blaise's dream. There's other news too. The Hardback has promised us a Friday night. Us, Wormdevil. He says we need to be ready. "The guys have discussed it, and we think it'd be best if, during this big show, if you just sang 'Wormdevil' to all the songs, rather than reading your thingies."

I am silent.

"What you sometimes don't understand is that the speed imposes certain limitations. There are some words you just can't sing to some songs. That's why 'Wormdevil' is so great. It fits anywhere, anytime."

"Is this an order?" I say.

"That's the deal."

He holds out his beer, just above the cup holder, and narcs out. His body slackens and the beer drops right into the holder as his arm falls to the console. I lock the doors and shut him in—he usually wakes within an hour—and walk, realizing after a while that my Post-it pad is gone, no doubt lost somewhere in the woods.

At home there are some insurance notices from the Stryker bed company for Marigold and another letter from Biodad in the mailbox. They arrive daily now. In one he was a guru of some yoga movement. He got into it because he was having severe back problems, then ratcheted up the whole pussy profession, which now knows him as "Power-yama." In another he wrote that he was a small-town mayor whose aides had tracked me down. He sits atop a raucous board of city councilmen, and he is planning a parade in my honor when I come to visit. The letters are all casual, mentioning his profession and the family he does or doesn't have. Standing there on my stoop, I tear the new one open. Now he is a radio DJ. He includes his number "at the station." He writes that he wants to take my call on the air. He wants to share our first phone call together with his listening audience. He thinks that would be a really "far-out" way for us to do things, taking the pressure and weirdness off us both. *We need to take the opportunities in life which life presents us for taking pressure and weirdness off ourselves. Your call to my hit local radio program, Morning Man Dan, a news, sports, and fishing show, can effect that for us.*

I take the letter and sit down in the driver's seat of the Ghia. I haven't driven in months. I fish out my keys and start the engine. I look at the return address on the envelope: Morning Man Dan, on a street called Orchard in Columbus, Ohio. I think about going there and destroying him. Now siblings don't mat-

ter. Now I want to see what kind of person finds this funny. I
wonder which version—if any—is the real Biodad, and what
does that mean about me? I could find him, just head north and
a little west from Florida and eventually hit Ohio. I could hook
up a Rand McNally at a gas station. I put the Ghia in gear and
let off the tricky clutch. It stalls. I sit there for a minute, then
snatch the key from the ignition and go inside.

Summerside
plush

Marigold is in the other room half napping and half reaching for pages in the crappy magazines she is suspended over. A little earlier I brought her white bread smeared with Marshmallow Fluff and she let it sit. Left camps out underneath her. I sit on the couch watching Discovery and listening to Slayer.

"Hey, When," she shouts from the room. "Can you get hard?"

"Likelihood," I say. "Can your screw handle it?"

"We'll have to be careful, but I want to. Turn the crank."

I crank the Stryker hammock sling until she's facing upward. I help her out and she unbuckles the bottom of her storm-trooper brace. She drops it to the floor, where it bounces with a hollow plastic sound like a Wiffle Ball bat. She's standing in underwear and these slipper socks with treaded polka dots on the soles.

"Let's use the bed you got me," she says. I arrange the Mombasa netting properly over the canopy and she comes over to the mattress, eases onto it, winces as she slides across. "Do we have some kind of a board?"

"I think there's one in the shed."

"Maybe I could lie on that."

I look for a reasonably clean piece of plywood in the shed out back. I sort through the scraps me and Blaise use to cut out transitions for launch ramps. I take my time because I understand that I have here a problem. Before Marigold left we weren't doing it much with her on the couch armed with the baseball bat, but when we did, it was in what was then still technically our room. The barber chair business ended long before she even moved in. Suddenly she didn't like the idea of getting hair all over her. Suddenly she didn't like itching. I became so bored I had to figure out some way to get into it and settled on watching my ass in a full-length mirror I positioned against the wall in our room so I could see it—my ass—from the bed. I didn't know why watching that way did it for me. I didn't have a nice one or anything, hairy and flat. Maybe I'd gotten used to watching her ass all those times we did it in her barber chair. Or maybe it gave me the illusion I was watching two other people go at it, which did something for me in the way me and Marigold going at it didn't anymore.

I can't think of a reasonable excuse to get the mirror, and so return with a roughly Marigold-size board. She is standing at the window in the dark and her eyes glint at me just like the marbles in all the skulls. Her body is curved, the shape of a question mark. *What it is she's asking?* This is a line to make note of, I think. Try and remember.

I pull up the fitted sheet and slide the plywood onto the Summerside Plush. Its splintered edges catch the threads in the mattress. I cover it with the sheet and approach her, cautiously. She does the same thing, each of us aiming to miss the other.

But we hit. The taste of her is so strange by now, milky. Our

mouths, which used to fit, can't seem to catch. We used to play
follow the leader with our tongues in her barber chair at Wild
Hair. All this *used to* is all over everything. Now our tongues
dodge each other, probe around each other's cheeks.

My mouth flits down her neck, where I used to dwell but
now skip, to her third nipple. I tease and coax it, but while her
regular nipples stand to, the third remains squishy. I circle it
with my finger, blow on it, nothing.

She reclines on the board, props her feet on opposite poles of
the canopy, and says, "Don't pressure me."

I'm gentle and slow. I try not to jostle the bed. She is silent
and tolerant. I picture her as the full wineglass on one side of
the Summerside Plush and me as the bouncing bowling ball.
Our eyes are open, but we look past each other. I can faintly
make out our reflection in the window glass, but then some
cars drive by and it's just enough of a distraction. I start going
soft. She adjusts her butt. She looks at me, smiles. I push stronger, trying to bring myself back, and kind of forgetting and
kind of on purpose, I grab her by her hips and pull.

She flinches and her pupils widen, her hands flash to her
sides and she scrapes a finger on the board. It's a look of pure
fear. I've never seen anything like this look. Her mouth con-
torts into the Q shape. I stop.

"Did I hurt you?" I say.

"No," she says. "I'm fine. It's just that . . . it's just like in my
dream."

"You dream we have sex now?" That sounds like progress
to me.

"No. You grab me like that, hold me down like that." She
puts her hands over her face. She sucks on the cut down the
side of her finger. "Then you bind me to the Stryker using dirty
aprons as rope. You leave for a second and come back with a
giant box of Kleenexes. You take me by the hips and pull me

to you. You lean way over me. One by one you rip a Kleenex from the box and push it into my mouth. You keep cramming more and more, until you couldn't possibly fit another, then you keep cramming and pushing and the wad is backing down my throat, which burns with that dry paper taste. I can't breathe. You have that same look you just had, a look of determination. Everything goes black."

We stay like that for a little while, let the image of her dream hang in the dark between us. Then I get up and pull my shorts on. I help her off the plywood. I help her fasten the brace and assemble her into the Stryker, crank the Stryker around so she's facedown. The Stryker is a one-man. I move the board to the floor and lie down on the Summerside Plush, listen to the trampoline-like sounds the Stryker makes as she adjusts herself.

"I'm not going to kill you," I say.

"I know. I just can't convince myself of that."

X

It's five a.m., and I'm trying to remember what it was I wanted to note. The blank Post-it pad stares at me in the dark. My sleep rhythms are all off. Normally I've been passing out about this time every night, sleeping until four in the afternoon, when I have to get up and get ready for my shift again. Once Marigold's asleep, I slip away to the bathroom and discover the Kleenex box empty and nothing but a cardboard roll where the toilet paper should be. She's gotten to the paper towels also.

The phone rings, too early for Prep Dog calls, and I brace myself. But it's Blaise, all somber. We didn't have to wait long for news from Shaka, Blaise says. For fact he is news. Blaise tells me he can't talk about it, that I should go get the *Sun*. I ride the regular skateboard through the twilight, down the block until I see a newspaper on a neighbor's front porch, steal it.

He made front page, bottom left, our local Bra. He didn't go down in any glory, getting his war on. He didn't even make it out of basic. The *Sun* says, *Local man Stephan Goulet, known by his friends as "Shaka," died Tuesday at a U.S. Army basic training facility from a chest infection caused by a wound to his pectoral area.* There's an investigation into how no military medics had caught the problem during his physical.

I read the article a couple times, then roll the newspaper back into its plastic and return it to its lawn. I sit on the curb and scrape my special restaurant shoe on the nonmotorized shortboard's grip tape.

THE ROB II

The amount down here

I've stolen from every place I have ever worked except for my first job at Maxie's Better Burgers. The Manager who hired me there was this balding guy named Rudy, and what was he thinking? I come in stinking of pot, barely sixteen, fading tattoos all over my arms, a virgin, and he takes me on. Grill! Three-sixty an hour.

I'd roll over there every day after school in the orange paper aprons they gave us, matching orange visor, polo, and name tag. The only good thing about Maxie's Better Burgers was that it was only a drive-thru—no dining room—so no one could see me. I'd stand behind the industrial grill handing over burgers to the bun station, calling out, "Hot meat, hot meat." There is nothing more embarrassing than fast food.

But Rudy wasn't the least embarrassed. He treated the job and his power over us as Manager very seriously. "How clean does this wall have to get?" I'd ask, and he'd say, "Clean-clean."

He had several different power trips going. The bottom-rung employees—that's Cash-Outs, Stackers, Fries, Dish, and Grill (me)—were nothing to him. He considered himself our boss and elder because he owned us for forty-hour increments of our teenage weeks. He thought we all looked up to him, when we considered him an absolute tool. He treated the Assistant Managers as close friends he was letting in on a good secret. And the customers—he was so nice to the customers. Whenever a customer made a complaint, he pinched his eyebrows together and got a totally concerned expression on his face. He nodded and put a greasy hand on the complainant's shoulder to comfort her. He shook his head at what a shame it was that she didn't get extra pickles on her double cheeseburger. I couldn't believe anyone could be so nice to a woman complaining about the inadequate toasting of her bun or a guy who didn't believe his burger weighed a full quarter pound before cooking. But Rudy would return these people's money. He'd replace their orders and manage to convince them the rest of their day would be better because they'd been through the Maxie's Better Burgers drive-thru. Sometimes at Piecemeal, pretending to be Manager feels like pretending to be Rudy, a frightening sensation.

I couldn't go out after working at Maxie's. I couldn't go out smelling of hot meat in those nylon pants and that ridiculous orange polo with the ridiculous name tag. I had to go home, shower, and change, and by then all my friends who didn't work were bumming me out because they were already drunk. Blaise had a job at the skate shop because those jobs just went to people like him.

Rudy was thirty, going bald fast, skinny, and basketball-tall. He always wore a suit and tie and sat in a tiny office in the back of Maxie's from which he popped out every hour to weigh the produce and meat, count the buns and patties, calculate sales percentages and employee cost and fax all that crap to some main Maxie's franchise office somewhere. He buzzed around the place, picking out the charred ends of french fries from between tiles, tsking, "Sweep-ity, deep-ity, guys!" Once he pulled me by my arm into his office. I had been changing the fat fryers for the new girl on fries. Rudy presented me with a little yellow sticker that said: *Caution. This chair is equipped with hard wheel casters for use on carpeted floors only. Use on hard surfaces may cause unexpected rolling and can result in injury from tipping or collision. Soft wheel casters are available for use on hard surfaces such as wood, linoleum, tile, and floor mats.*

"I pulled this off the bottom of my chair," he said. I looked at the chair he was pointing at, the one he sat in calculating store figures, an ergonomically shaped chair with armrests and butt indentations. "I phoned the main office to ask for these soft wheel casters. They say I don't need them. Do you see this floor?" He crouched down and touched the floor.

"Tile," I said.

"A hard surface," he said. "Floors are the cause of more injuries than any other surface in the restaurant industry."

"I think you should demand them," I said—I wanted to be on his side. "You're General Manager."

"They said no. They said it's a standard warning only so the chair manufacturer doesn't get sued and really, they said, it doesn't mean anything. But why is it there? There's got to be some reason it's there—because they don't want to get sued when some fast-food General Manager tips over at his desk and rolls out of the office directly into the path of a grill cook hauling fat-fryer grease. Sploosh!"

"Yes," I said.

"Why were *you* taking out the grease?"

"The girl on fries, she's small," I said.

"Watch it. That's sexist—sizeist, but we won't get technical. You've got to let her fulfill the duties required of her position. All right, buddy?"

"Can I just finish dumping this vat?" He was worried about his chair tipping over but he ordered this young girl to carry out a couple gallons of hot grease every night, a vat I could hardly carry, and which splashed all over you, raising little welts, and if you slipped, would wash your skin right off. All for $3.60 per hour.

"Let's let her do it. You brush the grill and sweep *your own* station. Head on up there. Fries!" he shouted. "You'll be up to $3.75 in a couple of weeks at the rate you're going. I'm ordering up some soft wheel casters. Fries!"

I was out of there within a week, graduated to Taco Bell, fast food with an actual dining lobby. And where did they put me? Drive-thru. But that's when I started to figure things out.

Generally, Restaurant Worker assesses the weaknesses of a given system and exploits thusly. But sometimes, like at the chains, a system has no weaknesses. The chains lock down the raw-product-to-assembly-to-customer-payment system tight. Exploiting thusly may incur collateral damage. At Taco Bell, Maxie's, and most other chains, the Manager weighs the beef quantities in the steam table every hour and any significant discrepancy—even the disappearance of a single taco's worth of beef—can result in immediate firings. You assess and adapt. You work hard, and look for opportunities to present themselves. I figured my shtick out by accident when I misread the screen one day. Guy's total was $3.25 and I read $3.75. He forked it over, didn't even flinch. So my tactic was to overcharge everyone fifty cents. Do that forty times a night and slide your very own twenty out at the end of the shift. I'd keep a little Cinnamon Twists wrapper by the register and keep track in roman numerals. If anyone asked what I was count-

ing, I said, "Hot chicks." Sometimes a customer would notice
the overcharge and I'd say, "My bad." But most of the time
they paid whatever I told them to pay. That's how customers
are. (Sometimes I'd fuck with them, tell them we were out of
tacos—at Taco Bell!—and they believed me. What can't you
tell customers?) Nowadays they have those readouts at the window that display the total. There's a number to call if you're
charged more than "the amount shown here." These readouts
are in most Taco Bells across the country now. Because of me, I
like to think. At sixteen I'd already had an effect on the world.

There are three types of workers in the restaurant industry:

The Specialists, those who understand the concept of the
line, who are flexible, who can come into a restaurant, briefly
observe a position, then start copying, adding their own style,
making the position their own. These are the people who
approach their positions as either sport or art. They can handle the big rushes even if they swear a lot and are generally
unpleasant people to have around.

The Grunts are the masses. They can pretty much handle
one or two positions. They are not fast, because they are either
a little too careful with the food or disgusted by it. A lot of
Grunts are vegan. Grunts you generally keep because you don't
want to go through the hassle of training another person in the
hopes he or she will be the upper tier, because, usually, you get
another Grunt.

Then there's the Jafaris. These people are told how to do
things twenty-five times and they refuse to understand. They
forget to Ajax the sink. They laze. They ask to take a smoke
break during dinner rush and their hands shake when carrying
slices of pizza to and from the oven. They burn themselves a
lot, which comes with the job, but then they whine about it

and use up all the Bactine from the first-aid kit. I worked with a Jafari at the Barbie-Q who needed gloves to scoop fries. They came straight out of the fryer dripping scalding grease, and he picked them up one by one, shaking his fingers out and hooting in pain. I showed him the double-handed scoop. "Just dig your mitts in there," I said. I did it once for him, letting the fries sizzle in my hands for a moment before dropping them onto the plate. "But it's hot," he said. "It's like anything else," I said. "You callous up." Instead he bought plastic gloves at Wal-Mart and the grease ate right through. He quit after a week. They replaced him with an old woman named Beaches who couldn't even feel her hands. She'd scooped fries and handled baked potatoes direct from the oven her whole life. Beaches was no Jafari.

Often the Jafaris are kept around because you feel sorry for them, and the Specialists, it being their nature, will take up their slack.

So when I get a surprise visit from Jafari the day after Shaka died, at my home—as in that wormy motherfucker on my front porch, patchouli-ing up the place—I am momentarily thrown off my game. Specialists and Jafaris are not the type to socialize outside of the place of work. Standing there on my porch, he has this serious expression on his face. Marigold is doing something in the kitchen, her back brace knocking against the counter. Left is going wild, wants to tear Jafari apart. I hold the dog back but stroke his head and whisper, "Good man." Jafari asks me to step outside for a private chat. He says the word "chat." There's none of the slowed-down cool guy in his voice, no hippie drawl. I'm shocked to hear him talk like a real person.

"You've been avoiding me," he says.

"Have I? Huh. Did not intend. What can I do you for?"

"You don't have any idea what you can do for me?"

"Everything all right in terms of van living?" I squeeze Left between my legs and manage to shut him behind the door. I stand on the stoop across from Jafari.

"Van living is great. But we never finished our discussion the other day."

"Oh yeah. Yeah, well just forget about that. I was a little out of it still. Freaked."

"Why would you be freaked?"

"All that craziness with the rob, and then, well, the health inspector, and the unfortunate moving of yourself from that cozy place on the roof, which, just—it wasn't right, man."

"We were all pretty wasted the night it went down."

"Yes we were. You're saying something there. We were."

"How wasted were you exactly?"

"Wasted good."

"Wasted good enough to rob Piecemeal yourself maybe?"

I laugh out loud, but my stomach drops. I don't know how he knows where I live. I assume that he followed me at some point. And if that is the case I should have noticed something like that and I wonder what other threats I'm missing. "Never been that wasted," I say.

"There's one thing I never mentioned when Skordilli kicked me out of my pleasant roof home: Greg couldn't have come in through the hole up there, because I was up there, and I would have seen him."

"You were wasted too, hombre."

"I never get so wasted not to know when somebody's coming through my space. And unlike some folks I don't need little notes to remind me about my drunken deeds."

"Sure about that? Me and Skordilli came up there the next day. He kicked you and you didn't budge."

"Playing possum and for very good reason." He looks down at my feet. "It's interesting," he says. "After this money disappears, you suddenly show up with hundred-and-fifty-dollar restaurant shoes."

"Skordilli gave them to me," I say. I move my feet while we're both looking at them and they make a crunching sound on the cement.

I start to think, he knows he knows he knows. And then I think back to that night and there is a faint image, another still frame, of me standing next to Jafari in the office, the black box open, the drawers on the table in front of us, the whole place wavy. *We can't stash the money on the roof, for obvious reasons. You take it home, we'll even out later.* And that's it—precisely there is where the night ends for me, at least with any certainty. It won't fast-forward or rewind, just that one moment. But I don't trust myself. It's like a memory of a dream and you're not quite sure if that's the way the dream even went, like how positive I was Marigold had come home weeks ago with those babbling hedgehog skulls when she was still multiple states away. Was it possible I'd been so trashed I conspired not only to rob Piecemeal but also to include the person I think least of in the thing? The whole idea riles me. If it's true, he had to have been the instigator. I never would have done it on my own. Or would I have? And the fucking suggestion is so infuriating . . . I don't buy it, I don't believe him, but somehow he knows, and I have to play like I don't. With the money spent, it's my only defense.

"What happened that night?" I say.

"You and me, we had some ideas."

"What kind of ideas?"

"Ideas about sticking it to The Man. You really don't remember these discussions?"

I'm quiet for a moment, thinking politic. It doesn't make any sense. I was already sticking it to The Man, in my own way. I didn't need Jafari.

"I don't know what you're talking about."

He rolls one of his dreadlocks between his thumb and pointer finger. "I'm due a half," he says. "I can wait a little bit longer. But soon, or my lips go a-flapping."

He removes an American Spirit from behind his ear, lights it, and drops the match on my stoop. He strolls away, looking back at me over his shoulder. When he walks his left leg twitches between steps. I remember Blaise's suggestion to refund the Summerside Plush, but it's seen some damage because of the board and . . . it doesn't matter. I won't take back the bed I gave to Marigold, even if she won't use it.

Then I'm back inside and Marigold's screaming into the phone and when she pauses I can hear the dude through the phone saying, "Drug seeking behavior. Drug seeking behavior."

She slams the receiver and stands in front of me cradling a bovine skull and petting it like a puppy.

"That was the pharmacist," she says.

"Oh yeah. What did the pharmacist have to say?"

"They're not giving me my painkillers."

"How can they not give you your painkillers? You're in pain. You need them."

"I know I'm in pain. I know I need them. I'm almost out, too."

"Our medical situation in this country is totally screwed up."

"You're the only medical situation I've got now," she says. "They're saying the prescription was tampered with."

"The prescription was tampered with? How could that be? Who would tamper with a prescription?"

"They say there are no refills on Percocet, yet my Percocet prescription designated a refill, one refill."

"One refill."

"Do you know anything about this, my love?" she says.

"Maybe the doctor made a mistake, babe."

"Even better, the pharmacist called the doctor in Long Island, who will no longer prescribe me anything stronger than Tylenol codeine, and the doctor is good buddies with my dad. So it's all great news."

She places the cow skull on the TV. She applies some glue to the back of a marble and inserts it into an eyehole, holds it there for a beat, then moves her hand away.

"Do any of those skulls come from a Tasmanian tiger?"

"You mean Tasmanian devil?"

"What's that one right there?" I point to a weird little skull, about the size of a pear.

"An otter, North American."

"All right. It was just a line, hardly even a one, more like a lowercase *l*. I wanted—it'd be good to have extras around in case you relapsed, or the pain got too bad or something."

"Do you ever stop to think?"

"When moving there is no time to think."

"I have one painkiller left. Tomorrow, you'll be getting me something from your little buddies."

"I'll do that," I say. "I will definitely do that for you, Marigold."

It's just about applying heat to something

Business is so dead I help Brain grease the thick-pie pans. We pass this yellow spray can of lube back and forth. I give the okay for everyone to get complimentary on-the-clock Newcastles. Brain and I stretch out the thick doughs and arrange them in the greased pans. When they rise we pass them off to Rick for prebake.

"Do you think cheese should count as a topping?" Brain asks.

Brain just got out of the army, where he was a welder. They didn't want him in Iraq, a fact he blows off: "Nothing to weld," he claims. He's gangly, eats lots of pills, and has been going out with one of Mea's fellow piercers from Second Skin. He's the kind of guy who will ask you out of the blue what you're doing under there. You say, "Under where?" and he just nods his head. I go along with him because I can't figure him out. It's hard to say if he's fucking around or making fun of you.

"It doesn't sound like a topping," I say. "It sounds like it's what should be there. Like you say, 'pizza' and there are certain things included in that: sauce, dough, and cheese."

"And think about this," he says. "What goes into a New York Cheese pizza? Eighteen ounces of dough, right? Flour, yeast, water—cost? Maybe one cent per pizza. Two spoonfuls of sauce: a nickel, maybe. Two cups of mozzarella. What's that stuff cost us, ten dollars a box? With the quantity this place buys in, one whole pizza costs us maybe a dime, say fifty cents with labor and utilities. We sell that motherfucker for two bucks a slice or twelve a whole pie. How many of those do we go through in a day?"

"About a hundred and fifty, New York Cheese alone."

He passes the spray can to me and I coat a rag with it, smear the stuff all around the bottom and sides of a pan so nothing sticks. I pass it back. He says, "Skordilli's the one robbing. I wish Greg had gotten more from him. How about this for a song: 'Bossman, you suck.' He covers my per-shift wage with three New York Cheeses."

"Greg is a true American hero," I say. Whenever the topic of Greg comes up, I laud him. It's the best apology I can do. "The next line," I say, "after 'Bossman, you suck,' should be 'You suck, Bossman.'"

The hours pass slowly. I jam the jukebox with quarters from the registers. Me and Brain huddle in The Hague smoking this kind bud with cocaine sprinkled on the top. Then I send the crew in two at a time to get their hits, ordering them to be stoned with us. "You must face an international criminal tribunal," I tell them.

"Yes, bossman," they say, and scurry.

I'm standing out back with Gutter Boy, who leans against the wall. As usual, the fake chameleons, the anoles, have come out.

He's hitting the weed and rubbing his chin. The lizards mimic him, pushing out their throats.

"I really like this girl," he says of Mea. "I mean, I really like this girl, Thinfinger." His eyes get watery. He seems to be saying that Mea holds the promise. For her he won't lie around the house covered in porno magazines anymore. For her, he may shave his neck. For her he would go by "Steve." "I really like her," he says.

The fake chameleons scurry back into their crevices. He sells me a bottle of Percocets for cost.

Jafari appears from the kitchen with this gaunt look and sudsy hands. "Ultimate Frisbee tournament," he says, "descended . . . as if out of nowhere." He holds the door for us. He points at his watch and says, "Ticktock" as I go by him.

We go right into full rush mode. Brain is up front helping Mea and Ashley, so I fall in at thin pies, but I watch him. I note, Manager material. The dining room is standing-room only. No one warned us about this. We're packed with dreadlocks and Umbros.

"Frisbee dog lickers," Skinhead Rick says loudly.

Our rush thing is like a trance. As fucked up as we are, orders go out. Ultimate is not such a demanding crowd. They come hard, but while they have volume they also have patience. (Softball would be another story.) Ultimate players sit at their tables and play Steely Dan on the jukebox. Me, Brain, Mea, and Ashley run their orders. Ashley overturns a bowl of pasta fagioli on three of them and they shrug it off. Free garlic rolls. We rock the line in half. The doors close again and people don't stand in the street anymore. I tell Brain to leave the front and start closing down his station, then I walk through the lobby nodding at people, asking them if they're enjoying their meal, trying to do it in a cool "Hey, man" kind of way and not the high-pitched "What can *I* do for *you*" voice Rudy used to use at

Maxie's. I force the question through gritted teeth.

When I return to the kitchen, feeling low about myself for asking dog lickers how their meals were, Brain's eyes are bugged. He finger-wags me to the walk-in. He's holding the yellow can that we greased all the thick-pie pizza pans with.

We wedge ourselves back behind the cheese and he shoves the can in my face. I read *Easy Off*.

"We have a problem," he says.

"Grease," I say. "So what."

He shakes his head. "This is what." He holds the can closer to my face and with his finger underlines a warning label at the bottom: *CAUSES BURNS TO SKIN AND EYES ON CONTACT. CONTENTS UNDER PRESSURE. HARMFUL IF SWALLOWED.* "It's not grease," he says. "Easy Off is the shit for cleaning ovens, not greasing pans. This stuff melts through carbon deposits on the oven brick. We soaked those pizza crusts in steel-eater."

"Why do they both come in yellow cans? Why give cleaner a name that sounds like it's lubricant?" I start counting in my head, all the thick-pie slices we must have turned out. We may be murdering the entire Southeastern College Ultimate Players conference.

Me and Brain zombie-walk back into the kitchen. And then there's another surge. More teams line up in the doorway. The Front Girls are shoveling out slices and Rick is drowning on oven. Rick scowls at us, the two dudes standing there shell-shocked. He thinks we're just too fucked up. I snag a tray of New York Cheese from the line and we retreat to the office.

"Some help here," Ashley hollers as we disappear.

I set the pizza on the counter where I count the Piecemeal drawers. We both look at it. "I've got to eat it," I say.

Brain looks at me. "You have to make a choice," he says. "We can shut the place down, admit what we've done, or keep quiet as blood brothers and ride this thing out. This could be our My Lai, my friend."

I peer out at the restaurant and scan: everyone is eating slices, slices, slices. *Easy come Easy go / As I let this feeling grow / Get some / Don't bum / how about speed? / If you don't like the rush / this is all you need.* I cram a slice in my mouth, pushing it down my throat with my finger and thumb. The taste is off, detergenty, but that could be the sauce. "You eat one," I tell Brain.

"I won't die for this country, bossman," he says.

I take him by the apron. "You eat one." I yank another slice. He shakes his head, but takes it. He inhales quickly, dutifully, filling his cheeks.

"Painty," he says. "Acidic. Chemical. No doubt."

We both get instant stomachaches, but that's not reliable because of the anxiety, and the dope, and the beers, and the fact that we eat so much of this shit it always gives us stomachaches. With this kind of business pouring in there's no way I can take down the pizzas without admitting to something, and damn if I'm doing that. People do time for that.

"It was an accident. That's all," I say. "We ride it out. But if anything happens, we never caught it. Without intention, the worst we get is manslaughter."

"You, you mean," he says. "You're Manager."

"I'm not manning this Bassmaster alone, hoss. Anyone else know?"

"Negative."

"Then go throw this can into the bottom of the dumpster and help Gutter Boy. Throw and go, go."

I jump on front, but let the girls serve. I handle the register and watch the slices go out and people gobble them down. I sip Newcastle to iron me out. I see through the pasta rack that Gutter Boy is wolfing down a Veggie Surprise slice.

"Don't eat that," Brain is telling him.

"Why?" Gutter Boy says.

"We'll get subs later," Brain says. "Don't you get tired of eating here every day?"

"It's the only reason to work here."

Over at the café Uschi munches the Hawaiian. Skinhead Rick finishes off a crust. He scrapes a broken calzone off the brick as crumbs fall from his lips. Whatever happens to them, I think, will happen to me. I'll be right there with them. I mow another New York Cheese, choke it down like a snake.

The phone rings and Ashley snags it. I can get rid of all the pizzas tonight after work, just say we had a really busy night, all thick pies, no pasta—the expensive stuff. Skordilli will buy it. I'm his man.

"Thinfinger," Ashley says. "There's some guy on the phone who can barely talk. He wants to speak to the manager."

Brain peers out at me from between microwaves. I start to think of a way out and for some reason joining the Coast Guard comes to mind. It is not like the real military. There is likely lots of mopping of boats and docks. Somebody must cook for them.

But this is the moment my life's been leading up to. The diabetic-Coke incident was nothing. This is the Manager's duty, not mopping the floor every night, not pushing around a mop bucket while your crew sits out back. Time to step up.

"Make food, not war," I say.

There is gargling at first, indeterminate, neither male nor female. And as I wait for another sound, an indication of the poisoning, I look out on the dining room, still filled with people who just ate our slices. They're starting to trickle out. If they make it home, then there's the chance they won't see the Piecemeal connection. If none of them talk to each other, or maybe if the effects are so—maybe they'll think it's pneumonia, massive group pneumonia. The voice on the phone swallows, barks.

"I got no pepperoni," he says. An old man.

"You ordered pepperoni, sir?" Just old.

"Pepperoni and sausage." His throat fills again and he coughs and gags. I take down his name and add him to the credit book, tell him I'll give him a whole-pie credit for next time. I'll put him down for two, I say. He thanks me.

Later, I sweat as I count down the drawers. I write on a Post-it, *Riff Idea: Poisonuss pizza / I'm a eatcha.* I count the drawers and lose count and start again and lose count. Then I count all the way through and come up with $3,114 and on my double-check count come up with $3,243. I add those two numbers together and divide by two, then I deduct my personal $20 for a total night of $3,158.50—a stellar night. Stellar. And not one customer died, so far.

I wash my dirty hands in The Hague. How many people do we cook dinner for every night? Cooks like me and Gutter Boy and Skinhead Rick. Even Jafari gets his paws on a baked ziti now and then. And people dig into it. They don't even question. People—and not just college kids but professors, business fucks, stewardesses, and pilots—just stroll in here and pay us for it. We might sop their pizza crusts with oven cleaner every night.

And cooking—it used to be such a mysterious thing. Then I learned it's not as complex as I imagined. It's just applying heat to something. Maybe everything is simple once you figure it out.

I join the crew on the back patio as usual. Brain and I quietly agree to meet later to dispose of all the poisoned pizza. Jafari is dismantling a failed attempt at a mini–porch swing atop the fountain pedestal.

The slam has everybody rattled. Skinhead Rick is so bushed he's calm. He sips Newcastle and spins his grenade on the glass table, making a clinking sound. Once, when we still worked at the Barbie-Q, a waitress called him a "little big man" because he wouldn't give her extra fries on her employee meal. He reached out over the pit and took a bone-in pork butt like he was palming a basketball. His hat fell off, revealing his shiny bald head, still decorated then with that ponytail. A low growl came from his gut. Customers gathered, their faces pressed against the wall-sized pane of glass that divided the pit from the dining room, so they could watch us like we were in an aquarium. He held the meat in his outstretched left hand and pummeled it with his fist, firing little bits of gristle in all directions. Scalding gristle stuck to my cheek and I took cover behind the door of the steak cooler. He drew back in a stubby pitcher's stance and winged it at the glass. The customers fled from the window and the pork butt burst through, spitting glass across the dining room.

By this time most of the waitresses had huddled together at the drink station and the one who'd instigated it all froze, unable to move, standing only inches away from where the meat contacted the glass. I'm not sure if he was aiming for her or not, but no one was hurt. He stormed out and I was left to finish up, though not many more dinner orders came in. The customers, having returned to their tables, believed they'd pushed him over the edge and most of them changed their orders to salads and left big tips for the fiery little cook.

None of this was caught on tape.

Just before eleven p.m., Mea stands up and takes my hand. "It's time," she says. I know it doesn't look good to the Gutter, but I'm pleased enough by how it looks to everyone else to not say anything. She leads me across the patio.

Jafari announces, "I still haven't figured out what kind of monument this place deserves. When, maybe, since you're Manager and all, you have some good ideas. Before you cut out, we could confer over by my van."

I pretend I don't hear.

"A skull and crossbones," Brain says. I laugh, and punch him in the chest with the hand not caught up in Mea's sweaty little grip.

"When," Jafari says, "do you want to talk to me about this? I think you should."

"Jafari wants to ask you something," Mea says as we step into the parking lot. I look back to see both Jafari and Gutter Boy glaring at me. Gutter Boy is stroking his swollen throat. Jafari is leaning against the blank pedestal in the fountain. I wave and walk on.

Blackout

Second Skin is located right beneath
Video and Tan on the main drag. Video and Tan rents movies
and tanning beds. Second Skin tattoos and pierces. Five or six
kids—I recognize them from the Hardback—are inside the
shop with their feet on the coffee table, smoking cigarettes,
playing cards, looking through comics.

One of the kids says, "Brother in struggle"—showing a lot
of respect either because he recognizes me as the Manager of
Piecemeal or because he thinks I'm Blaise, champion of the
local skatepark movement. Mea leads me straight through the
lobby toward the buzzing. She tells me she has one appointment to do and then we'll get started.

She drops me on a couch in the tattooing area and disappears
behind a curtain. There are three empty tattoo stalls separated
by partitions, each with its own leather dentist's chair. In the
stall across from me a fat tattooist covered in green dragons
is etching a schematic of a circuit board on a man's chest. The

man is reading *Computer Shopper*. The tattooist has a sketch on the drafting table next to him that he's using for reference. He pauses and moves a steel ruler and protractor around on the drafting table, figuring out angles before he inks them on the *Computer Shopper* guy. The entire facility is immaculate, more like a doctor's office than the house I got tattooed in. I anticipated the smell of mold and carpet.

I hear Mea's voice behind the curtain. I stand and move the curtain aside just enough so that I can see her. She is standing between the legs of a squat little dude in a Gap baseball hat, her hands buried in his crotch. His arms are propped back on the table. He stares nervously at the ceiling. She takes a device like surgical pliers and his retreating dick in her latex-gloved hands.

"Relax," she says, then whispers something in his ear. She thumps his dick, and the guy laughs but his eyes are lemons. She says, "Relax your cremaster. Suck this beauty up and what will I pierce?" He goes white. Her wrists make two quick, technical motions—it reminds me of her spatula technique. He jerks and there is a popping sound like a wet suction cup. She fiddles around there a little more, then takes some gauze and wipes off his balls with Mercurochrome. He shakes his head and touches the new silver hoop through his dick. She lights a cigarette.

"Relish this technique," she says to the curtain, snatching off her latex gloves and dropping them in a medical-waste bucket.

"To relish, I'd need a closer look," I say.

Gap Boy stares at his crotch, stands. His shorts and boxers are around his ankles. I had my ear pierced when I was eighteen but I was working at the Bell then and the manager made me take it out the same day. (I added fifty cents to eighty orders that night, and took forty bucks for myself at the end of my shift, a personal record.) Gap Boy pales and staggers sideways, trips over his pants. I come out from behind the curtain and catch him. His dick is stained yellow and he has an old-man ass. I steady him.

"Let's get tough guy back on the table," Mea says. "You need to lie down"—she pushes him down—"for thirty minutes." She puts a rag on his dick, puts his hand on the rag. "Keep the pressure," she says. Then she takes my hand and leads me through the curtain into the tattoo area again. Her hands are powdery from the gloves. The tattoo guy ignores us. We stop at the entrance to the lobby.

"I actually kind of fucked that up," she says. "It's crooked, but he probably won't notice."

"I thought you were a pro," I say.

"Technically, an apprentice. Ready for yours now?" She is maybe showing off for me a little bit.

"My penis likely requires a larger gauge jewelry," I say.

"Oh we have bigger rings," she says. Then she just looks at me like I might have something else funny to say. But I don't.

"If you really want to know who you are, a genital piercing is the answer. Believe me, it's the answer."

"What did you whisper in his ear, right before you did it?"

"A magician never divulges her secrets," she says. "Put it this way: I told him what he needed to hear."

The green-dragon tattooist is finished with the *Computer Shopper* guy, who bounces out the door. Mea introduces me to the tattooist. His name is Fester. He produces a small grunt. Maybe he's mute. He looks at my arms and rolls his eyes. Mea puts her hand on the back of his neck. She reminds him that he specifically needs a black piece, that maybe it will get him in the magazines, a show-off at the conventions. "It's way conceptual," she says. "Tattoos are so much about line and shape. This defies everything. Pure form."

Fester grunts, which seems to mean: Anything's better than this.

"Blackout," she says to him, then turns to me. "There's nothing to this," she says. "Fester will just scribble on your arm for a while, like working on a coloring book, except for no pictures and all fill. Imagine all-black pages."

Ten years have passed since Blue got to me. I've played it over in my mind thousands of times. How I could have woken up. How I could have willed myself to stay awake. How Blaise could have stopped him. They are all pussy thoughts and I am one true-blue pussy because I can't do anything about thinking them.

I sit in the dentist's chair. Fester coats my arms with transparent blue gel and shaves them with a straight razor. I admire his equipment, a sixteen-needle gun that makes a smooth *buzzzzz*. I remember Blue's instrument, the little model-train engine with a pen casing electrical-taped to it, a single guitar string running through. It hurt, that guitar string. These sixteen needles, when he touches them to my wrist, don't hurt at all. It's more like a lullaby. I get the sense that I'm drifting—the buzzing and whittling circling my wrist . . . and then I'm installing hand sinks at the Piecemeal counter, beneath the registers, but Mea won't use them. I tell her she needs to wash her hands before she touches anything. She refuses. "They're weaned as thistles," she keeps saying and licking her yellow fingers. Greg comes in, grinning, a dent in his head, but I look closer and see his head is actually a partly deflated and pushed-in beach ball. "You punch out now," he says, then dips Mea tango-style and kisses her on the lips. Jenny Raygun hovers into the room. She is wearing only her purple panties and I see that she is dangling from a piece of fishing line. Marigold appears in her storm-trooper gear, her hand at the base of her spine, grasping with the other hand at Jenny Raygun's panties. Greg releases Mea and looks at me. He takes a needle out of his pocket and holds it up to his temple. "This is me doing a you," he says. Then he sticks the needle into his temple and his head explodes . . .

I wake up with my head in Mea's hands. At first she has orange spots instead of eyes, but they fade back to her drippy brown. Then Fester's face appears behind hers, little red pterodactyl talons clawing up his chin. And behind Fester's face is the dude in the Gap hat, who's recovered and smirks at me smugly now that the tables are turned. "We've only just begun, my friend," Fester says, speaking for the first time.

"I'm here now," I say. "I'm in this."

"Thanks, lady," the guy in the Gap hat says to Mea, and strolls out of the shop.

And I am sturdy after this. The pain only gets bad under the arm. I grab Mea's shoulder. "Yeah," she says, "squeeze me." The absolute worst part is the fleshy white skin on the underside of my bicep. Fester makes me lie down and his sweat drips on my new arm, one whole black sore. Mea finds a red rubber dog bone and puts it in my mouth. "Bite down," she says. When I think he's finished, he wipes me down with a wet paper towel, then realizes he needs to darken some spots. He comes at me and I faint again.

When he's really done I stand in front of the mirror. The lengths of my arms, from wrists to the tops of my shoulders, are the color and texture of black construction paper. They're like bracelets running the lengths of my arms, ending in circles around my wrists and shoulders. Mea sets up a photography studio around me with high-intensity lights and reflective screens. She stands behind a tripod and discusses with Fester the best angle to shoot me from. I hold in my stomach while she shoots until I'm out of breath.

"Is there someone to take care of you at home, Thinfinger?" Mea asks.

"I don't know how to answer that," I say.

"Then I'll take you."

There's still time before I have to meet Brain at Piecemeal and deal with the poison pizzas, and she says her apartment is only a block away, at the edge of the student ghetto. It's a sparkling duplex in white and fluorescent, medical like the tattoo shop, just softer. There are cherub figurines on the walls and paintings: a naked woman with a rat on her head, a little boy and girl seesawing while a pack of wolves encircles them, a painting of Mea's face fading into a dark black watercolor night.

"Who did these?" I say.

"Me," she said. "I do have skills other than putting holes in people and serving pizza. Are you interested?"

"I'm interested," I say.

She shows me her studio, a small extra room in back with a drafting table like Fester's, dirty canvases, paints, lighting equipment, newspaper all over the floor, and a red mechanic's toolbox, the drawers overflowing with brushes and paints, X-Acto knives, measuring tools and straightedges, sandpaper.

"Oh," she says. She picks up a pen. There's a long strip of paper, like a Christmas list, taped to the wall over the drafting table. She scratches out the number 20,974 and writes 20,973.

I sit down on the couch and worry about bleeding on it. "What's that about?" I ask. Her tongue ring clicks across her teeth.

"How many days I have left to live," she says, "assuming I live to the average life expectancy of women today—seventy-eight—and die on that year's birthday." She closes drawers on her toolbox, knocking over brushes and tubes of paint.

"Countdown," I say. She unfolds a roll of her drawings for me, mostly abstract polygons in bright colors. They're all right, I guess.

"Exactly. One day I sat down and figured it out," she says. "It's surprising how short it all is. Twenty thousand is dick. Sad people think about existence in years, and fifty or so as forever, basically. Figuring by days gives a much clearer perspective. When the Egyptians were building the pyramids, dragging tons of stone miles through desert, they looked back and understood that distance of five hundred feet like we never will."

She opens a door in the cabinet below the television and takes out a bucket of Neosporin. She bear-hugs it over to the couch, uses a flat head screwdriver to pop the top.

"What about you, Thinfinger? What do you want? Oh wait, let me guess, to be Manager of that stupid fucking restaurant your whole life."

"No," I say. "I don't like all this Manager business. I'd prefer to just be Ovenman. Even Dish Dog."

"And trade all this power?" she asks and thumps my hand. She goops my arms with the Neosporin. It mixes with the ink and my blood. She takes it all the way up to my shoulders, then down again. She passes my wrist where the tattoos end and rubs my fingers.

"I'm going to make you my relative," she says. She pops a safety pin out of her lip and stabs her finger, then presses it to my blacked-out wrist. "Now," she says, "you can never fire me."

I zone out, calculate. I was always better at math than spelling. Realistically speaking, I can count on another forty years tops, which comes out to something like 14,600 days. Not even 20,000. Not even 15,000. It's nothing. And I cannot remember most nights. I specialize in fucking people over and forgetting it. I could still have possibly murdered an entire restaurant full of people tonight and am here now, tattooed and, maybe, about to get laid.

When Mea takes my pinky in her mouth, I'm already standing up, aiming to start paying a bit more attention. Even if this happens, I know that I can't handle her. I force myself to think, I have thrown in my lot with Marigold and I need to start working on that lot. I force myself because the last thing on my mind right now is Marigold. What is on my mind is Mea's wet mouth and the fact that it has never encountered the by-product of animal, an incredibly attractive notion. I almost can't believe it, but I retract my finger.

"Is that your sister?" I say, pointing to a photo of a hottie on top of the TV.

"It's my mom," she says. "She had me when she was fifteen." She grabs my hand back and pets it. "Look at these delicate fingers," she says. "Beautiful."

"What's she like?"

"When I think of her, I think of tofu. She used to spoon-feed me tofu."

"My mom was young, too. She once helped me steal a book on tree frogs from the public library."

"Did I mention I can do you a penis ring on the house? It'll keep you hard for eons."

"I've got to get back to the restaurant," I say.

"Yuck," she says. "Tonight?"

"Yeah, I mean I have to go."

"Let me dress you first." I don't understand the statement until she starts wrapping Saran Wrap around my Neosporined arms, like black kielbasas. "You're going to need to protect these arms for a couple days. Do you have a long-sleeved shirt? Can you stay out of the heat?"

"I don't," I say. "Can't," and flee.

At four in the morning I unlock the back door to Piecemeal. I quietly close it behind me so Jafari won't hear. Then there's a tapping on the door, and I hold my breath for a second, until it opens and Brain is there. We stand in the dish room.

"You some kind of superhero?" Brain asks. "Saran Wrap Man?"

"They call me Blackout," I say.

"Is that what you've been doing all night? Going partially African American?"

"I'm in the middle of rectifying some things. Check one."

We get right to work. Open all the reach-ins, stack the poisonous pizzas fifteen high on dough trays.

"No more gut ache?" I ask.

"The cleaner must have burnt off before the crusts absorbed too much," he says.

"We still should get rid of them, just in case."

We carry the dough trays and set them behind the dumpster. Frozen Piecemeal pizzas are like brittle cardboard. They snap in half. We double-bag them in Heftys, then restack the dough trays and Brain takes them back inside. When he returns I am in the dumpster, standing knee deep in the shit of Piecemeal. I clear some space. Brain tosses me the bags of poisonous pizzas one by one. I line the bottom of the dumpster with them and cover them with the other trash.

"Do you think I'm a cool boss?" I ask Brain.

"I don't even really think of you as a boss," he says.

"But in a way, I'm a pretty cool one, right?"

"You don't tell me what to do. Back there in the office, well, that was an extraordinary situation. You said eat the pizza, I said fuck you, you said eat the pizza, I said fuck you, eat the pizza, fuck you, eat the pizza, fuck you. Then I did it. Not because you told me to, but because it was the right thing. You got lucky and were right. There's cool boss in that. After the army, I don't handle authority so well. You're the one in the dumpster."

Brain is not giving me what I'm after, but he's not not giving it to me either. A cool boss is what I want to be if I have to be a boss, maybe because my bosses have been such true-blue cocksuckers.

I climb out of the dumpster. My arms are hot, sweating tattoos under the plastic. I pat Brain on the back. I stand for a moment outside Jafari's van, listening to see if he's heard us. There's only silence and the splashing of the fountain.

X

My new tattoos ooze and stain the sheets pink and gray. Like Mea taught me, I slather myself in Neosporin, then dig out my long-sleeved shirt for Shaka's funeral. Yesterday Marigold informed me that she has gone back to her life against doctor's orders. She's working full time at the salon again and she invites me to Rhododendron's show that night with a cutesy fridge note: *Dear Night Manager, Your presence is requested at The Covered Dish for a rock 'n' roll performance.*

The funeral is at this Hare Krishna temple across town. Shaka's dad is greeting people at the door wearing black shorts and a black T-shirt with black socks and sandals. His clothes match his tattoos. Now, mine do too. He is shaking people's hands, looking serious, but not sad. You can't imagine this guy crying.

He takes my hand, squeezes my fingers together, and cups his hand over mine. He lifts my sleeve, admires the work on my forearm and then turns my arm around. "You look good," he says.

I hear someone in back whispering about what a stupid way it was to go out. "Pathetic," he says. I glare at the guy, one of Shaka's surfing buddies from St. Augustine. The fact is I agree with him. The only way a guy like Shaka should die is by shark attack, or a nuclear bomb—something big and dramatic. Dying from a self-inflicted wound infection is something I would do.

Instead of one person getting up and saying something

about him, we stand in a circle and pass around this seashell necklace Shaka always used to wear. The deal is whoever holds the necklace speaks about him, then passes the necklace down.

When it gets to me, I don't know what to say, so I just say "Shaka Bra" a few times and it seems to be the right thing because everyone repeats it after me like an amen.

X

The Covered Dish is the anti-Hardback. It is a wide space that can accommodate radio-style bands. They don't sell King Cobra. There's no Slayer on the juke. The kid at the door is a frat boy wearing a button-down and pleated shorts, K-Swiss minus socks. Rhododendron rules this place. Their pop song covers have captured the hearts of the teenagers and college kids throughout the city. They get paid to play.

"I'm on the list," I tell K-Swiss and lay my hands flat on his little podium, hiking up my sleeves so the Blackout shows.

"Name?" he says.

"Thinfinger," I say. "When Thinfinger."

I can see my name, but he looks a couple times to make sure it's really there. "You're on the Eternal Guest List," he says, impressed. He stamps my hand and says respectfully, "Cool tats."

"True dat," I say.

The Dish has this long hallway. You can feel the thump of the bass drum and sense the muffled jugga of the guitars as you approach. I stop in the hallway and close my eyes, trying to recognize Marigold by the feel of her vocals in this muffled space. It's a pop song I recognize from the house: her in white plastic storm-trooper get-up bopping around in front of the mirror, the same one I used to watch my ass in when we had sex. I feel a tinge of embarrassment for her and for myself as I come around the corner and get my first glimpse. She looks like an action figure in her back brace, a yellow floral-print skirt, black cloth ninja shoes with silver buckles. The sorority girls are eating it up, bouncing off one another in a pillow-fight version of a mosh pit. Relentless ponytailing.

The guys, each of them copies of the door guy, pogo amid the ponytails. They grab waists and tits and spin and push, and everyone is holding a drink in one hand, spilling cranberry and vodka all over chests.

Marigold is twirling around, looking not at all like someone with serious back difficulty. She has one of those medical chairs on stage beside her, white plastic, hospital looking. She sits down in it between songs. I order a nickel Jell-O shot and wait. At intermission she descends and comes my way with Serial Bitch. She doesn't see me, but Serial Bitch does.

"Wanker alert," Serial Bitch says.

"You should call yourselves the Storm Troopers of Death," I say. "Oh, wait. Taken."

"You came," Marigold says, and wraps me up. She laughs, screeches. What a sound. "More Jell-O shots for this character," she tells the barman, "but not too many more."

I hike up my sleeves and show her the arms. She gasps, runs a finger along the top of my forearm.

"Why'd you do this?"

"It was a long time coming."

"I never said anything, but I always liked the way those faded things made you look. They made me think of getting old with you. These won't trouble my father nearly as much."

"They've earned me the nickname Blackout."

"I like When. And hey, when do you think you'll get the pills?" I remove them from my pocket and pass them to her. "Oh goodie," she says. She shakes the bottle. "There's not so many here."

"Do you even hurt anymore?" I didn't like the idea of her

becoming an addict. With some girls—in some bands—it would work well, but with Marigold, in Rhododendron, it'd be laughable. What was not laughable was that, even with all my empty efforts, she was slipping away faster than ever.

"Oh yes, I fucking hurt, When. It hurts more than you can know." She twists off the childproof top and swallows two. One of those could put down a horse. I smile and order us more Jell-O shots. I pass over some money and she says drinks are free for her and her people.

"Isn't Jell-O technically food?" I say.

"Food is free for me also, to an extent. I'm nervous, When. Any advice, one professional to another?"

"Flare the nostrils. Scare them."

"You could use yourself a trim," she says, catching my hair between her fingers.

"Serious question," I say. "Important."

"Okay," she says.

"Why don't you make your own songs? You could write about your dad's bunting, or your skulls, or our abortion."

Serial Bitch calls her to the stage.

"I don't like to think about that, When," she says. "Besides, people like to hear songs they already know."

Marigold pops back up onstage. She starts swinging around, real loose, singing, "Blame it on the rain . . ." Watching her, I realize the whole thing is pretty much dead in the water. She is moving her nose weirdly, trying to flare her nostrils, but either she doesn't know how or the Percocets have deadened any feeling. "Another Jell-O shot," I say, "on the band."

all
systims
go

I wake up in the Ghia at a BP I don't recognize. The interior light is on and the tape deck plays the Descendents in slow mo, *Sour fucking grapes*. A highway map is upside down on the passenger seat.

I roll out and do some waybacks, look around. Beyond the road, it's pitch black. There appear to be fields or woods, a highway absent of cars, and the BP. I knock on the window glass and the cashier, a kid, pushes the drawer out without looking up from an issue of *Juggs*. I say, "I'm not buying anything."

He points at a speaker on the wall.

I say into the speaker, "I'm not buying anything."

He retracts the drawer, continues reading.

"Where am I, dude?"

"Off Interstate 75," he says, doesn't look at me.

"What city?"

"Valdosta."

I think. Where is there a Valdosta? I can't think of it. "*The* Valdosta?" I say.

He sighs, closes his magazine, grabs a pack of smokes and joins me in the parking lot. "You, stranger, you're in the city of Valdosta, in the country of the United States of America, the county of Lowndes, the state of Georgia, the Peach State. Where you coming from?"

Now he wants to chat, but I'm done. I hold up my hand. "Talk into the speaker."

I go back to the Ghia and check the map. I find Valdosta, three hours north. It's the middle of the night, and I'm unsure where I am going or for why. I crank the Ghia but nothing's happening. The alternator maybe, voltage regulator, probably something that on any other car would cost forty bucks but on this one will cost six or seven hundred. The Ghia hasn't gone over five miles in five years.

A truck goes by on the interstate below me, a straight shot home down I-75. I gather the contents of the Ghia into an old Taco Bell bag. I scrounge up about seventy-two cents. I look around the inside one last time, see a Post-it I hadn't noticed before stuck to the underside of the steering column. It says, *all systims go*.

The kid is back inside reading *Penthouse Forum*. I say into the speaker, "I'm ready to buy." He pushes out the drawer. "How much for a Mountain Dew? Twelve ounce—I only drink from a can."

"Ninety-eight cents," he says, again without looking up.

I drop the change and the Ghia key into the night drawer. He pulls it in.

"That's seventy-two cents," I say, "and the key to that disabled Karmann Ghia. It's yours."

He looks at the car. "It run?"

"It's good business for in town. I wouldn't take it on any trips though."

He nods like, 'kay, he'll try that. He counts out the seventy-two, then counts it again, puts it in the register, goes and grabs a can of Mountain Dew, drops it into the night drawer and pushes it back at me. I have a sip and toast the Ghia, which procured me many a parking ticket in my pre-motorized-longboard, pre-Haro days.

I walk the southbound entrance ramp and stand in the dark with my thumb out. Few cars are out at this time of night, and I can't even see, in the glare of their headlights, who is passing me by. I walk backward on the shoulder. Finally an eighteen-wheeler passes, then slows way down the highway, like he was first going to fuck me off and had a change of heart. I take what I can get.

I run to where he pulled off and step up to the door. He's leaned over to open it.

"I'm taking this highway straight down to Miami," he says. "If you want anywhere from here to there, climb on in."

"Thank you," I say. I sit on the leather seat. The truck rumbles back onto the highway. A painted sand dollar hangs from a rosary around the rearview mirror. The radio blares a news station. It says that an Iraqi Scud missile hit a U.S. barracks in Saudi Arabia, killing twenty-eight soldiers. I think, That could have been Shaka. What a better way for him to go. The radio also says that Saddam announced the Iraqi withdrawal from Kuwait, but the trucker clicks off the radio midsentence.

"I only picked you up," he says, "because I was starting to fall asleep. If you don't talk, keep me awake, I'm not sure I've got any use for you." We both stare at the highway.

"I was driving somewhere tonight with no idea where I was going," I say. I am disappointed. I know exactly where I was headed when I stalled in Georgia in the middle of the night: to see that lying motherfucker in the Midwest. How I'd got the idea the Ghia would make it there I can't figure.

X

Dr. Bob calls me in again on Prep Dog recon dawn raid, a few hours after I walk in from the highway, where the trucker dropped me off. I curse the Prep Dogs, who show up less and less, but the fact is I don't mind it so much. It gets me my alone time in the restaurant, the way I like it best, dank and quiet, an awesome and silent machine in which I am the driveshaft. It's almost as good coming in hungover at six in the morning as coming in wasted at four. Piecemeal is a different place like this, empty in a relaxing way. It smells like me.

I make dough. The Hobart is a beast, with a murderous reputation. Its steel arm has been known to eat people. I imagine day crew finding me broken in pieces and mixed into a taut dough ball. The motor would still be going, and the arm spinning, snapping what was left of the pieces of my bones.

The recipe is so simple: a bag of flour, a half-inch square of cake yeast, some sugar, some oil, some salt. I add in a certain percentage of wheat flour to get the health factor up. That's it. The only hard part is keeping the yeast alive. You have to put the salt in last, on top of the flour, because salt kills yeast. The water temperature is important also: above one hundred and forty degrees, the yeast will die, while cool water decreases its growth and if the water's too cold the yeast goes dormant. Ideally I want between ninety-five and one hundred and fifteen, which is a water temperature I know with my finger, just like I knew at the Barbie-Q the exact doneness of a steak by pressing on it.

Once the Hobart gets going, you stand around eyeballing it. You can tell by the texture what the dough needs, a shot of water or a shot of flour. If you did it right, it pulls right off the Hobart arm, no stick. You get down in a crouch, tip the bowl toward you, and grab the dough like a perfect sinking ass. Then you stand, seventy pounds of dough in your arms, firm, yes, but still goopy enough to ooze down your gut as you transfer it to the cutting boards.

Today my arms are sore and the long sleeves stick to the dough ball. Once it's on the cutting board I pause and roll up my sleeves, check myself out. I use the reflective side of the dishwasher as my mirror and pose. The reflection is unclear, but you can make out what is standing there: one badass Ovenman.

I take out a nice serrated knife to cut off the dough segments. Some people use a scale; I weigh them by feel: fourteen ounces for a small pizza, eighteen for a medium, twenty-one for a large—and seven ounces for calzones. I wrap them in baggies and transport them to the walk-in, which I have to hip-check to keep open with my arms full of dough tray. I wander in sideways, absolutely in the dark, because I can't reach the switch.

Ordinarily I go right to the dough racks on memory. This time I hit something with my cheek. Some kind of cold frozen thing in the middle of the walk-in that swings away from me when I hit it and then swings back. I try going around it but hit another one and step in a dough tray on the floor, splashing liquid on my foot.

I set down my tray and fumble for the light. At the same time the walk-in door slams shut behind me, I recognize the smell of raw meat. You don't know you have this caliber of bitch scream in you until you're bitch-screaming it. Two skinned dogs hang from the ceiling, pink and blue bodies, cloudy eyes aimed everywhere and at me at once. I back away, screaming, and slip, fall to my ass. Blood is dripping into the trays on the floor, splashing pink on my white sock.

You can tell they're fresh, the meat is pink. It goes white after a while. I'm thinking they're some Satanic shit, some kind of Greg retribution. I push the plunger to open the door and it pushes but nothing happens. I hit it again, and the latch clicks but no movement.

I stare down the dogs. They have stubs for tails. I push one in the side, hard and cold. If I had my knife, I could cut them up right here. I learned at the Barbie-Q how to disassemble mammals into the parts humans like to eat and I know how to scrape the rest into a hot dog bucket. Then I'm banging on the walk-in walls with a twenty-one-ounce dough ball.

The door rips open and I fall into Dr. Bob who is all, "What?"

"Dogs," I say, pointing.

"Dogs?" he says. "What are you talking about, Thinfinger?"

He's looking at me and into the walk-in like everything is perfectly normal. And I think for a moment that I'm going nuts, that I'm seeing things. I point at them.

"Don't you see them?" I say.

"The lambs?" he says. "Those are lambs."

"Lambs," I say.

"We're having a family feast. Something wrong with the walk-in latch?"

"Must be," I say, looking back at the skinned things, hanging in my walk-in, the same one I steal kegs and buckets of pickles from. "Must be."

"You look kind of pale, Thinfinger."

"These things have affected me," I say.

"Well, get a grip."

"One question," I say. I am out of breath. "Are you doing anything with their skulls when you're done?"

A little later, I'm tearing into heads of lettuce again, thinking the lamb skulls may be the key to the whole thing. Marigold has always brought home skulls as a message to me. Never have I presented her with a skull. And why not? Granted, a lamb skull is fairly ordinary compared to her collection, but it's the thought that counts. Her reaction should pretty much tell me all I need to know.

Jafari walks in, his clothes shiny, covered in shellac. "I meant to tell you, last time I worked on that cooler door, I had some trouble getting the mechanism to open from the inside. I just couldn't find the problem. It'd be tragic if someone got locked in there, wouldn't it, Night Manager?"

Dr. Bob bumps by me, sticks a twenty in my hand and mutters thanks for coming in on short notice. The back door slams behind him. I hold the twenty in my hand. Jafari snatches it. "I'll be taking *that* for now."

X

Marigold is on the couch in her storm-trooper brace, watching TV and weeping. She doesn't look up when I come in. I stand next to her and watch.

"Are you crying about this cartoon?" I ask. It's Tom and Jerry.

"I never understood it like this. It's awful."

"Maybe you're a bit sensitive."

"Yes, When. Maybe. Excuse me for being touched."

I have to excuse her for being touched. I have to excuse her for enjoying the sensual pleasures in life. I have to excuse her for singing covers. I have to excuse her for being addicted to pills no doctor will give her anymore because of me. I have to excuse her for being unable to use the bed I bought her because she needs a special medical bed with cranks and hammocklike supports made of superfibers. I have to excuse her puking up all over the toilet. And I have to excuse her dreaming that I murder her. I have the sense, for the first time since I've become Night Manager, that things have completely slipped out from under my control.

So I leave her there and go back to work, walk right into

my tenth hour there that day. I call a box-fold meeting. Before punch-in—that's off the clock—everyone meets me in the prep room with a small stack of boxes.

"It has come to my attention that there are customers leaving the restaurant with inferiorly folded boxes. Boxes with edges that don't maintain, boxes that lack structural hold. It's necessary that when customers leave here with Piecemeal pie, they can be confident that their boxes will not fall apart en route."

I speak loudly so that Skordilli and Dr. Bob can hear me in the café. I'm not doing it for them, but since this is the kind of thing they want to hear from me, let them hear it. Gutter Boy, Skinhead Rick, Brain, Ashley, and Mea stare at me. They have never seen anything quite like this. They're more used to me ordering them to smoke up in the bathroom than to fold boxes correctly.

"I am serious about this, guys," I say. "Now do what I do." I take a flat box, bend the flaps at each perforation, and loosen them so that they move. "You are doing this so they move, so that you can better tuck them in," I say. I fold up the sides, then insert the ends from the front, pulling up the back and lowering the top, so that a finely formed, sturdy box sits before me.

The others twist and tuck and set theirs alongside mine, leave the prep room shaking their heads. I examine the results, all of them, indeed, pretty fine, except one, which is coming apart before its maker has left the prep room. Ashley's box is a disgrace, a pitiful specimen.

"Ashley," I say. "What is this?"

She comes back into the prep room. "It's my box."

I direct her attention to the inside back corners of the box, where the flaps have been crammed, not tucked, into the edge.

"Does this seem satisfactory to you?"

She pops gum. "I'm never going to get this part, dude."

"How many slices did you drop last shift, Ashley?"

She laughs, "There's so much cornmeal on those crusts it's a real balancing act."

I ask her to meet with me outside and she follows me out back, where we're out of earshot. "I don't think this is working out," I say.

"What don't you think is working out?"

"The arrangement of your employment at Piecemeal."

"When, speak English to me, I'm not following you here. Are we breaking up?"

"This is really hard for me, Ashley. I like you. You're a good person. You have the qualities of many individuals which are good: kindness, nice hair, being kind—you have all those things."

"That's all very flattering. I swear to God. What gives?"

"I've never done this before. So, it's like, there are all your good things, but then there are the things that have to do specifically with the job that are not exactly so good. You take cigarette breaks at bad times, fling slices and whole pies to the floor, you can hardly reach the boxes, forget about the actual box-folding technique, which is a separate thing, but it's in there, within the number of things which are not exactly good."

"'Fling' implies that I drop those slices and whole pies on purpose, which I don't. They fall," she says. Ashley is a hard girl, which is one of the reasons I'm going with this idea, to make her my first fire, figuring she can take it. But she tips back against the brick wall, her face soft and hanging. "Are you firing me, When?"

I can't think of anything to say. "I am fulfilling my responsibility as Manager."

"Okay," she says. "Okay, okay, let me go punch out—no actually forget that." She pulls the string on her apron and it falls. She reaches in her pocket, pulls out a cigarette, and lights it, then tromps off, throwing her head back in what I think is triumph.

X

Dr. Bob and Skordilli linger this night. Ordinarily they chill for a cappuccino or two, then duck out. But they've been hanging more often. Stoned and stone-faced they camp out at the café, Argus-eyeing. Dr. Bob doesn't say shit. Ignores me except to criticize something, too many stems on the spinach, the Sprite dispenser in disrepair, a stray meatball on a straight mari. I worry that Jafari has said something. He stands at the dish sink and when I walk by he glares and smiles at me. He'll then leave just as we're out of forks and go work on his fountain statue.

I make sure the crew knows about Dr. Bob and Skordilli by clock-in so we're all on our best behavior. Some guy comes up to the counter, stands there with his face literally three feet from the menu, looks into Mea's eyes, and asks her what it is that we serve here. She golds: "What do we have? Sir, we have dough, sauce, and cheese. Name your combo. We got open-face sauce and cheese on dough, we got sauce and cheese inside a dough ball, we got dough strings with sauce and cheese over them, we got thick dough, thin dough, extra-thin dough. We got long-string, short-string dough, wheat or white. We got meat sauce and nonmeat sauce. Name your flavor, sir. We're here to please."

"I'll have some pizza."

"Slice or pie? Thin or thick? New York Cheese, Stuffed Veggie, Mexican, Greek, Pepperoni, Portobello White, Vegan, Sister Seafood, Ready Freddy, Mama Jamma, Barbie-Q,"—my inspired invention!—"Szechuan. All ready to go, sir. Hot in a jiffy."

Night Manager, of course, has nothing to do. I circle the place, circulating, then hover around the kitchen. The grease in the fryer is black, so I decide to clean it. To clean the fryer you have to fuck it. Other than mopping, there is no greater satisfaction under the Piecemeal roof. But I've hardly got the shit drained when Dr. Bob taps me on the shoulder.

"Come here." I come there. "Look, When, you're the Manager. Let's have Gutter Boy or whatever you call him clean the fryer. Some advice, you could be more managerial in ways. Firing Ashley was good. She was worthless. The crew needs to know you're not their buddy and not their coworker. You're their boss."

"Well, yeah. Gutter Boy's on pasta."

"He can clean it in between pasta. And also, I don't want to hear about you mopping the floors at night. That's not Manager work. You should walk around and ask customers how's their meal. Give kids a free boat of garlic rolls. You've got other things to worry about. Worry about them."

He wants me to stand there. Just stand. Not run oven. Not fuck the fryer. There is always something to wipe down, but Dr. Bob doesn't even want me wiping down. He wants me supervising other people's wipedown. Manage. My tattoos have begun to peel and I'm under strict orders from Mea not to pick them unless I want faded spots. I defy her, scratching the raised scabs on the top of my wrist.

I order Gutter Boy to fuck the fryer. He does it but he won't speak to me other than to say he's really sorry, his supplier can't get any more Percocets. He'd suggest extra-strength Tylenol, and I understand this is retribution for the fact he thinks I stole his girlfriend. The white skin under his neck trembles when he says the word "suggest."

I stand at the front, smiling, doing nothing, watching Gutter Boy with my peripheral. He's hopeless on the fryer. He tries to wipe away peanut oil with a wet rag. He won't listen to me. So I go bother Brain, try and show him a more effective way of covering the thin pies in pepperoni. I snatch the pepperoni tray and stick it in the freezer for five minutes. Then I deal pepperonis out like poker chips. You want the same amount of ronis on each slice. You place a final layer of ronis on the cheese layer and you guide the Ovenman where to cut by your roni placement, by positioning the cheese layer in a six-pointed star. Brain keeps asking me, "Are you serious under there, man?"

I don't bite. I check the dough stockpiles. Plenty.

I assign everyone to tie off garlic rolls and I stand there watching them, thinking about the proper way to fuck the fryer, the way I do it. I imagine it step by step: twist the esophagus extension onto the drain, then pull the lever, but no grease runs out, another thing our health inspector ignores with the help of Dr. Bob. Only I know what's holding it in there. There is a layer of sludge, about an inch thick, made of flour from the calamari, cornmeal from the catfish fettuccini special, and fried dough skins. There are two tools for this business. One is a long wire with a bend for reaching into the grease and probing the clog from the inside. The second is a coat hanger that enters the machine at the other end, the drain. It requires a simultaneous reaming with both before a torrent of boiling grease runs out, congealing then flowing, congealing, flowing, filling the detergent bucket, which I then lug out back and carefully spill into the already overflowing third grease bin.

Gutter Boy's filling the fryer back up with new peanut oil but he forgot to close off the valve and a gallon rushes quickly across the kitchen floor before he realizes or I can get to it. Then he's all, "Fuck, fuck, fuck," and trying to mop it up with the wet mop.

"Stop," I say, dropping dirty aprons around the puddle of grease to keep it from spreading. "Get a new mop head, and we'll clean this right." He doesn't move. "Go."

"Shinola, sayonara," he says. He throws the mop against the walk-in and walks out.

He slams the door behind him and I go punch out his time card. I stick a new mop head on the mop and soak the oil up with a combination of mop and dirty aprons. I fill the fryer the rest of the way. In between I'm covering pasta and slinging some pretty maris to our Thursday-night crowd, sprigs of parsley crowning each meatball. I could do every station here better than anyone else in the place.

"You were rough on the Gutter, bossman," Brain says to me.

"Where's the competence, man?" I reply. "That's what I want to know."

X

Do I feel bad afterward? I feel bad. So I try to blame it on someone other than myself and I pick Dr. Bob and Skordilli, who are coming around too much, loafing around the place with Jafari, who could be telling them anything at any minute, and acting like I'm not on their good side so much anymore, like maybe I'm not their guy. How am I supposed to keep my head if I can't regularly mop the floor to my satisfaction? How am I supposed to steal kegs and wholesale buckets of pickles if they're around, because kegs and wholesale buckets of pickles, let's face it, are not after all grapefruits?

I can't stand to watch Rick lazily mop the floor anymore. He neglects to change the water or even rinse out the mop head more than once or twice, leaving a film of dirt. I approach Dr. Bob at the café and ingratiate, "How do you get into dentisting?"

"Dentisting?" Dr. Bob says. "Let me tell you about that, When." He drapes his arm across my shoulder and walks me around back, to the same place I fired Ashley. He puts me against the wall. When he talks he hunches over, his big body blocking me from all sides.

"I had this girlfriend—she was an artist, a sculptor—and things were going bad for us. Then there was a period when I would wake up with chalk in my mouth. I slept hard."

"Uh huh," I say, latching on to a point I can agree with. "When I sleep hard I too awake with a kind of chalky, dry feel in my mouth."

"She was also a hygienist, When," he says. "It was actually chalk, a chalk of sorts, a dental molding chalk or putty or whatever you call it. I haven't practiced in eons. They're probably calling it Mouthform by now, names change all the time."

His stale breath is right in my face. I blurt out, "I find it very difficult to not do anything. It's work and at work you should do something."

"Listen to this story. My girlfriend was casting my mouth in the night. I found out why, and also why my lamb chops seemed shorter and shorter every morning, when I attended an exhibit of hers, several weeks after she vamoosed. I still remember the title: A Nice Place to Keep Your Things.

"There were these little jewelry boxes, about half the size of those wholesale butter sticks we buy. The boxes were lined with molds of my teeth in gold casting, which she'd made while I was sleeping. I recognized the bite. The trim on the boxes was little wisps of my hair. She titled them, unoriginally, Jewelry Box Made from My Ex-Boyfriend's Teeth and Hair I, II, III, et cetera.

"They were selling like bonanza. Two hundred and fifty a pop. That's why I became a dentist. But it's not all it's cracked up to be."

"Did you buy one of the boxes?"

"I didn't. They were mine anyway. She had stolen them from me. I should have sued the bitch."

He gets this look in his eye like the story has taken him back. He fishes a one-hitter out of his pocket and puffs it. Then he turns away from me, looks up at the sky, and strolls around the corner. I follow him because it seems like he's about to say something else. Jafari is standing in the fountain, sopping his statue with a paintbrush.

"Just the two I wanted to see," he says, stepping out of the fountain and gesturing dramatically. "I present to you my achievement."

He has completed, finally, the fountain sculpture. For months we've gazed at the blank pedestal through clogged eyes after shifts. We've stood atop it dropping tiny balls of mozzarella in for the guppies. The statue is such an odd thing that at first your eyes can't process it and you think it's a squashed barrel cactus or some other disfigured succulent. Then it becomes clear. It is the same thing that sat on my table that bleary morning after The Rob: a pizza box, a Piecemeal pizza box, with fake money fanning out the sides. The bills—rectangles of newspaper cut into thick, tidy stacks—sticking out the sides of the box, dripping with the overcoated shellac as if there's tears or raindrops falling from them.

I hold my breath. "That's beautiful," Dr. Bob says.

"My work is almost done here," Jafari says. He stares at me, picking crusted shellac off his chin.

I've got a new habit of tossing Rick's grenade in the air while I count the drawers. It makes me count one-handed. I set the twenties in a pile on the counter. Then I count as I move them one by one into another pile. Then I do the tens and fives and ones. Bill by bill. I toss the grenade because it helps me count and makes the drawers take forever. I need forever since I'm not allowed to do anything else.

When I'm done counting, I reach for the Post-it pad to write the night's total, but there is already a message left for me on the top note of the pad. It's written in a scraggly style: *Consider this last call. They'll know everything come tomorrow.* It's unsigned, but I know who it's from. I wonder if he's serious.

I continue tossing the grenade, wondering what kind of hole it would make in Piecemeal and how would it sound. I watch myself in the reflective steel of the counter, seeing how wide I can flare my nostrils.

"Who said you could touch that?" Skinhead Rick says, appearing in the office doorway.

"I woke up in Georgia the other night," I say.

"That's why you're getting all dickhead on us? Georgia is a good state."

"Let me ask you something, Rick," I say. "Do you ever have a problem with the idea of, say, a woman shitting?"

"No. No I don't have any problem with that."

"All right," I say, "I see."

"Wait now, one of them flimsy bitches you go around with, okay, it'd give me trouble, the thought of one of them growing a tail. That's how I choose my women, though. Look at Katrina. You just look at her and you know: there's a woman who takes a shit."

He's right, I think, about Katrina. You do know that. "There's something I've been trying to ask you about that," I say. "How do you reach her?" He looks at me like I might have crossed a line. "I mean she's, well, she's beautiful, man. I can't imagine the mechanics of it. She's a tall girl."

"Don't imagine those mechanics. It's disrespectful. But I'll tell you this, there's plenty of tricks, and in missionary, my face is right at boob level the whole time, and that's a beautiful thing. Nothing makes me happier."

Rick unfolds a tabloid page from the local weekly. There's an advertisement for a bare-knuckle fighting circuit coming to town. He points at some fine print at the bottom: *Criminals and felons welcome*. The winning purse is twenty thousand dollars and a spot on the circuit.

"It's my chance," Rick says. "All I've got to do is wreck one of these titans."

"You're going to do this?"

"I'm going to win this."

Imagine the most dangerous-looking person you can, and

then picture him excited on Christmas morning. That's how Rick looks when he says this. I am happy for him, but it shows the real difference between us. He yearns for the top. I'm the opposite. All I think about is the simple joy of mopping floors, of Ajaxing the sinks, of scraping burnt-to-a-crisp ronis off the back of the oven brick.

"I might go see my dad," I say. "He owns a batting cage in Ohio."

"I thought he booted you long ago."

"Another one."

"Two dads?" This kind of paternal look comes over Rick's knobby face. "Which one's real?"

"The one I might see. Never met him before."

Rick's all nods. "Do it. Go. I'm telling you, you'll see things. I don't know what, but it's a good way of figuring out what's you and what's something else."

"I want to ask him what kinds of health problems he has. I want to see if he has all his hair."

"Your hair is great, man. If I had your hair, I wouldn't have to go skinhead."

Rick folds his ad and slides it back into his pocket.

"You really think you wouldn't be a skinhead if you weren't bald?"

"I know."

I nod like I understand. "Another thing: I might need you to take out the hippie for me. Haven't decided yet."

"Say the word, bossman."

My crew is fractured as we cut out; Mea rides the Haro but holds my arm with one hand, slapping at me every time I pick the tattoo scabs. We have a little while before the show, and I could go home to Marigold, to sit and watch Discovery or

cartoons and pop Percocets, however many are left. Now that
her back is a little better and the Percocets deaden the pain
enough we might even try to have sex on the Summerside
Plush again. Or I could go home and fire her like I fired Ashley,
and maybe, if I was lucky, she would accept it and straighten
her posture in triumph too. I want to do all that, but I like the
feel of Mea here. The rest of the crew is behind us a ways. I
steady her on the Haro, then bury my head in her neck, where
she's marinated in the sour stink of pepperoni and cheese, the
closest her body has ever come to meat and dairy.

"Eau de Piecemeal," I say.

We pause for free drinks. We swoop into the hotel bar, a
place we'd never go if we weren't hooking up a certain barkeep who is one of those freaks that likes pineapple on his
pizza. I announce, "My favorite, my man, Mr. Hawaii Five-O."
The barkeep lines them up. And I start tearing them down. I
am into my third pint when I notice none of the crew is sitting
by me. They're all clustered around the dartboard near the end
of the bar. I think I hear Brain say my name, then he looks over
his shoulder at me, and I don't like his look. I scan the room for
Mea and see her, attached to the barkeep, who should be taking
her order and hurrying back for my refills. She takes his throat
in her hand and he laughs. I can't hear what they're saying.
Then he turns around and lifts his shirt for her. Tattooed across
his back is a giant tsetse fly. Mea traces its wings and spindly
legs. I look across the bar at my reflection, sitting there alone. I
hold up my black arms so I can see them in the reflection and,
in spite of the fact that Mea's interest has already shifted, I feel
better about myself.

Then we go over to the real show, mine, where the wormy
door guy has a pitcher waiting for me. He hands it off to me
and holds the door. I remove the nonmotorized skateboard
from my Quest pack, where I keep it when I go out on bike. If

the Haro goes missing again I want to have a way home. Mea U-locks the Haro to a telephone pole. I swill the beer and hand it to her. She steps inside and turns to watch. I back up for some runway space. The opening band is in full swing.

"Hold the door," I tell wormy door guy. I kick the nonmotorized skateboard and ollie into the Hardback, blazing into the pit, snatching back the pitcher from Mea as I fly by. I pass Jenny Raygun, who is owning it, throwing fists like a pro. Queen of the pit on this night. She sees me coming and swivels at the hips. She catches me in the chest with a solid punch. I fall on my back, shooting the board through the air into the singer's shin. The pitcher showers beer all over the crowd and the floor. It bounces and someone kicks it into the wall.

"Goal!" the dude says.

The crowd lifts me by my shoulders and heaves me back toward Jenny Raygun, and my momentum topples us both. I land on top of her, her skirt hiked up around her thighs. I catch Blaise's glance over by the juke, think to myself, Not the way to repair things. Then some slickdicks I don't recognize pick up my legs and jackhammer me on top of her like we're fucking. Jenny Raygun pushes me off and I laugh and everybody sweats as the opening band's set dies out. Then I go run recon with Blaise.

He double-fists King Cobras.

"I haven't seen you in beers, my friend," I say. "You never even stop by for a garlic roll or two on me."

"I'm on skatepark duty daily," he says. "We've got the *Thrasher* people scheduled for the big opening."

"Any luck on the serpents?"

"Did you ever imagine it'd be this hard to find a rattler in Florida? You'd think that by now, just by accident, one would have crawled into the shower with me."

"If you wanted mice, I could help you."

"I doubt very much you can help me, Thinfinger."

"What do you think?" I say, holding out my arms.

"Uh huh," he says. "We're on." And he brushes by me.

When we take the stage I remove my shirt. The crowd gets throaty. "I'm Blackout," I say. "We're Wormdevil." They are amped, yelling back, "Murderphonica," "Free Pizza Man," "Devilworm," "Cut the cheese." It's never been like this. Even the bass player and guitar player pat me on the back. They don't say, "Try not to embarrass us too much this time." They don't say, "Just sing the word 'Wormdevil' to every song." The guitar player duct-tapes my mic plug into the amp.

Then it's on, war zone. Rick and Katrina are barreling through, punching each other in the face. I sing "Wormdevil" and it goes off. The bartender stands on the bar and dives into the pit. Rick kicks him down while the gutterpunks charge the taps. From the back of the pit, Mea flicks me off, then licks her bird finger in a way I am certain I cannot handle. The quote marks on her shimmying shoulders are telling me everything I need to know. The view from stage is the perfect one.

But in the quiet after the first few songs, someone in back is screaming, "Bossman." I stand on my tiptoes and see that it's Brain. It's the song we wrote about Skordilli. The only lyrics are *Bossman, you suck / You suck, Bossman.* I step back and confer with the fellas.

"Can I sing one I recently put together?" I ask. "It's to the Duh-duh-duhduhduh-daaa one."

They look at each other.

Blaise shakes his head no. "Do it," the others say. "Let's hear your thing."

Blaise shakes his head again, wrinkles his unibrow, then starts the bass kick and I'm all, "Bossman, you suck." It whips the crowd up right. But Brain is still at the back shouting even when it's over, screaming "Bossman" over and over and pointing his finger at me. He wasn't making a request, he was calling me out, but I'm the only one who gets it. He shouts again, punctuating and pointing at me from the back of the pit: "Bossman, *you* suck."

I know I need a bold move, something to set things right. I don't want to be Night Manager, but I'm embracing it in spite of myself. In my head, at that very moment, I start working on a song, and I know there's only one place where I can get into the right space and concentrate.

At the end of our set, I leave the stage. I ignore the encore. I get on the Haro and start pedaling. Then I realize I don't know where I'm going. Then I open my eyes and I'm there.

X

Suddenly I'm in Piecemeal, by myself, just how I like it. I turn on the prep room bulb. There's a mouse on the floor eating a shiitake. It looks up, not worried enough to stop eating, but ready in case anything funny goes down. I admire that.

I bust open the reach-ins and decide on a slice of the Greek, a pizza I've never eaten enough of for some reason. I check the rise on the skins and they're all a little short because Brain was slacking. He didn't leave them on top of the oven long enough. There's scraps of receipt paper and cup lids all down the front counter. I fill a draft then sweep the scraps up. I turn the dial on the oven up to five fifty, careful to duck when cars roll by on University. I crumple up a tray paper, then light the end and jam it toward the pilot. A big blue flame singes the new growth of arm hairs up to my elbow.

I return to the prep room, where I hop up on the steel table, almost exactly the size of a twin mattress. I prop back on two fifty-pound bags of flour. The mouse is still eating the mushroom and eyeing me. "It's okay, my friend," I say. "You've beaten greater men than me."

Then I fall asleep. And when I wake up, my underarms are sticky and wet. I have tipped the beer across my chest. The timer has turned all the lights out. There are no windows in the prep room and the dark is pure black. Something squeaks across the floor, the flit of fur on paper flour bags. I reach out for the light. Then I stop. There is a clunking sound from the Naked Woman Poster Corridor. I hop down eye-level with the table, hoping I don't land on a mouse. I try to shake my tired. The sound is coming from Jafari's nailed-shut ceiling panel. I can hear the panel groaning as it's pulled up, the nails easing out of the wood. A spotlight of moon shines on the floor of the Naked Woman Poster Corridor.

Then a pair of black boots appears in the light, dangling there. The feet hang, kick, and a body drops into the restaurant. It crouches, slowly stands, and walks forward, toward me. It turns to inspect the porn posters on the wall and runs a hand over the *Hustler*'s bitties. A scrawny profile with a flat-backed skull. It caresses the poster, then lights a lighter. Greg. He kisses the poster. The flame gives enough light that I can see he's got a crowbar in his other hand. I am crouched on the balls of my feet. My arches begin to sting. He turns from one wall to the next, carefully examining the porn, then steps into the prep room and flips the light switch.

We're looking right at each other, my eyes just above the prep table. He doesn't even flinch. "Hey, spooky," he says.

I blink and hold my hands in front of my face to shield the light. "You're standing in the Piecemeal kitchen unauthorized," I say.

"Yes. One-hundred-percent right. Unauthorized." He hunches, leans forward onto the table, cigarette unlit, hanging from his mouth.

"Crazy running into you here," I say.

He comes around the table and I scoot away. He points to his forehead, to what I think is a big forehead crease until my eyes adjust a little better and I see that it's a scar.

"You cut your hair," I say.

"Why do you keep telling me shit about myself?" We move in a circle around the prep table, me stepping away as he comes toward. He shifts direction and I do too. He stops again, plunks the crowbar on the prep table, and lights his cigarette. I could grab the crowbar.

"I'm sorry," I say.

"Why would *you* be sorry?"

"I'm sorry that happened to you."

Greg turns around, puts his hands on the prep table, and then scoots his butt up. He leans back on the flour bags I'd been sleeping on a few minutes ago. "I haven't had any of that awesome veggie lasagna in so long." I move away from the table and he kicks off his boots. One of them lands on a sticky trap. I stand there for a minute, then I go warm him up a plate.

When I return his eyes are closed. I am relieved he is still clothed. I nudge him and hand over the plate with a fork, a knife, and a napkin bundled in the little cutlery pack we do. He devours. I refill the pitcher and bring a cup for him.

"Don't expect too much," I say. "The new Pasta Dude leaves much to be desired."

"Rarely do I expect too much," he says. "Too little is my default. I didn't rob this place, you know."

I stare at the shabbily mopped floor. I rub out some blackened mozzarella between the tiles with the toe of my special restaurant shoe. "What'd you come here for?" I ask.

"And that?" he says, pointing at my arms.

He starts kicking his heels on the steel prep table, and I crouch down, thinking it's a Prep Dog's truck. I don't know what time it is but I tell myself I'm too fucked up to care. I know that if it's anywhere close to time for Skordilli or Dr. Bob to open up, I don't want to be found here with Greg.

"Yes!" he says. "Yes! *Those* are tattoos, Thinfinger. I thought you were wearing long sleeves." I run my finger down my arm. The scabs have a strange texture; it's like my arm hairs are growing out of a thin layer of black mold. "I've taken heat for stealing money," he says, "and since I've had me some heat, I believe I should have me some money."

"Things are more complicated than that."

"For example?" Greg says, a carrot shred stuck to his chin.

"You won't get in the black box. There's a new combo. If you steal again they'll come after you again. They'll know it was you."

"Any other problems?"

"I'm here," I say.

"You are here," he says. "And you have neither kicked me out nor called the cops yet, Night Manager."

We're standing there in that kitchen silence. The only sounds his chewing and the far-off drip of the walk-in's condenser. "Come here," he says. I glance at the crowbar. He sees this. He kicks it off the table and it clanks to the floor. I step toward him. He swallows hard. He takes one long, thin, bony finger, one very much like mine, and pulls his cheek aside, points into his mouth. I step closer and he turns his head to the light. In the back are two empty square spaces, one on the top and one on the bottom, where teeth should be. He lets go of his cheek and eats another bite of veggie lasagna.

It's quiet except for his chewing. Then he screams, "You fired. You punch out now!"

Suddenly I am risking my job, the only real connection I have to anything in this life. I am entering the combination on the black box, the new one that I can only remember because it's sequential: 34-5-6. I am removing the money from the drawers. As I am leaving, I see Rick's grenade in the office and without even thinking, I slip it into my pocket. Then I'm handing over to Greg half the night's take bound with Piecemeal twisties.

"What did you say to Skordilli to make him fire you?"

"You really want to know?"

"I do."

"I told him that the restaurant looks like a kindergartner designed it. I told him that Jafari was conning his ass, making a laughingstock out of him. Anyone could see the place looked like shit. I was trying to help."

I shake his hand. "Take the money and run," I say.

"Wiser words never spoke."

He goes out the way he came, through the old hole in the roof. He even tries to half-ass replace it, knocking a few of the nails back in with his crowbar. I listen as his footsteps tap across the tin roof, then disappear on the alley side.

I go out the back door and lock it behind me. I pause outside Jafari's van and go through all the good things I could do with the other half of the money: buy Blaise some rattlesnakes, get Rick the hair job so he wouldn't have to be a skinhead anymore, buy a china cabinet for the display of Marigold's skulls. This makes me even madder about doing what I'm about to do.

I yank aside the curtain to Jafari's van and step in. He's asleep naked across the driver's and passenger's seats. He's covered in junk. He's sleeping with a hacksaw, a claw hammer, a window from an old house, and seven or eight wood screws. He sits up and the screws roll off him.

I throw the remaining stacks of cash at him. "There's your dough. There's your *cheddah*."

He wipes his eyes, then reaches for a stack. He holds it up with his left hand and with his right he fingers a wood screw from his bellybutton.

"This looks like trouble," he says. "Good morning, trouble."

"Just one thing, Jafari, one thing and we're square."

"Shoot."

"In terms of your life, make shit out of shit, make all the shit out of shit that your heart desires. Stick to what you're good at, well, what you do, your *art*. Do me a favor. Don't work in any restaurant. Period. I want you to promise me. It's a disgrace."

"All right," he says. "You're good at the restaurant part. I wonder which one of us is worse off?"

"I know," I say. "I don't need you to tell me what I know."

You wanted
it this way

Marigold wakes me up on our doorstep, smelling like the blue liquid hairstylists use to store combs. It's morning. She is jostling my shoulder. She does not seem pleased. Her amp and microphone kit are parked at the bottom of the steps, like she's going to practice. "Get up," she says. "There's something you should know."

"I like used to," I say. "But I don't know how good I am at awareness."

"I enjoy painkill," she says, pulls away. She descends the steps and picks up the amp and mic kit.

I pull myself up by the handrail, the same handrail I used to do acid-drop railslides down at my peak—I'd come barreling out of the house and jump free-willy-style into the air, sliding all the way down the rail and riding out of it. I try and lean comfortably, to look as though I'm in absolute control. I wonder if she should be carrying the amp. It's a little one, but she's still in her storm-trooper getup. "How's your back?" I ask.

She sets her gear down again and unsnaps the brace. She turns around and lifts her shiny blouse, her orange fluffy hair bouncing. There is one thin fleshy pink line. The color is the exact same as the skinned lamb from the Piecemeal walk-in.

"I like your purples best you know," she says.

I look down and realize I am only wearing my purple briefs and the special-tread restaurant shoes. I glance at the driveway, where I see my shorts but no sign of a T-shirt anywhere. Now a guy emerges from the house carrying a box labeled, *skulls.*

"Hey," he says.

"Hey," I say.

The guy walks by me.

"It's starting to get warm," I say.

"Yeah," he says. Marigold resnaps the brace and carries the amp to a Ford pickup truck parked in the driveway. The guy is arranging the metal poles of the Stryker around the skulls box.

I tap at my chest, nothing. Then I run my hands down my body, searching out the Post-it. I look around the porch, feel my head, eye Marigold.

"Did you take my Post-it?" I say as she goes by with a milk crate of toiletries.

"What Post-it?" she says. "When, we've been stepping over you for half an hour."

"I always have a Post-it."

I got a feeling that something bad has gone down, and I work myself into a panic, run over to my shorts in the driveway. They're heavy and it's because Rick's grenade is in my pocket with my pen and Post-it pad, blank. I see the Haro with the kinky triangular frame leaning against a tree a few houses down. I search it and, blessedly, stuck to the front tire, is a torn and wilted note. On it, I have written, *you wanted it this way.*

Rarely do memories crystallize for me like this one does, which is one thing to be proud about in this moment. I'm standing here in my purple briefs and restaurant shoes, looking at this tire-marked Post-it. It doesn't matter now. It's done. One rob can be forgotten. Things can return to normal. Lingering suspicions linger for a while, then they linger out. After a second rob everything changes.

I walk the bike down to the house with my shorts slung over the handlebars. Marigold and the guy are fitting more boxes into the truck. It is a nice truck, new, with whitewall tires, and a Milli Vanilli sticker on the rear window.

"Reggie," Marigold says, "this person standing here in his underwear is the boyfriend I'm moving out on."

"He's cute," the guy says. He's familiar, and then I realize why. He's the guy whose station we used to screw at in Wild Hair. He doesn't look like the fat gay guy I'd imagined from his pictures. He looks completely different, embarrassed to be in the middle of this. I'm panicking, have to pee in a bad way.

"What about Left?" I ask Marigold.

"You two are made for each other, When. But I will miss that mister."

"Just a problem all of the sudden?" I say.

"I thought you'd come around. I tried getting on with my life, so you could see I'm not just that girl who can't wheelie. I even quit the puking and put on seven pounds."

"Bunny hop," I say.

"Now you can't even get me the painkillers you made it so that I can't get. Reggie can. He's from Miami."

She shakes her head. She thinks I'm not getting it, but I get it. I want to say a lot of things here. I want to confess to not knowing what happens all the time, making it hard for me to apologize for any of it, and even harder to feel responsible for any of it. I want to confess to having apparently made a conscious decision to go above and beyond the boundaries of typical employee takey-takey. Though I can't say it was for her, to her went the spoils. I want to confess to not understanding why all the things that make her human are the things that disgust me about her. But I don't work that way.

Before I've come up with any of it, she startles me by saying—in the same way some women would say, "Pass the toast"— "You have blood on the front of your underwear."

I don't even look. It wouldn't be the first time. Blood—hers, mine, someone else's. I cup myself and, besides a dull sensation of soreness, I feel something strange, a pebble maybe, in my underwear.

She slips a little business-card-sized flyer into my hand with a picture of a rat's nest and the name Wild Hair. It says, *Good for One Free Haircut* and *Love, Marigold* at the bottom in her flippy handwriting. Reggie watches in the side-view mirror and buffs his front tooth with a Handi Wipe.

"You should expect a letter from me at least once a year," I say as she walks away. I am already composing the first one in my head: *Have gotten shit together, am rocking the USA. You can see me on MTV, but in real life you'll find me in the back of the restaurant, where I belong. I take restaurant jobs in random towns because I like the work (don't really* need *it anymore) and I like the people. I am honest and trustworthy, can be relied upon, come home and remember where I have been, what I have done.* She looks back, then disappears around the side of the Ford. It pulls away. I will not lie about myself in these letters.

I remember something about Marigold. It comes to me with the same clarity as last night's rob. It was early on, right after one of the first times I tried to teach her the bunny hop. She hadn't succeeded of course but I hadn't yet recognized it as the problem it was going to be. We were sweaty and thirsty. She asked me for water, and I went to the kitchen to get it for her. As I returned through the hallway I had a perfect view of her sitting on the couch. She pulled off a shoe—she had these bright white sneakers—she put it down, hesitated, then picked it back up. She held the shoe up to her face, stuck her nose in, and breathed deeply. She didn't know I was watching her. She dropped it to the floor and leaned back, looking happy and satisfied. It seems so simple now. All the unanticipated things—the panties on the floor, the third nipple, the puking, even a quickly acquired addiction to Percocets—were so in contrast to the kind of girl she seemed to be, and that was the attraction. I have been mistaking all the things I love about her for flaws.

As they pull off, I am left there in my purple underwear cupping myself. I got what I wanted: she's out of my life. But this time there is no prime time, no solid gold. The college kids walk by with backpacks and notebooks on their way to the university. They try not to but stare at me anyway. They are maybe thinking about first times, impotencies, fights, classes, protractors, projects, incompletes, essays. I am right now providing for them an anecdote to start conversations with people. They will never look at this little house the same way again. I step into my shorts, one special-tread restaurant shoe at a time, for all to see.

Inside, Left circles toward me. He sniffs at my crotch. I magnet the free-haircut card to the fridge. I look around and feel very alone without all the skulls and their marble eyes on me. I walk around the empty house. I start in my room, which is the only one that hasn't changed much. My shoe box of Post-its pokes out from under the bed. I sit Indian-style and flip through some of them. They are so shabbily written, covered in beer and other liquid stains, wrinkled and wet from the humidity, that I can't read most of them, but they make me happy just looking at them. I make a mental note to try and sit down with the shoe box next time I'm blasted because supposedly when you encounter something that you've written in a

similar state—drunk—you can better understand what the hell
it was you were trying to say. I find a Post-it longer than the
others and realize it's that notice to appear for peeing in public,
the date now hopelessly long past. I read the fine print: *Failure
to appear will result in a warrant issued for arrest*.

This reminds me that I have to pee, but I walk right past the
bathroom into Marigold's room. It's cleaned out except for the
magnificent canopy bed with the Summerside Plush mattress.
No sheets. I stand there until I almost piss myself I have to go
so bad, staring at the bed, Piecemeal's two thousand dollars, the
fruit of my foil. I pit-stop briefly in the kitchen: a pile of knives
drips in the dish drainer.

The bathroom smells like Scrubbing Bubbles. The toilet rim
is polished to an astonishing white. She Windexed the glass,
even the flusher. I get off on standing there, so close to the
toilet, about to burst, but holding it, standing there for a long
time, admiring that flusher. Then I lift the lid and go. The relief
is accompanied by a slow, steady burn. I stare at the ceiling as
my finger finds the pebble again. I don't look but feel further, a
metal thing protruding, soreness. Pee runs down the underside
of my hand. I freeze and close my eyes: moments like this ter-
rify. Then, I look. Winking back at me, out of the head of my
dick, which is swollen to the size of a plum, is a silver ball on
a hoop.

"Oh, fella," I say.

I'm afraid to touch it. I turn around and sit down, pee like
that, bearing the sting and the burn. When I'm done, I inspect,
twist my dick upside down and examine the new hole on the
bottom from which small drops of urine trickle. I realize this
is the new way I—Ole Two Dickhole—pee. I can be sure of
at least one thing, committing the second rob was not the last
thing I did last night and, though I have zero recollection of

it, things seem to have gone further with Mea than they ever have before.

I shake, wiping off my hands on the toilet-paper roll. I try to figure out how to take the hoop out, but I have no idea. It's not like an earring; there's no clasp. I remember from my brief experience with the pierced ear—the Taco Bell general manager made me take it out before it healed—that you're supposed to slide the ring around the day after, so it doesn't stick or become infected or something else awful. I reach down and slowly spin the hoop like they spin that wheel on *The Price Is Right*—come on down.

A slurred speech
creeps like a
fat lip

I **remove** my meager savings—a little more than a hundred dollars—from under the mattress. It might have been advisable to pocket a percentage of the second rob to get me out of this. The phone could start ringing any sec, or they might just show up here. I stuff clothes into my Quest pack and locate the address on the first letter Biodad sent. Ohio. As I head out I notice the grenade where I left it, on the TV where one of Marigold's skulls used to be. I drop it in the Quest too.

I mount the Haro with the kinky triangular frame and make for the Greyhound station. The morning is coming on strong and with it the scent of patchouli, the sway of dreadlocks. I'm dodging hippies at every intersection. Like the lovebugs, they come out every spring. The lovebugs, manufactured at the local university, some genetic breeding experiment, fill the air with their rutting bodies. They plaster grills of cars and bike reflectors. Their blood eats through the paint on cars and crusts on the reflectors. You need mayonnaise to get them off. The hippies arrive for the Rainbow Gatherings in the Ocala National Forest. More than ten thousand of them descend on the city. They attach themselves to dumpsters and street corners and restaurants, corroding customer base and bleeding laziness. Skordilli takes great pleasure in booting them off Piecemeal property with his porous-tread breathable sheep-hide restaurant shoes, except when they're named Jafari.

I take the long way to avoid Piecemeal. I fly, my Quest pack bouncing on my back. At the bus station I bunny-hop the curb and when I plant my tire the front fork buckles. I do not land on my feet but on the side of my face. A group of black guys falls out laughing.

The bus takes forever to get there. What should be a twelve-hour drive takes a whole day and night. We stop at every Podunk town from Florida to Georgia to Alabama to Tennessee to Kentucky to Ohio. I don't get off to eat at any of the Hardee's they stop at. I try to put my seat down and sleep but the woman behind me kicks it back into the upright position. So I just lean against the window, watch her scowl in the window's reflection, and doze stiff-backed the whole way, clutching the non-motorized skateboard in case anyone gets any ideas. Once in a while I use the bathroom to slide around the penis ring.

We're outside of Cincinnati when I realize I've never been anywhere before. Me and Blaise tried to drive to Colorado once to snowboard, but we only made it to Kansas. We stopped in the emergency lane near Plevna to fix a windshield-wiper blade and a cop who had it in for skaters pulled up behind us. He asked Blaise for the registration and since Blaise couldn't remember if the pipe we were smoking off was in the glove compartment he tried to pull the car door shut all stealth so the cop couldn't see.

"Boy, if you try and close me up in that door again, I'll see you good," the cop said, as he snatched the door. We didn't know what that meant. He told us we could save ourselves a lot of trouble by just giving him our stash. He could smell it, he said. I was the stupid one. I gave it to him, but just our driving stash. He made us go stand in a ditch while he found the rest. We had an ounce and some cocaine in the back. Another cop car pulled up and helped him search.

When he found the baggie of blow he held it up in the wind between his thumb and forefinger. "Who's is this?" he said. Blaise didn't say anything. I was about to cry.

"Mine," I said.

It's the closest I've ever come to going to jail. It would have been bad all around. Underneath his jacket Blaise was wearing one of his cop-equals-suckass-loser T-shirts. I could imagine what the Plevna police department was going to do to us when he got to the jail in that number. I kept thinking, Strip search, nightstick.

Then the cop told us to load our stuff back in the car and sit in it. We did. He sat in the other cop's car talking with him. When he came back over, he asked me to roll down my window. He poured out our weed. It blew away, three hundred dollars, kind. "That marijuana might not be so bad for you. There's controversy surrounding the issue. But this stuff," he said, holding up the coke, "will kill you." He poured it into the wind.

"I don't want you guys coming back here. I don't want to see you guys in Kansas ever again."

We couldn't understand why he let us off. He probably could have booked us on interstate trafficking or something. All we could figure is he'd illegally searched us. It didn't matter, we slid away. Without any drugs we wouldn't be able to pay our rent in Colorado. So we took the long way home, through the Midwest. We went through Ohio, I guess, but we didn't stop. We kept moving the whole week.

I figured once the Greyhound arrived in Ohio, I'd put things back in motion, resume my natural velocity. But there are No Skateboarding signs everywhere and walking around downtown Columbus is slow going, big blocks of corporate buildings and I can't tell what address goes to which street number. I ask someone where the city hall is and he points me down a street called Town. But my envelope says Orchard. When I get to the city hall, I ask the rent-a-cop out front for Biodad. I figure even if there's an APB for me out there—for failure to appear or for robbing Piecemeal—a rent-a-cop won't know anything about it, so I'm safe. I point to the name on the envelope, thinking for a minute, wouldn't it be something if Biodad actually was the mayor.

"This is a city of six hundred and some thousand," the rent-a-cop says.

"Thanks," I say and try to walk past him.

"Let me see that envelope," he says. "This ain't Orchard Lane. For fact, I know that address. It's nowhere near city hall. It's nowhere. My sister's got a preschool over there. Bad kids in that school. Bad motherfucking kids."

I walk a mile until I get to the end of downtown and then I put the nonmotorized skateboard down for the next two. I find a street that looks a lot like mine, on the outskirts of the university, with small houses, halfway between student ghetto and real-thing ghetto. I walk until I come to number eighty. There's a mailbox in the shape of a manatee. I lower the manatee's jaw and pull out a Columbia House bill to Dan Smith, an absolutely ordinary name that could have been mine.

There's a porch swing I sit in and look through the windows

but the blinds are mostly closed. I try to figure how I want to be when he pulls up. I stand and lean against the door. Then I recline in the porch swing, legs spread wide, deciding to seem pissed.

I realize I stink. I smell like pepperoni. The only change I brought is socks, so I pop off my restaurant shoes and get as far as one sock when a red Honda Civic pulls into the driveway. A guy who is taller than me gets out and walks straight for the house. He's wearing a black apron, black slacks, and a black polo. He looks at me. I have one sock on.

His hair is curly and kind of long, looks gay. "I know who you are," he says. "I hadn't quite pictured you showing on my doorstep though. Where's the bulrush basket?"

"Mr. Mayor, I presume," I say.

"How should we do this?" he says. "You want to shake?"

"We could try."

"Let's shake." He steps forward and offers his hand. I take it and we exchange a couple of wet fish. His hand is soft, a little bit moist, cold.

I follow him in. It's all Rent-A-Center inside. I sit down on a white couch and look at the white walls. He goes to the back of the house and bumps around. I pull on the other sock. I pack the others into the Quest and the grenade plunks out. I freeze.

"I wish I'd known you were coming," he shouts from down the hall. "I'm covering a shift for someone tonight. I owe. He covered for me while I went to get my cholesterol tested. They're putting me on reducers. Too much grease fat. How's your diet?" I put the grenade back in. He reappears in the living room, wearing a fresh set of the exact same black apron, polo, and slacks he was wearing when he arrived. They're a little stiffer, the black a little more pronounced.

"I eat pizza every day."

"Every day?" He looks at me like he's considering a fatherly

lecture. "They wanted to do a polyp check too," he says. "I'm
. . . well, technically late forties and never had one. But I said
no way."

He stops talking for a moment. I scan the room, absolutely
nothing on the walls, no decoration, completely blank.

"You're just like me but younger and better looking," he
says.

"Can I use your bathroom?" The bathroom is also white.
The mirrors are Windexed, and he wasn't expecting guests.
Admirable. I spin the little hoop in my dick around and around.
It sticks in spots, but in a weird way feels kind of cool. I sit to
pee and then wipe the dribble off the seat with toilet paper.

When I come out he asks if I want something to eat. "What
do you have?" I ask.

"I have a job," he says. "Come on."

I watch him while he drives. It's scary. He uses one hand, like
me, puts it at the bottom of the steering wheel. He leans forward when he checks the side mirrors, to eliminate the blind
spots. He uses his tooth to clean under the fingernails of the
hand he doesn't use to drive. These are all things I do. We
pull into a joint called Ferrarini's. It's going on dinner shift.
He walks me past this blonde and says, "Wendy, meet When,
an old friend in need of something to eat. Think we can score
something?"

He trots to a back room, disappearing and leaving me with
this chick who's looking at me, up and down, stopping on my
arms. "Let's see," she says. "Where can I put you?" She's wearing a short black dress, showing clammy bare legs. I follow her
legs into a separate back entrance than the one Biodad went
into and we emerge in the kitchen. "What do we have for the
scrubs?" the blonde says to a fat Mexican guy in a white T-shirt
behind the line.

"We are in luck," he says. "One guy sent the good stuff back." He produces a plate of bright yellow and crisp fried squid. Takes a ring himself before handing it to her.

"It's the Employee's Old Friend Special of the Night," she says, not passing it to me but walking right by.

"What kind of oil do you use?" I ask.

"What kind of oil do I use?" he says. "Peanut oil, my friend. Only the best for you."

"All right," I say.

"Here," he says and hands me a slice of lemon.

"Muchos," I say.

I look around for the blonde's legs and see her standing in the back corner of the kitchen, at a little round table with a stool, holding my plate of squid and looking annoyed.

"Will you be my server this evening, Madam?" I say. The cook laughs.

"In your dreams," she says and clip-clops away.

I serenade her with some Beach Boys by way of the Descendents: "Wendy / Wendy left me alone / Hurts so bad . . ." She flips me off and keeps going.

I squeeze the lemon on the squid and sit there watching the guy work. Two other Mexican guys come in but he's clearly running the show. It's a complex operation, over my head. No microwaves. I don't fully get it, but one of them seems to do the main dish and the others prepare the sides. They meet somehow at a plate in the middle and it all comes together.

Biodad appears and hands an order off to the cooks. He stops to check on me. "You all right here?" he says.

"I'm all right," I say.

"If you want I can give you the keys to the apartment. You can go back there and crash for a while."

"I think I'll just stay here," I say.

"Have it your way. Doesn't seem very interesting, though."

I pick at my squid and watch how things work. When it

starts hopping, I stand in the doorway and have a look at the dining room.

It's the kind of place I'd never even walk into, all groomed waiters and waitresses. It reminds me of a dog show, except no judges checking if anybody's balls dropped. You can hear some sounds from the kitchen, but they're all mannered clinks and clanks. The Mexicans back there are probably making half what the dolled-up waitstaff out here are, Biodad included.

I scope him out and watch his game. He's all yes-sirs and no-sirs. He makes a big production out of bread, how exactly people should rub it around in a saucer of olive oil and weeds. Pours wine in a glass and waits for some dipshit to swish it around, waits while the guy swirls the wine around his tongue, waits for his okay, for the guy to tell him that it's all right and he can continue pouring the wine. When Biodad joins a group to sing the restaurant's personalized birthday song—which is not the actual "Happy Birthday to You" song that everyone knows and loves because they are too proper to violate the copyright—to a crowd of sorority girls, I go back to the little circular staff table in the corner of the kitchen.

They've only got one dude busing, and he gets behind pretty quick. So I carry my empty plate of squid into the kitchen and start in on the dishes. They've got a nice semiautomatic, so you just rinse, load up the racks, slide them into place and drop the box for a two-minute clean to kick in. When I'm done I start wiping down surfaces.

The busser comes back and asks me who am I, and I say, "I'm your pinch hitter."

The Mexican cook, the main one, laughs again. I see Biodad's face as he picks up three ornamented plates. He looks at me for a minute, balancing the plates on his forearms.

"We conscripted your comrade, Dan-o," the Mexican says.

"Don't piss on him like you piss on the food," Biodad says.

"Your mama seems to like it," the Mexican says. Biodad disappears into the dining room again.

After the busser clears out the rush, I give him his job back.

"What do you think of that guy?" I ask the cook.

"For a dipshit, he's pretty cool," he says. "What, you guys brothers or something?"

I don't have any answer for that, and the cook thinks I've misunderstood him.

"No, seriously he's one of the all-right ones," he says. "Carries all his plates, don't fuck up orders. Eats his mistakes. Just got to put up with his mouth is the thing."

I try to see Biodad as one of the all-right ones, but don't get it. I don't see how. He's the kind of dude I could see Skinhead Rick winging hot meat at.

X

Biodad sets me up on the couch back at his apartment. He sits in a recliner. I lie there with my feet on the armrest, covered in a light blanket. I'm pissed at myself for coming here. At least Luke had the balls to tell me my existence served only to remind him that my mom had fucked other men. What would this Biodad say? All he can do is serve people. Despite the shit Luke did—pissing on my feet in the shower, ridiculing me for following him around the trailer trying to mimic the way he held his hands slightly curved (mine were straight), inflicting his name on me then discarding me into the world with it—he never served people. Even he was above that.

Biodad turns the TV to some twenty-four-hour news channel, then goes to the kitchen and loads our water glasses into the dishwasher and turns it on. "I noticed you have some tattoos," he says.

"They're new," I say.

"Are they talking about that war again?" he asks. I can

hardly hear him over the dishwasher motor. Some high-school basketball player is explaining why he turned down a chance at college ball to enlist. "What was that war about anyway?" Biodad says.

"I'm not sure. Oil, I think."

He sits down in the recliner again. We're as far away from each other as possible. We're there maybe for hours staring at the tube. Then I catch myself tracing the edges of the TV with my finger, and I look over at him and he's doing the same thing—two people who don't even know each other sitting in a room tracing the TV as they watch it.

This was a mistake. I sit up and put on my restaurant shoes. The Quest is always ready. I put it on my shoulder and stand up.

"What are you doing?" he says and stands up.

"Why did you send me all those lies?"

"They were all true at the time. I go through careers like you couldn't imagine." He smiles, a familiar smirk.

"Guess I'll cut out now," I say. I'd come for two reasons: to have a look at this guy and to get the fuck out of Dodge. I had. He couldn't do anything for me.

"Really," he says. "They were real, as real as anything is, I guess. What else is there to say?"

"I've fled from my work. My best friend has a skateboarding event. I feel the need to go back. We're preprogrammed, okay. I get it."

"It's the middle of the night," he says.

"The buses start early."

"Wait a second, let me tell you something: Don't ever take nothing for granted. Always hold your hand. I'm trying to speak your language, man," he says. "Like, let's say you're talking to a guy, a friend or an acquaintance, about a girl. You're expressing to him your impression that she wants you. And he's

all, 'Oh yeah, yeah, man. Oh yeah?' But here's the thing, this
guy has actually fucked her before. In the middle of it she was
whispering in his ear what a dope she thinks you are. You're
sitting there spilling your pile, thinking you're giving him to
understand that you're desired by women. He's holding his
hand. He's not taking for granted that you're bullshitting, that
you didn't fuck her and have her whisper similar somethings
in your ear—which if you did then you're maybe playing this
thing exactly right and I don't need to tell you nothing. But,
let's face it, more than likely you did not. Now he's up on you,
maybe in his own mind, and maybe it's even more important
that way. You see what I'm saying?"

He's too pathetic to blow up. I consider pulling my wig-
out on him while he's taking his one opportunity to play dad,
his one shot. I wonder how this cellophane pops would react
to his loin output jumping around screaming he is Satan. His
fatherly advice, the one thing I'm incapable of doing: you've
got to know your card to hold it.

"And why wouldn't you just sing 'Happy Birthday to
You'?"

"There are royalties at issue there. The restaurant has its own
birthday song."

"I see what you're saying," I say to Biodad.

"No one likes doing that, When. We just do it because that's
our job."

X

I ride the nonmotorized skateboard through the night and
when I get to the Greyhound station I find that the next bus
going my way doesn't leave for four hours. I scrounge enough
change from the bottom of the Quest for a cheese sandwich
and camp out on a bench.

On the bus home I realize I'd forgotten to ask him all the

important things: Where are we from? Are there any health liabilities—heart disease, brain aneurysm, memory loss—in the family? I never looked hard at his hairline. I can't even remember what he looks like. When I try to conjure his image in my head all I see is the back of his head and his finger tracing the TV and in my memory it looks just like me from behind. All I can clearly visualize about him is that hand resting at the base of the steering wheel as he drove, a hand with fingers of perfectly regular width, stable and agreeable, nothing like mine.

It was pointless to go there. I understand that now. And there's only one redeeming thing left to do: face the music at Piecemeal.

I write as small as I can until I fit my whole song, the song that would change Wormdevil forever if they would give me the chance to sing it. I write it on one Post-it note, front and back. The rest of the way home I hum it to myself, mimic my punches and facial expressions, the way I will never surf out into the crowd as I never sing it:

> *As the sticky, stained rug absorbs my feet*
> *And the gray ash of a cancer stick drops*
> *I slug my luke warm brown bag as if it were*
> *To make me un-beat*
>
> *The consistancy in my guzzul awakes me*
> *As the conditioned stimulus consolodates me*
> *I sip another aluminum lid*
> *While another one awaits me*
>
> *A slurred speech creeps like a fat lip*
> *And I accept a bit of shake to be the last hit*
> *I stagger toward Munchville were the beer is kept*
> *Mind puzzled, forehead wet, physical shit*

I begin to focus in on horizontal state
Oblivious to shirt, shoes, or light, bed is fate
Awakened by sunlight and bad breath
What happened last night?

Snakes
are not
a crime

The Haro with the kinky triangu-
lar frame is waiting for me at the Greyhound station in far
worse condition than I left it. The world has interpreted it as
junk. Coke and coffee have been poured on the seat. It looks as
though it has been beaten with blunt metal objects. The bolts
and sockets are single-butt ashtrays.

I leave it there and ride the nonmotorized skateboard. I
know now that no matter what the consequences, I have done
right by Greg, and fuck Jafari—a guy like that you can't do
right by even if you try. I did what I had to do.

I ride direct to Blaise's skatepark. I am right on time. Three
blocks away, I catch the sound of skateboard wheels over
wooden surfaces and Slayer, the good stuff: *Auschwitz, the
meaning of pain / The way that I want you to die* . . . I find Blaise
sweating under a party tent. Jenny Raygun is beside him holding pillowcases that flutter, full of, maybe, butterflies.

"Thinfinger," Blaise says, "there's more than a hundred and twenty thousand rattlesnakes in this state, and we can't attain a one."

"Did you see the guy?" Jenny Raygun asks. "The *Thrasher* photog." She points across the crowd to a dude looking way too nerdy to have such a cool job. How does that happen? I think. He lazily shoots the kids carving around the bowl and looks around. He seems bored, ready to split.

"What's in the pillowcases?" I ask.

"Garters," Blaise says. "Petland. We managed wholesale pricing. There's a couple full-growns, but the rest, they're still technically babies. Mean for nonvenomous."

"We tried painting diamonds on the backs of some of them. It didn't really work out," Jenny Raygun says. She grabs a handful of small, thin, baby garter snakes. Black paint smears her hands. Several attach themselves to the sides of her fingers with their little mouths and she laughs. "You can't even feel them."

Blaise droops. I reach my hand over—one of the benefits of growing up in Florida, if you've lived right, is that you've been bitten by enough weird critters to not be scared of anything's bite. One of the garters clamps on to my arm and it tickles, like when we used to hang anoles, those bastard fake chameleons, from our earlobes.

"Enough already," Blaise says. "There comes times in lives when we don't have much of a choice."

A couple thugs shoo the kid skaters out of the bowl, and I stand by Jenny Raygun while Blaise takes the mic. The DJ kills the Slayer. Blaise goes into his opening speech, thanking city commissioners and blah blah blah. I actually hear the following come out of his mouth: "This is a bright day for skateboarding in Central Florida." Then I tune him out. I take a step back and check Jenny Raygun, wonder if she ever changes those purple underwear, or if she has multiples.

Blaise says, "As chief coordinator of the project and, in all likelihood, the most astute ripper in the state, I will officially baptize this bowl Left Coast–style—left if you're facing from the perspective of the map. There's some controversy about this, but you know what I mean. My assistant, please." He gestures to Jenny Raygun, who steps to the edge of the bowl, holds the squirming pillowcases up dramatically, then upturns the snakes into the bowl. Momentarily shocked, they clump together as they slide down the ply.

Jenny Raygun steps back from the edge, grabbing a fistful of my ass. "He's going nowhere fast," she says. "You two are made for each other." She releases my cheek and refills Gatorade jugs.

The garters break from their clump at once like they all share a brain, but they only make it up to the vert, where they lose their traction and plunge back into the bowl, tumbling down the transitions. The crowd gasps at the sight.

Blaise hoists a bottle of champagne over his head and drops in. He road kills two snakes immediately, pops a massive front-side air and breaks the champagne bottle on the coping edge as he reenters the bowl. This time, he is agile and carves around the garters, who get more frantic with the vibrations from his skateboard on the surface of the ramp.

He holds a long invert on the other side, as one of the full-growns—upset and confused by the scene—goes right for him. He's upside down, holding the board on his feet. He waits until the snake's almost touching his hand, then rides in again, barely missing it.

For a moment it seems Blaise might just pull this off, even with only mildly perturbed garters. He's ripping. But the thing with the full-grown and the invert, as it turns out, constitutes a turning point. I don't know if it gets the other snakes thinking or what, but suddenly they find it in themselves to clear the vert. It starts with the other full-growns. Four of them break for opposing sides of the bowl and speed-bump over the coping to freedom. The crowd spreads out to let them through.

Someone who must have heard about the snake thing beforehand holds up a PETA sign and screams, "Snakes are not a crime!"

Sensing abandonment, the baby garters again clump together in the flat bottom, looking as dangerous as a sewer cap. And to the crowd, rather than a feeling of excitement because Blaise might be in danger, it becomes clear that these baby snakes are terrified and Blaise is their terror. The bowl might as well be full of kittens.

Blaise misunderstands. He rides closer to the snakes, thinking it will bring the crowd back to him. He ollies them in the flat bottom. I don't know how to explain it, but they cringe. Blaise tries to make up for the decline in snake action by increasing the difficulty of his tricks.

He is setting up for a McTwist, an inverted one and a half revolutions over a vert bowl filled with snakes. I know what he's thinking: This is my shot. I glance around to see if the *Thrasher* photog is getting any of it. At first I don't see him, but then I notice Jenny Raygun laid out underneath a table not far from me. Some punks are pouring cans of Natural Light into a Gatorade tub and she's got her mouth wide open taking a continuous pour from the spigot. The *Thrasher* photog is not shooting Blaise. He is shooting Jenny Raygun, from every angle, and he's instructing the punks. "Get a skateboard into the picture," he says. While one of them pours in the Natural Lights, another one does kick-flips on the table next to the jug.

Blaise almost makes the McTwist, but by this point the wood is slick with champagne and glass and snake blood. The board shoots out from under him. He goes hard to the hip, slides face first to the flat bottom, losing all momentum as he gently butts into the clump of baby garter snakes.

The PETA guy applauds and dances. Someone turns the Slayer back on. As soon as the vibrations from the skateboard stop, the snakes unclump, trying once more to escape. Like before, they make it all the way to the vert then rain down backward onto Blaise, stranded in the flat bottom.

When I look up again the *Thrasher* photog is in my face. He's pointing the camera at me. "Hold out your arms," he says. I hold out my arms. The camera clicks away.

Thought I
was gone

After a day spent locked in my
house with the lights off, the phone and answering machine
unplugged, sleeping on the Summerside Plush, on top of small
plywood splinters, and eating all the old pizza left in the freezer,
I make sure that Rick's grenade is still in the Quest, find my
long-sleeved shirt, and kick on the nonmotorized skateboard
to Piecemeal.

I enter the Piecemeal parking lot and approach from the
back. Jafari's turquoise Westfalia has been pushed onto its side.
Skordilli's Infiniti and Dr. Bob's Mustang are there. I walk past
the cars, note the clean, recently waxed exteriors. Then I enter
the door I have called my own for many months now.

The smell and the pace come to me immediately. I can sense
there is a rush, and I can sense that not enough of something
was prepped. I peer around the corner into the prep room,
where a short man with hairy bare feet is pushing logs of
cheese into the shredder with his fist. The radio is blaring some

local rock station, and he is singing along with it. To whatever cock rock the radio is playing, he sings the word "minno."

"Excuse me," I say. He stops what he's doing.

"A-OK," he says.

"I'm When," I say.

"Minno," he says. He has a blue bandana wrapped around his head, not the Piecemeal kind, but the paisley pot-smoker kind.

"Minno, what you're doing here is very dangerous. There's a handle with a, like, pusher right under the shredder. You should use that. The blade sometimes slips."

"Oh no, man," he says. "Totally cool."

Just then, Dr. Bob and Skordilli are squeezing themselves through the thin corridor leading from the kitchen to the dish room. Their arms are outstretched and they're growling my name. I brace myself against the prep table. The two of them are caught for a moment in the corridor, then Skordilli pushes through. He crosses the room and has his arms around me. Dr. Bob squeezes me too, and I'm thinking, They're going to tear me apart is their plan. They're going to rip me in half. I close my mouth, grit my teeth. But they are not trying to disassemble me. They are hugging me. And the dick ring is giving me a hard-on. They cannot get enough of their hands and arms and sides of their bushy faces on me. And what they are saying, it is not condemnation, it is all apology. In rhythm with the song—whatever it is—that Minno was just singing "minno" to, they are repeating "Sorry, sorry, sorry"

When the surge is over, they step back and each keeps one arm on each of my shoulders. I am surrendered and have assumed they'll be killing me, that the facts of the second rob must be clear by now. But the looks in their eyes are not the looks I expected.

"Thinfinger," Skordilli says, "I am so sorry for word of mouth. I figured you would have known that you of all people were spared in this."

"I should have," I say. "I should have known." If my ass is saved, I will say whatever to keep it that way. Whatever. Minno busts through the two of them and hugs me. He smells of deet.

"I heard so much about you, man," he says.

Skordilli peels him away, suggests he get on the cheese and he goes back to pushing the logs with his fists.

"Let's just air it all," Dr. Bob says. "Let's put it all out there."

"Good idea," Skordilli says. "Let's."

"I'm still feeling confused." Then, going out on a limb, not wanting to start the airing, "I thought I was a goner."

Skordilli: "No no no. Just everyone else. Two robberies and that Gutter Boy and . . . no offense but . . . that Rick—did you know he was a skinhead? Brain was a casualty, sure, but I've learned something in my time in the restaurant industry, Thinfinger, sometimes you have to waste a little product. But not managers, not managers like you. I should have told you. I purged—I fired everyone *but* you."

Dr. Bob: "You suspected Jafari all along. Didn't you? Didn't you, fuckrod?" Dr. Bob jabs me in the chin.

I tread carefully here: "*Two* robberies?"

Skordilli: "It's what inspired the purge. I show up here, the black box is cleaned out, as is Jafari's van. Jafari's gone. It's no great feat of deduction. The Rainbow Gathering had split town that morning, moved on to some hippie grovel in Texas. The hole he used to enter by—reopened. He didn't even bother to cover his tracks. In all likelihood he did the first one too, and I punished that witch Greg for it. It's all clear now. We have people, our people, searching the Texas Rainbow Gathering as we speak. Scores will soon be settled. I'm only sorry that you heard through the grapevine that the employee purge included you. You should have talked to me."

"I wasn't sure you wanted to talk," I say, looking down at the brown restaurant shoes.

Call it—like spider-sense—kitchen-sense. I turn around just before it happens. Minno watches us, teary eyed. He is still singing his name to the cock rock. The blade slips, sure, but he follows through, a moron move, plants the big knuckle of his right hand into the shredding blade, which lops it clean off, his finger an empty wedge where the knuckle used to be. He pulls his hand back and covers it with his apron, keeps singing: "Minno, Minno, Minno, Minno."

Dr. Bob clutches the guy like he'd embraced me a moment ago. "Don't look," he says. "Don't look."

"Minno?" Minno says, then crumples in Dr. Bob's arms.

"No problem," Dr. Bob says. "Happens all the time." He slops him up on the prep table and ties his finger off with an apron string.

"Workman's-comp worthy?" Skordilli asks Dr. Bob for my benefit, though I know good and well they've got no work-man's comp, and Minno won't be seeing any doctor on their dime.

"I'm sure we can handle this here," Dr. Bob says. He opens the shabby first-aid kit on the wall and douses Minno's hand in peroxide. "A little nick." He wraps the finger in a rag until it's as big as a squash.

"I'm just glad we have it all straightened out," Skordilli says, turning back to me. "The only question is when can we get you back? Can you start now?"

I can't believe what I'm hearing. I pictured myself walking in here as the last thing I'd do. I was prepared to face up to everything and take what I had coming. Now I'm all giddy and thinking about the opening of the Ovenman position with Rick gone. For a second I play it all out like it could be: once again, I am Ovenman. That would be my condition: I'll come back, but only as Ovenman. It's a sweet idea. Then I understand it can't be that way. How would it look, me coming back to work for them after they canned everyone else? And they would eventually get their hands on Jafari. I wouldn't mind hosing his blood off the Infiniti but he'd surely say it was all me. "I've got some things I need to take care of," I say. "I'm still getting over the joyous fact I'm not fired."

"You could start tonight," Skordilli says. "The girls, and this sorry fish, could really use you."

"Wait a second, Thinfinger," Dr. Bob says. He blows by me and Skordilli out the back door, leaving Minno on the table still muttering his own name. One of the dykes comes back. She doesn't seem to remember me. She glances at Minno on the prep table, then picks up the bus tub of mozzarella with the knuckle in it. She runs it right past me, up to Thin Pies.

Me and Skordilli exit the back door. He won't take his arm off me. Dr. Bob is fumbling in the trunk as we approach.

Outside Piecemeal I take in all the smells. There's the faint scent of sawdust from what was Jafari's van, the sour ice from the walk-in, the bleach from the mop bucket, which hasn't been cleaned properly in days, algae coming from the fountain, and in between, the glue holding all those smells together, the rich perfume of dough and sauce. We are standing in the damp spot from the mop bucket hose snaking through our feet.

"We sure missed you, When," Skordilli says. I look up at him, realize that looking at him is a lot more like looking at a father than looking at Biodad. I am keeping one eye on whatever Dr. Bob is doing in the trunk. At one point he comes up with a badminton racquet and I drop to my knees, covering my head.

Nothing happens. "Shell shock," I tell Skordilli, who pulls me up and asks, "What's going on?"

"I'm feeling kind of light-headed," I lie.

"Here it is," Dr. Bob says. He hands me a lamb's skull. "I promised you this."

I hold the thing. "Thank you," I say. "Thank you so much."

"Come in a little later. We'll work on the schedule, hire some new blood. The mice problem is already clearing up."

"I can go now?" I ask.

"Okay," they say and I walk carefully away, looking over my shoulder, around the side of the building to the front.

As I clear the café, I ignore Uschi waving to me. I start running full speed down University, the grenade bouncing in the pack on my back, hitting my shoulder blades hard enough to worry me, the lamb skull tucked firmly under my arm. I drop the nonmotorized skateboard to the ground, and am going, going, gone.

X

On instinct I head for Blaise's pad and bust in without knocking. I stick my head in his kitchen sink, my face in the stream of water, above a sink of dirty dishes, gnats. He's home alone. He hikes up his shirt to show me his hipper. His hip and thigh are purple and black.

He limps back to his room-bed and turns on the TV. I grab us Natural Lights. We zone on the TV and don't talk about anything that's happened.

"I'm glad you came by here, man. I've been meaning to talk to you," he says.

Blaise's new plan, he says, is to concentrate on Wormdevil. And he tells me the first step of the new plan is concentrating on it without me in it. "It's an experience issue," he says. But I know what the issue is. He can do the math. And I'm the variable.

"I'm not going to forget you when we reach the top, Thinfinger," he says.

"I know you won't," I say. I think about showing him the song, but don't. "I took the Greyhound to Ohio, visited the Biodad."

"How was that?"

"I'm not getting any money," I say.

"Bummer," he says.

"I didn't really want any money though, not from him. Just kind of wanted to see what the dude is like."

"What's he like?"

I think about that and settle on, "He was everything his letters weren't."

We're watching some documentary on giant snails. I'm doing everything I can to resist tracing the TV with my finger.

"Hey," I say. "I found something out. Chicks dig these fingers." I open my hands in front of me as I say this. "Chicks dig these frail fingers of mine."

"You've got to be kidding me," he says.

I stay until it gets dark and he narcs out. Then I go out on foot. I have never walked the town. It's surprising how long it takes. When I walk into Second Skin, Mea has just finished a tongue and a young girl is sitting there with a mouth full of cotton balls. When Mea sees me, the first thing she does is grab my crotch. I am hard. "Was I right?" she asks.

"You date-pierced me," I say.

"I wouldn't call it a date," she says.

"Is there any way to get the thing out?"

"Steel cutters maybe."

"Precision steel cutters, I hope."

"I got it in, When. I can get it out. But not until I say so."

We are out of there straightaway, and I come clean with her: She is way too much woman for me. Way. For one, she'd constantly have some guy's genitals in her hands, and then there's all the trolling for wang. And the word on the street is she can ollie a speed bump.

"I know I am," she says. "Our relationship will be a purely professional one." I will be her pin cushion, her practice mat. What I will get out of it is I will be pierced on her plush white couch with garbage bags underneath.

We go inside and she applies Neosporin to all my injuries, then she removes the gear from her home autoclave.

"I want more holes in me," I say. I recline and feel still, like everything has suddenly stopped. I clutch the lamb skull.

"It's about time," she says. "Now where should we start?"

X

The piercings are tiny release valves. All the pressure of being Night Manager seeps right out of me. We strike another day from our remaining days to live and, she points out, she still has a good five thousand more than me. We open a bottle of whiskey and drink to women's life expectancy.

Within a few shots she is asleep on the couch.

I leave her apartment with the grenade, the bottle of whiskey, and the lamb skull in the Quest pack.

The first rob still bothers me. I wish I could remember it. And there is one possibility that keeps gnawing at me: that Jafari wasn't in on it at all. That Jafari had had me in the same way he had Skordilli, wrecking his restaurant and him all the while loving it. I couldn't even say for sure if he was in that office with me that night, my still frames can't be trusted like a Post-it can.

I make my way to Piecemeal through the alleys and emerge in the parking lot, empty of cars except for Jafari's abandoned van, still knocked over on its side. For kicks I try my key to the Piecemeal back door, but it doesn't work. So I wander over to the back patio. I apologize to the guppies, spit on the pizza-box statue, which is already coming apart from the rain and humidity. I sit down at a table and remove the whiskey, grenade, and skull from the Quest. I set them on the table.

I drink from the whiskey and look at the skull. Unlike Marigold's skulls, which are a crisp white, this one is yellow. There are spots of meat and blood on it like dried pepperonis. Either the whiskey bottle or the grenade has knocked a chip out of its jawline. Most of the teeth have fallen out. I consider going for my free haircut, giving the lamb skull to Marigold to see what kind of effect that might have. But I know I won't.

I leave the whiskey bottle and skull on the table. I stand at the fountain with the grenade. I only have a conceptual understanding of how this works, don't know the intricacies of timing or pull, but I figure if you come this far none of it really matters. I tug at the pin and it cuts my hand, soft from dish soap, like dough. Then I pull harder, and it releases. The pin pings across the patio. The grenade plops into the fountain, and I turn, tripping on the leg of a chair—part of me doesn't want to stand, thinks I should go down with the place. But I jump up, tear through the parking lot, hop the little brick wall and dive behind the grease barrel with the dead crow in it.

I hunker, watching the back patio. I lick my lips. I pump on the balls of my feet, ready to sprint at just the right moment. I don't have a watch. It could be seconds, but it feels like hours. I begin to suspect that all this time Rick may have been toting around a dud.

I slowly walk back to the fountain. At the edge of the patio, I peer around the corner, stare at the pizza-box-money statue. I step onto the brick walkway and approach. I swig from the whiskey. Then I look around in the fountain. I panic when I can't find the grenade and step in, immediately soaking my special restaurant shoes. I stomp around. It's hard to see through the splashes, and I begin to wonder if I've actually done what I believe I've done.

Then I find it, right in the middle. I pull a patio chair into the fountain and sit in it drinking the whiskey. I watch the fish circle the grenade. They nip little air bubbles off of it. I take long pulls on the whiskey until I have enough in me to accomplish what I want to accomplish. I leave the bottle in the fountain and the skull on the table. I make out a Post-it: *You blew it up. And the place deserved everything it got. Good fer you. Now dont go there again, take the sidstreets, better not to see or be seen. Dont be sorry.*

I sprint in the squishy restaurant shoes to the back of the parking lot again. I am breathing heavy, the arches of my feet burn. I stare at the back patio for a long time. I don't take my eyes off it. When I imagine the explosion, I imagine it vividly. I'm shot back into the alley from the force. There is a burst of the thickest cloudlike dust and fire, then guppies and chips of fountain and pizza-box-money statue are falling all around. The back dining room collapses in on itself from the force, the roof drops out first, then the walls fall. I can hear the pinging of detritus off the grease bins. And when it all settles I see an image like the CNN images from that one-minute war: mounds of rubble and a fog of dust. I replay it over and over. I focus on every fragment, especially the lamb teeth and flecks of bone, which rain down on the asphalt around me.

ACKNOWLEDGEMENTS

Thanks to Arthur Flowers, dogbrother, for so much support and good counsel. Thanks to those who read drafts early on: Ben Andrews, Aaron Burch, Adam Davies, Mary Caponegro, Elizabeth Ellen, Steve Gillis, Mikhail Iossel, Kevin Keck, George Saunders, and Tony Walsch. Thanks to the Syracuse University Creative Writing Program and Terri Zollo. Thanks to my fam, especially my sister Crystal, who reads everything I write, and Yulya, who puts up with me. Thanks to the Tin House crew, especially Lee Montgomery and Meg Storey, for their Argus eyes and steadfast belief in this book. And thanks to Ellen Levine for going to the mat with me.